This is for Teresa Chris,
a veritable tiger of an agent;
and for my hawk-eyed friend,
Avis Worthington.

My special thanks to
Dr. Louise Miller of Berkeley,
who was most generous with
her time and information.
If I got anything wrong,
it is my fault entirely.

D0188337

THE CRUEL
MOTHER

JANET LAPIERRE

WORLDWIDE.

TORONTO · NEW YORK · LONDON · PARIS
AMSTERDAM · STOCKHOLM · HAMBURG
ATHENS · MILAN · TOKYO · SYDNEY

THE CRUEL MOTHER

A Worldwide Mystery/August 1991

This edition is reprinted by arrangement with
Charles Scribner's Sons; an imprint of Macmillan
Publishing Company.

ISBN 0-373-26078-4

Copyright © 1990 by Janet LaPierre. All rights reserved.
No part of this book may be reproduced or transmitted in any
form or by any means, electronic or mechanical, including
photocopying, recording or by any information storage and
retrieval system, without permission in writing from the
Publisher. For information, contact: Charles Scribner's Sons,
an imprint of Macmillan Publishing Company,
866 Third Avenue, New York, NY 10022 U.S.A.

All the characters in this book are fictitious, and any
resemblance to actual persons, living or dead, is purely
coincidental.

® are Trademarks registered in the United States Patent
Trademark Office and other countries.
TM is the property of Harlequin Enterprises Ltd.

Printed in U.S.A.

ONE

SLEEP WAS RELEASING HIM, nudging him toward a consciousness he didn't want. The dying man lifted heavy eyelids, groaned softly and let them drop. There he was, Death, a skeletal old man in a white nightgown.

He inched his wasted body higher against its cradling pillows. Negotiate, he used to be good at that. Look, I'm not quite finished here. Maybe we could work something out. He opened his eyes again, looked straight before him and made a raspy little sound that would have been a chuckle had his throat not been so dry. Greetings, Mr. Death.

With unrelieved darkness outside and a shaded, low-watt lamp beside his bed, the huge square of glass before him was shiny black. He nodded, and lifted one hand a few inches; in the window the lumpy skull with its sparse wiry tufts of hair nodded, too, and a bony finger waggled . . . denial? admonishment?

He turned slowly, carefully, to look for the water glass on the bedside table. Watch out for the button, or you'll get a nurse and a shot of Demerol. Nothing working now but the mind, it's worth pain to hang on to that. For a while.

Soft footsteps sounded from behind him. "Shame on you, Michael, you shouldn't be awake. Let me get you . . ."

"No." His croak silenced her, and she came around the bed to peer into his face and lay assessing fingers on his wrist.

He gestured toward the glass; she lifted it and held its bent straw to his mouth. He sucked eagerly, sat back, let his eyelids drop. "Sleep," he said, in his tiny, old-man's voice. "Turn out the light."

She obeyed and padded away on rubber-soled nurse shoes. He opened his eyes and was pleased to find only a bare hint of reflection in his window. Something else he hadn't known about himself, that he was vain. The sparse hair, the fleshless eyesockets, the skin with the look of crumpled gray linen—all of it offended him.

Maybe a hint of light out there. One more dawn. He wondered whether it was cold, whether the old radicals and peaceniks camped across the road were shivering and building up their fires. His mother was furious at their audacity in coming to the very gates of this walled retreat. But they were his friends, his people. He'd been a leader, hadn't he?

Let it go. The phrase ran through his head to the tune of a song, some pop hit he couldn't remember. A genetic kink of some sort had given him a tall, lean body, an ascetic's face, a sonorous voice. If he'd been the stereotypical fat energetic little Jew like his father, no one would have set him up as a hero.

A cough surprised him; he tensed in anticipation of another, the onset of the infection that would give the coup de grâce in this war. Nice irony: the pacifist whose body was made a war zone, chemicals bombarding evil invaders until it became clear that not enough healthy cells remained to make the battle worthwhile, and the field was abandoned. Peace.

There was no further coughing. He relaxed, dozed, woke and saw pale streaks in the gray beyond his window. He imagined he could hear the sea crashing against rocks, washing up over the pebbles of the beach and making a rattly retreat. If the afternoon turned warm, he'd insist on having the side windows opened.

So, not a hero. But he'd loved a woman, hadn't he? Or been loved by her, mesmerized by her passion for justice and for him. He shifted his position once more, edging himself lower in an attempt to ease the ache in his poor bony ass. His eyes fell on his scrawny upper arm, smeared with the bruises that followed the lightest touch or sometimes none at all; and he pulled the sleeve of his nightgown lower to cover the ugliness. Strong as a horse, Maureen, prematurely white-haired but all smooth springy flesh over willing muscle, and she'd live to be a hundred, damn her.

Let it go. It was a Beatles' song, he remembered suddenly: "Let It Be." All he recalled of it was that one phrase, repeated; not much of a Beatles fan, he'd preferred classical music.

And he'd killed a man. Hadn't he? He stared at the dawn sky, where ragged strips of fog were turning a delicate pink at the approach of the sun. In a while he'd have the bed cranked higher so that he could see the surf, creaming over the black rocks that stood like sentinels at either end of his small cove and framed the enormous reach of ocean beyond. Unpeopled landscapes pleased him most these days, desert or sea or high cold mountains. He'd cut a man's life short, and now he knew how paltry and mean had been his remorse.

He had fathered a child. That he had indisputably done. Fucked his smooth hungry wife, watched the great lump grow in Maureen's unwilling belly, snatched a squirming slippery frog-child from between her blood-smeared thighs. Caught it in his hands; he turned them palms-up against his sheet. How did it feel?

Let it go. Outside his window the sky was turning blue and pink and gold. Sitting up to watch, he felt a sob catch and ache in his chest: so beautiful. Tears trickled down his cheeks; the ache flared, dulled and settled to stay, and he groaned. Pain in the bone itself, his sternum. Worse than yesterday.

He had to stay alive; he was waiting to see his child. No, replied the brutal imp of truth that had dogged him all his life. No, you're waiting to see your self.

(And Maureen, the imp added in a whisper. Maureen, because she can help you if it finally gets too hard. No one else would, but Maureen will.)

TWO

In the panhandle of Idaho, a hundred miles or so south of the Canadian border, the sky was high and clear, pouring hot sunlight over brushy fields and spindly pines. The tobacco-brown Mercedes sedan jounced along a rutted gravel road northwest of Coeur d'Alene, its driver wincing at small potholes and swearing at larger ones. Some years earlier an eager developer had bought this chunk of logged-over land and split it into ten-acre "estates," promising that the new growth would be tall and green in no time and the area would remain exclusive. The second promise had proved true; the few widely spaced houses were as ill-tended as the road, some of them bearing FOR SALE signs so weathered as to be nearly illegible.

The car slowed for a curve, then slowed still more as the driver peered through the windshield toward the right side of the road, where chain-link fencing was oddly modern protection for an old two-story farmhouse and its outbuildings. Four years earlier, with a healthy Michael Tannenbaum on the scene playing hippie carpenter, the place had had a spruce, energetic look; now the house displayed peeling white paint and sagging shutters, while daylight gleamed through the walls of the old barn. Maureen was having trouble managing on her own, Ben Taylor noted.

The Mercedes crept another twenty yards, eased onto a graveled drive bridging the roadside ditch, and came to a stop against a wide gate held shut by a serious-looking padlock. To the left of that gate was a smaller one, pulled tight but not obviously locked. Taylor set the brake, turned off the engine, pushed the door wide and stepped out, a long narrow man wearing gray flannel slacks and a white shirt with a plain dark tie. He settled his belt, inspected his shirt cuffs, then reached into the car to lift a gray tweed sports coat from its wooden hanger.

The smaller gate bore a handpainted sign, black on white: SHELTER. A bell jingled as he opened the gate. Its sound had hardly stilled when a man appeared from behind the house. Rawboned and of medium height, he wore tan workclothes and a carpenter's apron. A brindle dog trotted beside him, a muscular animal with a pink-tongued, squinting grin.

"Want somethin', mister?"

"Only to pay a call. I'm an old friend of..." His mind went blank. Maureen called herself Elizabeth now, but what was the surname she and Michael had chosen? "Of Elizabeth's," he finished lamely.

Pale blue eyes inspected the caller from shoes to hairline before the man nodded. "Miz Brody's in the house, might as well go on in."

A small enclosed porch gave directly into what had once been a living room. Wooden floors were scarred, walls smeary with fingerprints. The furniture might have come from half a dozen attics, a mix of worn upholstered chairs and couches with children's low tables and wooden chairs. A baby dozed on a couch; in one corner a flock of toddlers encircled a small woman who was strumming a guitar. Against the far wall was a desk where two women sat, one tall and straight-backed with broad shoulders, the other huddled low, face hidden against her outstretched arms.

"Elizabeth?" His voice rang loud in the uncarpeted room; every face but that of the sleeping child turned toward him. The tall woman rose; the woman beside the desk tipped back her head, looked at the intruder from the slits of two blackened eyes, reached out to grasp the other's skirt.

"It's all right, Annie, I won't be long. Go to the kitchen and have someone make you a cup of tea."

The woman, a girl really, got to her feet and shambled away; when a door had closed behind her, Elizabeth Brody turned and came across the room in long firm strides. Thick silvery-white hair was knotted loosely at the nape of her neck, incongruous frame for the smooth face with its broad brow and clean, taut jawline. It took a second or even a third look to note the roughened, darker skin around the brilliantly blue eyes, the lines bracketing the wide mouth. "Ben," she said with a nod but no particular warmth, "what a surprise."

Ben's face was an elongated egg, its shape emphasized by a receding hairline and a long pointed chin. Now his reddish eyebrows arched high, and he shook his head. "I hit forty, all of a sudden I'm an old, bald guy. But you, you're just a beautiful woman who decided to start over with white hair."

"Thank you, that's very nice. But I'm really forty-three," she reminded him, "and you're forty-five."

He winced. "Thanks a lot. Look, could you let me have the key to your gate? I don't like leaving my car on the road."

She took a large key ring from a desk drawer, selected a key, and held it out to him. "Park behind the house. I'll go make us some tea."

"Never mind, I have something better."

"At Shelter we don't..." He was away before she could finish; she pressed her lips tight and stood waiting in the open doorway.

"We don't permit liquor here," she told him when he returned. "Ben, isn't that the same car you were driving four years ago?"

"That Mercedes, lady, is a classic. You don't trade in a machine like that. And if you consider Glenfiddich liquor, suit yourself; for me it's what smooths the edges off a rough world. Magic medicine."

She eyed him silently for a long moment, then shrugged. "Come into my study; we can be private there."

The room was small and dusty, with a cluttered oak table, two tall gray filing cabinets, and a wall of bookcases filled with medical books and pamphlets. Elizabeth sat down on a wooden kitchen chair, her spine as straight as its back, while Ben cleared a space on the table for a leather case which he opened to reveal two bottles and two small glasses.

"Cheers," he muttered a moment later as he handed her a glass of amber liquid. He moved to stand before the open window, curving his mouth in a grin that had a pasted-on look.

"Cheers. Now please tell me what brings you here."

"Um," he said, and sipped and nodded and sipped again. "Well, I've been in Denver, looking into setting up a practice there, or joining one. L.A. can be a fairly depressing place to live unless you're a multi-millionaire."

"I see." She cradled her glass in her lap and fixed her unblinking gaze on his face.

"And Sweet has gone silent on me. He used to call every two or three weeks, but I've heard not a word for a couple of months now. I thought I'd better go up and pay him a visit."

"Yes, you should," she told him. "I don't see him often, because it's clear that he looks on me as just one more snoopy official. But I think his medication needs adjusting, and I *know* it's been far too long since he saw a doctor. For you he'll go." She took a sip of single-malt Scotch, and smiled briefly. "Good. Now what else?"

"Okay." He set his empty glass down and pulled a pack of cigarettes from his jacket pocket. "I saw Michael. Just last week."

"Is he . . . bad?"

"He's dying."

Elizabeth closed her eyes and moved her head in one up-and-down jerk of assent. "I managed to see a San Francisco paper; they'd printed that wild-eyed picture from twenty years ago and then this sad, sad recent one. One thing for sure," she added bitterly, "no one around here is likely to associate either version of Michael Tannenbaum with the man they knew as Michael Brody."

"No, I wouldn't think so."

"The story said he had entered a guilty plea in the policeman's death but received a suspended sentence, because his leukemia was acute and his family could provide the best care." Tears welled and were blinked away. "No more remissions?"

"I didn't speak with the doctor, but I think not."

She sighed deeply and held her empty glass out to be re-filled. "I have never known, not for sure, whether it was Michael who actually pulled the trigger or me."

"Elizabeth, there is nothing to be gained by reliving all that."

"Not for you!" she snapped. "You weren't there; you were always on the phone or in the toilet when the rest of us were ready to hit the streets."

"So I'm a physical coward. I've never denied it," he said with a flush that reddened even his ears. "But I was damned good at arranging bail and convincing juries."

"It was one of those hot summery days you hardly ever get in the Bay Area, the kind of day that turns life into a picnic..." She spoke in a reminiscent lilt, reciting an old tale mostly to herself. "People had their kids along, and their shirts off; everybody was chanting and singing. The cop who lost control of his bike was just a kid himself, he didn't mean to hit that little boy."

"Elizabeth..."

"Then nothing, nobody even breathing, just the earth turning silently in the sun. Sometimes I go back to that moment and make the rest of it different: the marchers stayed cool instead of freaking out, the cop didn't panic and start shooting. And I didn't open my nurse's bag and see that gun right there, where I'd put it the night before because I was making calls in west Oakland."

Ben took a long last drag on his cigarette and scrunched the butt out in the soil of a potted cactus on the windowsill. "Michael has confessed; I think what you should do is accept that."

She blinked, stared at the glass in her hand, then drained it with a shudder. "You're right, of course. So much waste already, it would be foolish to cause more. Ben, I do thank you for coming. While his father was alive, Michael managed to get occasional letters to me, but there's been nothing since the old man died in January, not a word. Mother Tannenbaum hates me; I've always suspected her of intercepting *my* letters to Michael."

"I think letter-writing would take more energy than he has to spare. Michael is...right now he is deeply involved in the process of dying."

"Yes. Yes, of course he would be." Elizabeth stood up, set her glass on the table, and pushed her hands into her pockets. She wore a belted dress with roll sleeves and a flared skirt, soft and blue rather than crisp and white; odd uniform, but uniform it was, with the RN pin over her breast and her shoulders squared.

"What Michael wants now, the only thing he says he wants, is to see his daughter. You and his daughter," Ben amended quickly.

"I know I should go," she said, and drew a deep breath. "But I'm like Sweet, not eager to go back to the world. This is a good place, and I'm useful to these people."

"How many patients...clients, residents, whatever... how many do you have?" Ben settled his shoulder against the windowframe and sipped his whisky.

"It varies; some stay a night or two, some for months. Right now there are fifteen women here, and twenty-three, no, twenty-four children."

"Don't you get into trouble, up here in he-man country, putting ideas in the heads of formerly obedient wives?"

"I no longer deal in ideas," she said sharply. "I try to mend bodies and deliver healthy babies. And to teach women how to avoid more babies."

"I didn't even know you'd had a kid until Michael told me. I thought you'd long ago decided to forgo motherhood in the interests of your profession."

Her mouth curled in a quick, bitter smile. "Michael had been so sick and listless that we rarely made love; I got careless. And he realized I was pregnant almost before I did. I tried to tell him that I was too old, that we couldn't run with an infant. But I loved...I love Michael. I couldn't go have his baby scraped out of me without his permission."

"I love Michael, too," Ben muttered, red-faced. "He's a fine man and it's a goddamned rotten dirty trick that he's dying. Does she look like him, your daughter?"

Elizabeth shook her head. "Tessa is an ordinary little blond girl; there are half-a-dozen others here just like her."

"Michael won't see her as ordinary."

She made no reply, except for a small movement of her shoulders that could have been a shrug or a shudder.

"Maureen . . . sorry. Elizabeth, I know the possibility of prison has always terrified you, but my best judgment is that the risk is small, they won't charge you with anything more than . . ."

"They could charge me as an accessory, before or after the fact! It was my gun, I did not have a permit to carry it, it could be said I gave it to Michael. So they could charge me as a co-conspirator, for murder. None of this sounds like small risk to me."

"They have their guilty person, Elizabeth, a man who is obviously paying for his crime. You will be coming bravely to the bedside of your dying husband, to bring him his child; the media will love it, they're hovering over Michael already. And if you think that's disgusting, I'd say you should be able to stand it if Michael can."

Definitely a shrug this time, followed by a brief and very reluctant smile. "Michael always said you were a good advocate."

"I am indeed, and I'll be pleased to put my skills at your service. In fact," he added, his face brightening, "if you do decide to go to California, I'll even take you there. The Merc is a real highway car; we could do it in two days."

She pursed her lips in thought. "We probably couldn't travel that fast with a small child. But . . . yes. There's a woman in town, a practical nurse, who'd be willing to come here on a half-time basis while I'm away; and Jack, my handyman, could deal with the garden and the livestock. All right, we'll go. Thank you."

"Welcome. While you make your arrangements, I'll deal with my baby brother . . . find out what he might need, arrange for him to see his doctor, give him a dose of human company. Beats me how anyone can stand to live all alone, completely out of sight of all the rest of humanity."

"He's not alone at the moment," Elizabeth said absently. "When I drove up to the cabin to see him six weeks ago, I had *my* brother with me, my eighteen-year-old brother. The two of them hit it off, and Sweet invited Buddy to stay."

"And you agreed? I'm not sure that was a smart thing to do."

"Sweet is not a danger to anyone but himself," she replied crisply. "And Buddy is an over-mothered, priest-ridden baby who'll be the better for a summer in the woods, away from city streets and city troubles."

"Okay, okay." He straightened, stretched, and grinned at her. "I'm ready to chill out after a long week, get down to business on Monday. Here's a deal for you. If there's a decent restaurant in Coeur d'Alene, with a respectable wine list, I'll take you to dinner. In return, you put me up here for the night."

"There are several excellent restaurants in town," she told him, "but I won't join you. I have work to do this evening. And I can provide a bed for you, but not mine."

He spread his hands and shrugged. "As you have cleverly deduced, I'm the same horny bastard I always was. But what about you, Elizabeth who used to be hot old Maureen? Michael went home almost two years ago; what do you do for fucking these days?"

"Sublimate!" she snapped.

THREE

VINCE GUTIERREZ FOLLOWED Mary Louise's directions without thinking about them; he had an old patrol cop's feel for city streets and these were drowsing in Sunday morning calm. Colorado Springs was very clean, he noted. Clean and rich. Just another playground for tourists and absentee landowners, the kind of place his own little California hometown was turning into; he could hardly wait to get to the wilds of northern Idaho.

He checked a street sign, turned right, hit a pothole and was pleased to note only the faintest twinge of discomfort in his left side. The bullet that had smashed through a rib and nicked his lung two months earlier was the first he'd taken in nearly twenty-five years as a cop, and it could have been a lot worse. He was not willing, not yet, to agree that it was time to find something else to do for a living.

Another turn. Mary Louise had said seven blocks, second light. The van was okay, no Cadillac but it had new bucket seats in front and he enjoyed being up here above the folks in their little cars. Be terrific for looking at the scenery. "On the road again," he caroled, and then sang the whole chorus, his Willie-imitation hampered somewhat by a broad grin.

He made the final turn, onto a street of slightly seedy older houses. Halfway down the block he found the number and pulled to the curb. Cottage in the rear, she'd said. Gutierrez remembered the split-level ranch house his sister had occupied during her marriage and wondered whether she regretted its loss.

He glanced at the mailbox, then peered more closely and read the words aloud. "Maria Luisa Gutierrez." Christ. She'd dropped the Gutierrez when she left home at seventeen, and she'd been plain Mary Louise all her life, through several "relationships" and three kids and then a ten-year marriage. As he picked his way along the lumpy asphalt path skirting the main house, he vowed not to ask what she was up to now. A cup of tea and a little exchange of family gossip, that was his agenda for today.

There was a low picket fence with a drooping gate, a small yard full of tall grass, two old tires serving as planters for scraggly petunias. The cottage was stucco, with a flat roof and a lopsided porch, and a lot of exposed chicken-wire at one corner where someone had started a patch job a long time ago. Gutierrez tried to remember how much money he had in his wallet. Must be close to two hundred; he'd leave it all and cash a traveler's check tomorrow.

He stepped onto the porch, and the door opened. "Vincente! Come in, *mi hermano*, come in!"

Mary Louise was only five feet three inches tall, and still very slim. In a white blouse and black skirt, with black hair looped softly back into a bun, she looked tiny and defenseless. Black-dyed hair, Gutierrez corrected himself. It had started out light brown.

"And did you bring your *novia*? I'd love to meet her, I can't believe you've been here for a whole week and just called me this morning."

"My...you mean Meg?" *Novia*—fiancée—was probably as good a word as any for Margaret Halloran, who had been the woman in his life for the past two years...although he was currently nudging her toward *esposa*. "Meg has been here for the week, at a conference for English teachers at Holy Names College. I flew in yesterday." Noting black-lined eyes and darkened eyebrows and a hovering-dove solicitude, Gutierrez got it: the new role was Latina, chicana, whatever. Unfortunately Mary Louise looked not at all like their father; she had Mama's neat-featured narrow face, pale skin, and gray eyes.

"Holy Names. I've heard they have a good ethnic studies department," she said brightly. "You see, I've decided to explore my Hispanic heritage. I'm almost forty, after all, it's time to find out who I *am*. I'm taking Spanish lessons, and guitar lessons, and..."

"...and working in a greaser bar and bringing home a big fat greaser boyfriend," said a voice from across the room.

"Hello, Cass." Another transformation, noted Gutierrez sadly. Three years earlier, Cass—Cassandra Hall, Mary Louise's youngest child—had been a pigtailed tomboy, clear-eyed and grinning, quick with a hug or a punch to the biceps. Now she had reddish hair that stood out around her head in long spikes, more black eyeliner than her mother wore, glittery green stuff on her eyelids. Clad in what looked like black tights under a gray sweater that reached nearly to her knees, she was propped against a doorway, arms crossed, watching.

"Not Cass; she's Amparo now, her middle name," said her mother.

"Bullshit. Emily's my middle name. Hi, Uncle Vince. We haven't seen you in a long time."

"I know. I'm sorry."

"That's all right," she said with a shrug.

"Amparo...all right, all right, *Cassandra*," said Mary Louise with an exaggerated sigh. "Would you please get your uncle a Dos Equiis? Here, Vince, this is the most comfortable chair."

"Don't fuss, Mary Louise. It's been two whole months and I'm in good shape, even my doctor says so." Gutierrez eyed the tippy-looking plastic recliner and then sat down in gingerly fashion.

"There's a tiltback lever on the side, I think it still works," his sister told him. "I still can't believe it, you know? I mean, a pokey little northern California town where nothing ever happens, and the chief of police gets himself shot?"

"Never happen again in a million years," said Gutierrez firmly. Old familiar phrase, he'd been repeating it daily to Meg.

"I heard about that." Cass slouched across the room to hand a longnecked brown bottle to her uncle. "My boyfriend saw the story in the paper. He says you killed a kid."

Mary Louise's "Cass!" was shrill, but Gutierrez ignored her. "Jerry Dooley was nineteen years old," he told his niece in even tones. "When his sixteen-year-old girlfriend told him she didn't want to go out with him anymore, he went to her house with a pistol and killed her and her father and wounded her mother. I went in to try to talk with him, and when he shot me, I shot back."

"Oh." Cass's voice was small. "I'm sorry."

"So am I."

"Now that's enough from you, young lady," said Mary Louise. "You can just go to your room. I need to talk to your uncle."

"Bullshit. You're going to talk about me; I've got a right to hear what you say."

"Oh for God's sake! Vince, she makes me crazy! Remember how she was, what a nice little girl? The diving team, and gymnastics meets, and the honor roll? Then all of a sudden she's dressing like a slut, cutting school, riding around all the time with guys in cars."

"It's called puberty, Mom," drawled Cass. "The biology teacher told me all about it, and then he tried to get his hands on my boobs."

"Cassandra! You never told me!"

"Cass, you're out of line," said Gutierrez. Lightning rod, punching bag, he wasn't sure what his role was here, but his sister obviously had one in mind for him. "Look, Mary Louise, I don't have a lot of time; Meg is waiting for me at the campground and we want to get on the road early tomorrow. We've had this trip planned since last summer, to the Idaho panhandle, but for a while there it didn't look like we'd get to..."

With an impatient shake of her head Mary Louise broke in. "She's been in trouble for cutting school. She got picked up by the police for being drunk. She was spending all her time with a gang of absolute hoodlums, kids who were proud of having big brothers in jail."

"Did you consider sending her to her father?" Gutierrez meant Fred Hall, the stepfather who had adopted Cass when she was three.

"He doesn't want me. If he'd wanted me he'd have kept me," Cass said coldly.

"He wanted you, I just wouldn't leave you." Mary Louise's tone held a note of regret. "Now she has a new boyfriend, this rich Anglo kid and his..."

"*Anglo?* Come on, Mary Louise." The big plastic chair was sticky and vaguely hostile; if it tipped back he'd be helpless as a beetle, staring up at two angry female faces. Gutierrez got carefully to his feet and tilted his beer bottle for a long draught.

"Actually I thought he was an improvement at first, this Jonathan Archer. He dresses nicely, and he has good manners when he wants to use them. His father is an attorney and his mother's an artist; they have a lovely home out in Pinewood Estates. But he's not a nice person at all, he's just an animal, he and his friends are animals."

"You shut up...!" Cass began, then lapsed into sullen silence under her mother's furious glare.

"Sergeant Akins from Juvenile told me about them. These boys from wealthy families, they come down to a high school in the poor part of town, or even a junior high, and they pick up young girls"—Mary Louise set her splayed-out hands on either side of her head, as if to hold it together. "Vince, they give the girls presents and take them out in their nice cars and they make 'love' to them and then they turn them out, they turn them into whores, for the money. A little extra spending money for rich kids."

"Mother, this is a pile of shit and I'm not going to listen to any more." Cass turned on her heel and stamped out.

"I called Mr. Archer and told him to leave my daughter alone, to tell his kid to leave her alone. He said I should be careful about slander and hung up on me. And Jon...Vince, he scares me. I've told Cass she can't see him, but Friday night he forced his way in here, when I was getting things ready for a party. He pushed me out of the way"—she lifted the wing of hair at her left temple, and Gutierrez saw the purple-black edge of a bruise—"and he took Cass off on his big motorcycle, he made her go with him. That's when I called the police."

"Mary Louise..."

"In spite of what the whole family thinks of me, the other two are okay, my kids. Star is married, did you know that? She's in Nevada. And Gabriel is living with Fred and going to UCLA. Cass, she was the happiest baby and the funniest little kid, the smartest one. But see, I've messed her up some way. It's like she's running into the street and she doesn't hear me when I call her."

Mary Louise's eye makeup had run and smeared down her cheeks, making her look like the little girl who'd once again fallen afoul of older, meaner kids and needed her big brother to help her. Keep out of this, Vincent, he told himself. Your personal life is shaky but mending, your body is the same, you're a fifty-year-old man taking your first vacation in years...

His own voice echoed ominously in his ears. "Mary Louise, just what is it you want me to do?"

FOUR

You'd think an intelligent self-supporting forty-two-year-old woman would have better sense, Meg Halloran thought to herself Monday morning as she climbed up the trail from the campground showers. Better sense than to get involved with—*screw* that, fall in love with, or what the hell was she doing here? Fall in love with a policeman. Who got himself shot and damn near killed. And then turned out to be such a soft touch that he agreed to take a delinquent teenager on his vacation. Their vacation.

And here she is, hallelujah. Meg stopped in her tracks, to finish plaiting her damp hair into a single long braid and to gaze at campsite 47, at a girl so small that Vince Gutierrez, a compact five feet eleven, towered over her.

Gutierrez's niece wore narrow-legged black jeans and a bulky gray sweater with something like a loose white tank top over it. In the bright morning sunlight her spiky hair glowed orange, giving her head the look of a ragged chrysanthemum on the narrow stalk of her neck. The bony structure of her face was clean and forceful under unblemished pale-olive skin; paint her three shades darker, thought Meg, and the resemblance to her uncle would be startling.

As Meg's moccasinned feet moved from silent dirt to crunchy gravel, Gutierrez looked up with a grin. The girl swung around, and her casual slouch stiffened to an uncompromising T of rigid spine and squared shoulders. Add narrowed ice-gray eyes and tight lips, and you had a picture of pure adolescent hostility. Oh, Vince, said Meg silently, I'm not sure I can do this.

"Meg, this is Cass, Cassandra Hall," said Gutierrez in the cheerful tones of a used-car salesman. "Mary Louise was sorry, but she couldn't . . ."

"My mom couldn't wait around," Cass broke in. "But she said I should thank you. For having me."

She said you should, but I'll bet you're not going to, thought Meg, and waited a moment before saying, "Hello, Cass. I'm Margaret Halloran."

"So I guess you and Uncle Vince aren't married?"

"That's true," said Meg. "Not that it seems to make much difference."

Gutierrez winced; Cass looked mildly puzzled and then shrugged. "Uncle Vince says you're a teacher." The curl of her lip was clearly visible to Meg, but not to Gutierrez. "Do I have to call you Mrs. Halloran?"

"Not unless you want to. My friends call me Meg."

"Meg." Cass tasted the word, then shook her head. "Maybe I could call you Margaret?"

"You may."

"So that's settled." Gutierrez shifted his booted feet uneasily, sending up little puffs of red dust. "So. I guess we should get moving, it's almost nine o'clock. Cass, I don't know where we're going to put all this," he said as he eyed a small mountain of gear.

"I packed it tight as I could, okay? See, I had to bring all my stuff. My mom decides to move, she'll either forget it or give it away."

He ran a hand over his close-cropped grizzled hair. "Well. Okay, but I tell you what, we'll stop in town and buy you a nice new sleeping bag to replace that monster."

"No!" Cass sat down on the huge khaki bundle. "This is Fred's bag, from the Marines. I always use this bag."

"It can go in the back of the van," Meg said. "Something soft to lean against. Let's hit the road, friends, we're facing at least three days of hard driving."

NORTH OF DENVER a hard wind blew, slapping at the van like a heavy hand, tugging at the trailer. Meg switched on her headlights and hunched over the steering wheel, peering out into a shifting veil of dust. At one in the afternoon the sun was only a muted glare from somewhere above.

Gutierrez slept in the back, his soft snore audible now and then when the wind slackened. Cass slouched in the passenger seat, her eyes on the road or the side mirror, her hands cradling the third diet cola she'd opened since reformed-smoker Meg had vetoed cigarettes in the van. Meg cast a quick glance at the stony profile and sighed. Half-a-dozen defeated attempts at conversation and two direct confrontations, that was the sum of her short relationship with this angry child.

A pickup truck pulled past, swung close in front, and sped away, several small pale-haired children waving from the back. "Neat!" said Cass, waving back. "Jon really likes little kids; he says when we get married we'll have lots of kids."

"Mm," said Meg. Jon was the girl's sole topic of conversation...not conversation, really, just comment. Jon was blue-eyed and incredibly handsome. Jon loved motorcycles. Jon's parents kept big ugly dogs, but Jon preferred cats. Jon apparently had a nasty temper, too, as Vince's sister had claimed; earlier, when Cass was changing from her big sweater to a tee shirt, Meg had glimpsed fading bruises like bracelets high on the girl's upper arms. Big bruises, from big hard hands. "And what about you? Do you like kids?"

"Well. Sure. Sure I do." Cass sank back into her seat and took a mouthful of cola. "Uncle Vince says you have a kid, a girl named Katy."

"That's right."

"How come you didn't bring her? Does she spend summers with her father?"

"Her father is dead. He was killed in an accident five years ago." Maybe when the number was twenty she'd be able to say that without feeling her throat tighten. "Katy's at camp, a horse camp in California."

Cass wound her window down and tossed the soft-drink can out. "Jon says the only interesting thing about camp was all the fucking. That's what the counselors were really there for. How old is Katy, anyhow?"

"Twelve," said Meg through her teeth. She took a cassette from the box between the seats, shoved it into the tape deck, turned the volume high; moments later came a glorious blast of twelve-string guitar. "Please don't throw things out the window," she said loudly, "unless you can afford to pay the fine for littering."

AT NINE O'CLOCK that night Cass slipped out the door of the campground rest room and around the corner of the building to the telephone booth she'd noted earlier. She shut herself inside, closed her eyes for a moment of concentration, then punched out a lengthy sequence of numbers, ending with the four digits of Jon's credit card. The Archers' housekeeper, who had practically raised Jon, had her own telephone in her own cottage behind the big house. At this time of night she should be out there with her feet up, watching television.

"Yeah?"

"Doris? Hi, this is Cass."

"Cass. How you doing?"

"I'm fine. How's Jonny? Is he still around?"

"Nope. Jonny took off yesterday with a friend. The pair of them headed for the woods on their motorcycles. All he said, he won't forget about the party."

"That's good," said Cass. Jon's eighteenth birthday was next Monday, August 17; the big family celebration was planned for the following week, upon his mother's return from Europe. "Doris, please give him this message if he calls. Tell him I'm staying Monday night in this little town in Wyoming about fifty miles before Casper, it's called Douglas. Tomorrow night I'll be in Montana, probably someplace around Billings."

"Jonny told me you was going to California."

"Yeah, but first I have to go to Idaho, northern Idaho. Listen, if he should need to get in touch with me, we're in an old blue Chevy van, California license 39772X." She paused, then repeated the number. "And we're pulling a U-Haul tent trailer, one of those fold-down things."

"I'll tell him. And you have a good time, Cass, okay?"

"Yeah, okay. Thanks a lot, Doris. I'll talk to you again."

"SHE'S BEEN GONE quite a while," said Gutierrez uneasily. He was stretched out on one of the trailer's two beds, a glass of wine balanced on his flat belly.

Not long enough, thought Meg. "The average time an average teenager spends in a single shower is forty-seven and a half minutes," she told him.

He grinned briefly. "Well, hell, she agreed to come on this trip and promised not to run away. Mary Louise says that once Cass gives her word she keeps it."

"Mm," replied Meg, as she reached across the table for the bottle of California chardonnay.

"Yeah, I called Mary Louise while you were out walking. She says things are quiet in Colorado Springs, no trouble from Jon Archer. She says she feels like an enormous weight has been lifted from her shoulders."

Yes indeed, right onto mine. Meg said "Mm," again, and took a healthy mouthful of wine. Probably she should have brought a case of the stuff along, instead of half a dozen bottles. A supply of good booze might be very important on this trip; could you buy good wine in Idaho?

"Then I called Port Silva, talked to Svoboda," he went on quickly. "Turns out I missed some interesting stuff, a riot for one thing."

"Riot?" Meg sat up straighter. "Have the fishermen gone after those oil-exploration ships?"

Gutierrez shook his head. "Not yet. What happened, on Saturday night some farmers from out in the county, some of the old hippies and peaceniks, were having a picnic in the city park, families and all . . . just playing a little music and probably smoking a little grass, but discreetly."

"I can't imagine Hank's getting upset over something like that." Hank Svoboda, Gutierrez's second-in-command on the Port Silva police force, was a stolid middle-aged man with the patience of a tree and the same strength. Svoboda was not given to easy irritation.

"*Hank* didn't." Gutierrez sat up and held out his empty glass, a hopeful expression on his face. "Thanks," he said when Meg had filled it. "What happened was some very emotional Vietnam vets came out of the Palace after one of the heavier war movies and spotted the picnickers' old VW van with peace symbols all over it. After that I guess things got a little hairy, and several guys from each side spent a night in jail."

"How nice that you weren't there," said Meg.

"Yeah. I'd probably just have been in the way," Gutierrez replied glumly. "Hank says he still wonders why we'd want to go to Idaho. He says Idaho is famous for being full of kooks: religious nuts and tax protesters and all kinds of people who don't fit in anywhere else."

"We won't bother them," said Meg firmly, "and they won't bother us." She looked at her watch and sighed. "I was going to call Katy, but it's too late; I'll do it tomorrow. Vince, did I see a little tent in that pile of gear Cass brought?"

"Yes ma'am, you did. Why?"

"Because, love, I am feeling selfish and out-of-sorts and lonely for my daughter. I need you to convince me that I am in fact wonderful and lovable. Let's encourage Cass to sleep in her own tent."

FIVE

"BUSY PLACE," Ben Taylor remarked Wednesday afternoon to the girl who had introduced herself as Carla and offered to show him around the Shelter. Now a dusty path took them from the barn to the rear of the house and then around to the west side, where a pair of locust trees shaded a small playground. "Is one of those children Elizabeth's daughter?"

"Tessa? Nope, she's ... Eddie! You get your ass out of there!" Carla sped toward the sandpile in a flash of long skinny legs. "You leave those little girls alone, hear? Or I'll get me a switch." She plucked a scowling five-year-old boy from his tricycle, half-tossed him onto the grass, and sent his vehicle after him. As he scrambled back onto the trike and pedaled away, Carla distributed cursory brushes and pats to three indignant small girls. "Tessa and the other real little ones are likely in the bathtub now, getting ready for bed."

"Should you be running like that?" he asked, eyebrows high.

"You mean in my condition?" The girl's wide mouth stretched wider in a grin, and she patted her enormous belly. "This baby's made it real clear he's staying right where he is for the whole nine months."

"That's good," he murmured, and glanced at his watch. "It appears that Elizabeth runs a tight ship here. How do *you* get along with her?"

Carla shrugged. "Elizabeth's okay; she don't preach at us and she don't pray over us. Besides doing our work and staying clean, only extra is we gotta be polite and keep our heads down when one of the real preachers comes to visit."

"Because they come bringing money?"

"Right, sometimes they do. And since this place is kind of irregular, they could find some rule to shut it down if they wanted. Then there'd be a whole bunch of dumb women and sorry little kids on the street, or back with guys who beat on 'em.''

One of the children in the sandpile began to whine. Carla bent to pick her up, then turned and cocked her head. ''There's Elizabeth now; I can hear the bad lifter on that old wreck she drives. If you was planning to make a donation, mister, she could sure use a new car.''

ELIZABETH ROLLED her old green station wagon to a stop against the gate and sat there for a moment, eyes blank. The idling engine roughened, coughed; she sighed and slapped a hand against the horn button, two quick bleats.

A figure came around the corner of the house. She blinked, then drew her mouth tight. Ben Taylor wore new jeans, old boots, and a white shirt with rolled sleeves. His nose and high forehead were peeling from sunburn; even his forearms were pink. He waved at her, unlocked the gate and walked it back.

''Is something wrong?'' she asked as she moved slowly through. He cupped one hand behind his ear and shook his head. She rattled along the unpaved track that led behind the house, parked her wagon beside his Mercedes, and hurried back to meet him.

''No change with Michael,'' he said as he saw her face.

''Ah. But—Ben, you haven't mentioned me, or Shelter, or our plans?''

''Absolutely not, I swear!'' Solemn-faced, he lifted his right hand. ''I came down from Sweet's place to phone my message service: nothing. Then I bought myself a straw hat and some sunscreen. And *then* I decided that after three days of unrelieved male company it would be a real treat to talk with a lady. How are you, Elizabeth?''

''I'm fine,'' she told him wearily, and turned her steps toward the house.

''You don't look fine; you look worn out. Come on,'' he said softly, taking her arm and matching his stride to hers, ''let's go have a small nip in the study, a little Scotch for the soul's sake.''

"Oh . . . all right," she said on a long sigh. "Just see that I stop at one, or maybe two; this was a miserable day."

"A girl I talked to, Carla, told me you were out, um . . ."

" 'Whoring' is undoubtedly the way Carla put it. I prefer to call it fund-raising. Or maybe begging. Good evening, Margo," she called to a buxom brassy-haired woman who was shepherding three sleeper-clad toddlers toward the stairs at the end of the hall.

"Evening, Elizabeth. I'm on nursery duty tonight."

"I hadn't realized it was so late," Elizabeth remarked with a shake of her head. "Good night Elena, Lisa. Good night, Tessa."

The tiniest girl, Elena, merely ducked her curly black head. Honey-blond Lisa and towheaded Tessa said, "Night, Lis'bet," in one voice.

Ben's eyes followed the departing children as Elizabeth unlocked the study door. "Don't you . . . that is, don't the mothers want to be with their own kids?"

"It seems to work best if we handle the children in communal fashion," she told him. "Some of the mothers work outside. Occasionally one is in jail, or has fallen back into bad old habits, temporarily we hope. This way, no child gets short-changed. Don't look so horrified," she suggested, and closed the door. "We're not rigid about it; we're always ready to adjust to meet individual needs."

"Sounds like *Brave New World*," muttered Ben as he opened his little portable bar.

"More like *Walden Two*, actually." She sank into the nearest chair and let her hands fall limply into her lap.

"Here you go," said Ben. He handed her a glass and took a sip from his own. "Elizabeth, I hate to repeat myself, but you look beat."

"Comes the revolution," she said, and paused to drink, "I will be given what I need to work with. I will not have to let some fat dandruffy man of God rub up against me while we both pretend it's not happening. Real whoring would be cleaner."

Ben set his glass down and moved behind her chair. "Here, let me work on your neck."

"Don't do that," she said, but the words lacked force. He began to knead her shoulder muscles with long strong fingers, to work his thumbs in little circles up and down her neck.

"Just relax. Sip a little whisky and let it go. Lady, let your head hang down," he crooned.

"Comes the revolution and they banish lawyers, you can support yourself by giving massages," Elizabeth murmured, eyes closed. "Lord lord *lord* that feels good. If I drop off to sleep, just let me lie where I fall."

"Why don't you come keep me company first?" His voice was absent, as if all his concentration flowed to his fingers. "I've about had it with your basic camping out; I crave soft lights, and a tablecloth, and something on my plate besides eggs."

COEUR D'ALENE, IDAHO, a town of some twenty-five thousand people, is connected to ten-times-larger Spokane, Washington, by a thirty-five-mile stretch of busy Interstate Highway 90. The Tamarack Lodge, a few miles on the Washington side of the state line, had begun life as a roadhouse with cabins. A two-story motel had replaced the cabins; the roadhouse had its original bar, ceiling fans, and highbacked booths, a scattering of tables on the former dance floor, and a house specialty of prime rib. "Eat!" Ben advised his companion. "And drink. Nobody here is likely to recognize Sister Elizabeth."

She took a second and then a third sip from her vodka gimlet, and pulled her salad plate closer. "I'm so tired I forgot to ask. How is Sweet?"

Ben shook his head slightly, his eyes on the cocktail napkin he was pleating around the bottom of his glass. "Not good. He wouldn't talk about his health even to me, except to say that the pills mess up his head and make his hands shake. I think he's stopped taking them. He's got a stash of grass, probably grew it himself; that doesn't bother me much. But I found some empty bottles, bourbon and rum. Buddy...I like your little brother, seems to be a nice serious kid . . . Buddy is obviously too young to buy booze, and anyway he says he doesn't drink.''

"He doesn't." Elizabeth sat straighter and spat her words out like bits of ice. "And neither should Sweet. He *knows* that liquor is deadly to a chronic depressive.''

"He's thirty-six years old and a free man; he can do anything legal and lots of things that aren't." Ben drained his glass, and signaled to the waiter for another. "But I don't know how much longer he can stay out in the woods on his own. One of these days somebody—couple of local teenagers, hunters, *somebody*—is going to wander by, catch him at the wrong time, and he'll blow them away. Then what?

"Or there's the alternative, that he'll blow himself away," Ben added softly. "That's what I think about every time he goes quiet." The waiter set a fresh glass before him, and he picked it up at once. "Ah, well, according to the rumors I'm hearing, some developers want to put a fishing resort up there. So maybe I'll be able to sell his land for enough to keep him in a good private place.''

He looked up, caught her astonished gaze, and flushed. "Well, I'm a lawyer. *I* sure as hell can't make a living in the woods, and he hates city life. How about you, would you consider taking him in?''

She sat back quickly. "At Shelter? No!"

He spread his hands in a palms-up gesture: what can I say?

"Most of my women have spent their lives being kicked around by one man or another. I'm sorry, but I can't bring an emotional basket case like Sweet into their home. Besides, he wouldn't come, not to a place full of women.''

"Believe me, I understand," he told her. "Look, we don't have to solve this now. He's agreed to let me take him to see his doctor on Friday, and I'm hoping the man can prescribe something different and give Sweet a pep talk about staying on medication. I'll tell Buddy what to watch for and what to do if things go bad. Then you and I and your little Tessa will take off Saturday morning for the coast to see Michael. Okay?''

Elizabeth pulled her elbows close to her body to contain a visible shudder. The waiter appeared and dealt a large platter to her and its duplicate to Ben. "Fresh horseradish," he told them, setting down a small bowl, "and a carafe of the house red. You want anything else?"

"Michael was...*is* a vegetarian," Elizabeth said when the waiter had left them.

"I know."

"I always felt guilty when I ate something like this, as if I were some kind of savage." She cut into the deep-pink slab of meat and put a chunk in her mouth.

"I don't think he wanted you to feel that way."

"No." She swallowed the meat and cut another piece. "Michael was never a sensual person. Oh, he was full of love. He loved forests, and mountains, and the sea. He loved working with his hands, or being out in the weather. I guess he loved people; certainly he could give a person such a great warm blast of total attention that whoever it was loved *him* forever after."

"Yeah."

"But physical indulgence didn't move him much. Not food, or grass, or sex. Necessary things, but not truly exciting."

"I know."

"Do you?" she murmured; she cut another piece of meat, put it into her mouth, chewed slowly.

"We've talked about it before."

"I suppose we have. I suppose I forget, or repress, the times I was less than loyal to Michael." She swirled red wine in its tall glass, and took a deep gulp. "The NO-VACANCY sign wasn't on when we arrived. We can probably get a room, don't you think?"

SIX

AT TEN O'CLOCK or close to it on Thursday night, Meg Halloran made a slight adjustment to the angle of her seat, sighed, and reminded herself that the day's journey was nearly over. She had made it safely through the hazards of the long summer twilight, surviving a drowsy spell with the help of coffee from her thermos bottle; now Coeur d'Alene, Idaho, was only minutes ahead, Coeur d'Alene and the junction of Interstate 90 with US 95 north.

Traffic was light and well-behaved, demanding only the edge of her attention. About to reach for a cassette tape, she changed her mind; with the others asleep, even the scrawny, flea-ridden kitten that Cass had found or perhaps stolen in Billings, Montana, Meg might have been out here in this lovely quiet world all alone. Peace and quiet, something she'd had very little of during the four days it had taken them to travel from Colorado Springs.

Hang in there, Maggie, she told herself once again. A grown woman shouldn't fight with a sixteen-year-old, 'tain't fittin'. Maybe you counted wrong and she didn't take a ten from your wallet; maybe the extra set of keys did fall out of your bag instead of being lifted, and anyway when you noticed they were missing she gave them back.

Another sigh: soon she'd be wringing her hands like some Victorian lady. The girl *was* being sweet to her uncle, who was loving it. Farragut State Park, where they would camp through the weekend, was a big place, room to spread out. And Priest Lake, their ultimate destination, was real north woods, practically within shouting distance of the Canadian border. Perhaps Cass would get carried off by a grizzly. No, no; make that a Mountie.

There was the sign for the junction. Meg slowed, made allowance for the silent and nearly invisible trailer she was pulling, and accomplished the turn neatly, waking neither of her companions. Big bright traffic lights, stores and gas stations claimed the landscape for a brief mile or two; then open space and the night took over, blackness eased by countless stars and a low moon not quite half full.

She rolled her window a little lower and settled her heavy wool cardigan more closely around her shoulders. The wind on her face was cool and sweet with the hint of hay, no taste there of cities. Maybe another half hour to Farragut, a few minutes spent setting up the trailer, and then she'd have a shower and a drink. She'd bought a 1.5 liter bottle of Bombay in Butte, the last one in the small liquor store and very dusty too. Probably no Bombay gin to be found up here, just clean air and big fish and beer.

Good reflexes brought her foot to the brake pedal before she realized what was happening, as she was still trying to read what she saw. Some distance ahead, on the other half of this divided and at the moment nearly empty highway, lights were doing something odd, tipping up and down, swinging from side to side. Headlights, and behind them, smaller lights outlining a long high shape. A truck?

No, closer now and she could see that it was a sedan or station wagon pulling a travel trailer. A tire had blown, or a driver fallen asleep: somebody had better get that thing under control.

The cones of light swung wide away, swung back. Another set of headlights appeared, something frantically trying to get past trouble. Didn't make it; she thought the trailer clipped it, thought she saw lights flash skyward and a dark smaller vehicle fly into the broad grassy center strip. Then a blinding glare hit her windshield as the station wagon swung left and came lurching across the grass, slapped forward by the almost lazy side-to-side swipes of the fishtailing trailer. Aimed at the northbound lanes, at some convergence point right ahead.

She stood on the brake with both feet, jerked the wheel to her left. God, she had no idea what was behind her, who she might be cutting off! She heard Cass scream, heard Gutierrez yelp, heard a thud as he hit something, the dashboard or the door. The bottom of the travel trailer was right in front of her now, wheels and axles, pipes and dark rectangles; and she could hear things breaking inside, objects crashing about. Her brakes weren't going to be enough, she had to make one more sharp lunge left and around.

She was on a grassy slope and felt the van tilt, knew its right wheels had left the ground. Then it settled back with a fat squishy shudder and a thump from the trailer, their own trailer; she thought it might have stopped the roll and kept them from going over.

"Vince?" She turned off the engine, opened the door to bring on the overhead light. "Oh, Vince, I'm sorry, I'm so sorry. Are you hurt?"

"That was a goddamned good job of driving, lady," he said through his teeth. Blood trickled down his forehead, and he had his left hand tucked against his right shoulder as if to hold something in place.

"Here, let me . . ."

"Never mind," he snapped, and took a deep breath. "I'm okay, nothing serious. Get out and see what you can do; I think somebody got thrown from that other car. But turn on the C.B. before you go, and hand me the mike."

She obeyed, then slid from the van's high seat to the ground. They were perhaps fifty yards beyond the point where wagon and trailer had doubled back across the road to block both north-bound lanes. Headlights from several cars limned that scene, and people swarmed over and around, their voices an excited babble. Meg reached behind the seat for her lantern flashlight, and found Cass at her elbow.

"I just yelled because I was surprised," the girl declared. "I had first aid at the Red Cross last winter, CPR and everything."

"Fine," Meg said, and handed her the lantern. Back-lit by the van's headlamps, they jogged along the center of the grassy trough which was the divider strip, toward a single light glimmering through a swirl of dust. "On its wheels!" said Meg in astonishment as she caught the shape of a squarish dark sedan.

As Cass shined their lantern on the car, the driver's door opened with a screech and a tall narrow man eased himself out, holding first to the upper edge of the frame, then to the door itself.

No interior light, it must have failed in the impact like the headlight; but the engine still ran, a fact which made Meg uneasy. "Is anyone hurt?" she asked. "You should probably..."

"I'll be all right in a minute. As soon as I can breathe," he added, fanning a hand at the dust-laden air. "God-damned farmer in that wagon, I'll sue his ass, this Merc is worth... Hey! Get out of there, what the hell do you think you're doing?"

"Taking reasonable precautions!" she snapped, and handed him the keys she had removed from the ignition as she turned it off. "Just a moment, I'll help you." These words she directed into the car's interior, where a silent figure in the passenger seat seemed to be struggling with door or perhaps seat belt.

"Oh, yeah. You okay, Elizabeth? Son of a bitch," the driver muttered as he followed Meg around the vehicle, one hand on the hood for balance. "Shit, look at that, and this machine was cherry!"

The rear door on this side was ajar, Meg noted with a chill of apprehension as she grasped the handle of the front door and pulled. "Are you all right? Do you need help?"

"Aah, no. Thank you." There was a rasp and click, the retracting seat belt. She swung her legs out first, and then stood, a tall woman with thick light hair loose around a pale face. She took a step away from the car and stopped, widened her stance and put a hand to her head.

"We've called for help," Meg said quickly. "The highway patrol, or whatever it's called in Idaho, should be here soon, but we thought... was there anyone else?"

The woman brushed a hand across her eyes, straightened, and turned back to the car. "Tessa."

"Meg!" It was a high wail, thin-edged with terror. "Meg, come here right now!"

Cass's voice came from the far side of the grassy trough, where light from her lantern glimmered through a stretch of tall weeds. "Meg!" she cried again, and Meg went from fast trot to all-out run.

"Meg, oh Meg, I think she's dead!"

A small child lay on its back, arms flung wide, head slightly turned. The round forehead was unmarked, the eyes almost closed, just a glint of white showing beneath the lashes. Curly hair so fair as to look white in the poor light was rumpled and pricked with bits of dry grass, but Meg could see no blood.

"Cass, I don't...I think I saw her chest move, I think she's breathing." Was she saying it because she believed it, or to reassure Cass? She pulled off her sweater and dropped it over the small body, tucking it around.

Hurrying feet sounded behind her, and she stood up. "We've found...your child? She's unconscious, and I think we should wait for medical assistance before moving her."

The woman brushed past and knelt. Distant voices, the rumble of a passing car, Cass's whimper, even the pounding of her own heart: all sounds seemed to suspend themselves and Meg held her breath to watch the utter stillness before her, the bent unmoving head and straight back. Then the kneeling woman drew a long breath and leaned forward. She cupped the child's head gently, drew her fingers along temples and jaw and neck; she slid one hand beneath the sweater to rest it on the chest. Then in one swift flow of motion she bent further and scooped the little girl into her arms.

So much for proper first-aid behavior, thought Meg. "I saw a hospital sign in Coeur d'Alene; I'd be happy to take you there," she offered, and then thought guiltily of Gutierrez and his injuries. "In fact, we're going there anyway."

"No need, I'm a nurse," the woman announced, and stood up with little effort.

"Oh Jesus." The man stumbled as he reached them, fell to one knee but quickly regained his footing. "Jesus. I forgot. Oh, Christ, Sweet must not have closed the door tight, you have to bang it. Elizabeth?"

She shifted her grip to cradle the child closer against her breasts. "It's all right, she's just unconscious."

"Sure. Little kids, they're made of rubber." His words came in a whoosh of relief.

"She's beginning to stir already," the woman assured him, and turned to Meg. "Thank you for your help. We'll stop at the hospital and have her looked at. But I'm sure she'll be fine. Ben, are you able to drive?"

"Drive? Oh. Sure, I'm in good shape. Let's get out of here."

"Oh, wait!" Meg called after a moment, but they must have lost her words in the slam of the car doors, the roar of the engine. She snatched up the lantern and stepped forward, waving; the car swung past her, climbed the grassy bank and set off to the north. "Damn it, that's my best sweater," she said to empty air.

A choking sound from nearby swung her around. "Cass?"

The girl was on hands and knees in the lantern light, fluid spewing from her mouth. She arched her back, gagged once more, then simply let her head hang. "It's all *right*," she mumbled as Meg bent over her. "Only I never..."

She sat back on her heels, spat, wiped her mouth with the back of one hand. "See, I really thought for a minute she was dead. I never saw anyone dead before."

SEVEN

AN IMPATIENT GUTIERREZ had tried to follow their progress from within the darkened van. "Anyone hurt?" he demanded. "I could see people moving, a man and then a woman, but I couldn't tell what was happening."

"It was a child who was thrown out, a little girl two or three years old," Meg replied as she climbed in beside him. "She was unconscious when we found her, but the woman, her mother, is a nurse and says it's not serious. Vince, what about you?" The bleeding, apparently from a cut in his scalp, had stopped, but he sat carefully, stiffly still, and his face was shiny with sweat.

"My own fault," he told her glumly. "Shoulder belt was hurting my ribs, so I took it off. Bam. Stupid." He blew a long, disgusted breath through pursed lips. "Shit, I guess I'd better see a doctor."

"Shall we wait for an ambulance?"

"Last ambulance I was in, I'd have been better off in a dump-truck. No, I'll crawl in the back and lie down against the sleeping bag."

They got him into the rear of the van, and Cass stayed beside him while Meg eased vehicle and trailer back onto the highway and headed north. "There may be a hospital in Sandpoint," she said over her shoulder, "but Coeur d'Alene is a safer bet."

She checked her mirrors, seeing only the lights of her own trailer close behind. Well back, at the scene of the pileup, one set of headlights separated from the general glare, and then another, as northbound travelers began to edge past the blockage. She gave a moment's unfriendly thought to the driver of the station wagon; then she dismissed him and strained her ears to listen to Vince's breathing, to try to read the degree of pain there. Darkness ahead, except for a few scattered lights, dwellings probably. Her headlights caught a car off on the right shoulder, dark and squarish.

"Aha!" The sign was on the left:

NO TURNING,
AUTHORIZED VEHICLES ONLY.

"I authorize myself," she said, and she drove across to the southbound lanes.

BIG BLUE SIGN with a capital H, and then just beyond the junction she said "Aha" once again, quietly. She'd tossed it an absent glance on their first pass, the large well-lighted building set in a big parking lot. Hospital, yes; and an arrow pointing toward the emergency entrance. She turned carefully off the highway, drove halfway around the building and pulled in beside an ambulance.

"Hey, lady, you can't park there with a trailer! Nobody could get by."

"I'll be happy to move," Meg told the white-coated man, "just as soon as you get us a stretcher or a wheelchair."

A wheelchair arrived in moments; ten minutes later Meg found chair and occupant in X-RAY.

"Have you seen the doctor?" she asked Gutierrez, whose face was greenish and weary under bright fluorescent lights.

"Yes ma'am, for about thirty seconds. Soon as they put my pictures in a folder I'll see him again."

Another white-coated person came through a swinging door and dropped a folder in Gutierrez's lap. "There you go now, doctor's waiting."

"What is this, self-service?" snapped Meg, and stepped behind the chair. "Which way, Vince?"

"Back down that long, long hall. Cass knows the way," he added, and the girl rose from a plastic chair, rubbing her eyes.

Gutierrez had a scalp wound, too small to need suturing. He had a lump on his forehead, no evidence of concussion. He had wrenched and bruised ribs, new and old. He had a broken collarbone.

"Travel? You mean in a car?" Dr. Wu rose thoughtfully on his toes, then let the heels of his Adidas hit the floor. "No. No, that would be foolish, and uncomfortable." He put his flashlight back in the pocket of his white coat and leaned his tall frame against the doorjamb. "And we can't be sure, yet, that there isn't some slow internal bleeding from your previous injury. No, Mr. Gutierrez, you should stay right where you are for at least two or three days."

"No." Muscles jumped in Gutierrez's cheek as he set his jaw. "No more hospital time. I'm going home, tomorrow."

Dr. Wu frowned, and did his levitation act again. "Well. Perhaps by air. As direct a flight as possible, and a check with your own doctor, and then several days in bed at home, with good nursing." He bobbed his head in Meg's direction, appointing her good nurse. "I will see you in the morning. Mrs. Gutierrez, there's a clean and inexpensive motel just down the street; you and your daughter would be more comfortable there than in our waiting room."

As the door closed, Gutierrez leaned his head back and closed his eyes, clenched them shut. Not in pain, Meg decided, but to prevent tears from spilling, tears of frustration and spoiled possibilities.

"Priest Lake next year, love," she murmured. "Tomorrow I'll put you and Cass on a plane for California, where it will be cool and foggy and wonderful; and I'll turn the trailer in and head for home. Cass can take care of you for the, what, three days the trip will take me."

"No!" Not Gutierrez this time, but Cass, lips stretched thin in her pale, dirt-streaked face. "No. What about my stuff? What about my cat? *You* go with Uncle Vince to take care of him, and I'll drive your van to California."

Meg stared at her, and she pushed her hands deep into the pocket of her jeans, hunching her shoulders. "I know I've only got a learner's permit, but I'm a good driver, I drive all the time. My mom's car, even Jon's dad's car with a stick shift; I drove that all the way to Denver once, on the freeway."

For perhaps five seconds Meg considered this plan, herself and Vince on a nice plane together hand in hand. Then reality intruded, first in the ghostly person of her insurance agent gnashing his teeth, and then in the voice of Vince Gutierrez. "Absolutely not."

"No," agreed Meg regretfully. "I'll bring all your belongings, Cass, I promise. And I will cope with the cat. Unless you'd rather have him fly with you; I'm sure that could be arranged."

"Cass," said Gutierrez, "I'd like to talk to Meg alone. Why don't you go down to the waiting room and find a Coke machine?"

The girl was out the door before he'd finished speaking.

"Vince," Meg began, "I do not want..."

"Lady, lady. Please."

She closed her mouth and bit down on her lips to keep them shut.

"Meg, you know how I feel about airplanes?"

"I picked you up at the airport a few days ago, remember? It took you half an hour to unclench your teeth. I still think that if you'll simply have a drink or two as soon as they bring the cart along..."

"I'd rather be just terrified than drunk and terrified," he said grimly. "Look, I fly when I have to, but my whole family hates it. Maybe it's genetic; more likely it's because Papa died in a plane crash when we were kids. Anyway, I know for sure that no prize in this world or the next would get Mary Louise into an airplane, and I guess Cass feels the same way."

"It's time she got over it. Maybe the doctor can prescribe a tranquilizer."

"Meg, I won't need her on the plane; I'll throw myself on the mercy of the stewardesses." He tried a quick grin. "And I can get help at home. Svoboda will pick me up and I'll stay with him if necessary."

He watched her for a moment. "I know, you hate it. But please do it. I'll feel better that you're not alone. And you'll make better time, get home to me faster, with somebody to spell you at the wheel. Which Cass can do legally, in the company of an adult.''

It was a curse, Meg decided, and there was no way for her to escape it. As punishment for past sins or just at the whim of some malevolent god, she was condemned to spend three days in the sole company of that pint-sized adolescent virago. Maybe two and a half days, if she drove fast.

She closed her eyes and took a deep breath. ''Okay.'' Then she remembered a notion that had crossed her mind earlier. ''Vince, what about Jon? Cass's Jon. Today I was watching her *watch*; she does it constantly. It occurred to me that she might be expecting him to turn up.''

He opened his mouth, closed it again. ''Okay. Possible. And here's what you do. If it happens, let her go with him. You couldn't stop it anyway; he's a big guy and he might hurt you if you tried to interfere. Just let her go.''

Meg remembered the bruises on the girl's arms. ''He might hurt *her*.''

''If he does, the responsibility is at least partly her own,'' Gutierrez said. ''Meg. Promise me.''

''Oh...all right, yessir Mr. Policeman. I promise. I also promise not to leave you to the mercy of nurses tonight. Presumably this place has nurses?'' She stood up and stretched. ''I'm going to order up a cot or one of those sleeping chairs and spend the night on the scene, the way I did when Katy had her tonsils out.''

''And I'll sleep in the van,'' said Cass from the doorway. ''There's lots of lights in the parking lot and even a guard.''

''Fine,'' said Meg before Gutierrez could get his mouth open.

''ALL SET,'' Meg said breathlessly to Gutierrez at something after eleven o'clock the next morning. She dropped into the bedside chair and stretched her legs out.

''You look pretty good for someone who slept in a chair. Or didn't sleep.''

''I slept enough,'' she told him. ''And I am really looking forward to getting home, by whatever means.''

He grinned at her. His color was nearly normal and his posture easier, as if he'd stopped fighting the device the doctor had called a clavicle splint. "Me too. Screw Idaho."

"Right. So, I found the U-Haul place and turned the trailer in. The people there were agreeable enough once they got over wondering how we'd lost so much kitchen gear from their trailer in only six days. Skillet, couple of pans, stuff like that," she added in response to his raised eyebrows. "We must have left something in every campground along the way. And whoever found the stuff is very lucky, because every item was apparently made of gold."

"Probably Cass or me, sloppy cleanup. Did you see Cass? She was here a few minutes ago."

"I ran into her in the hall and sent her out to the van to stow things for travel, all that gear of hers that was in the trailer. Okay, on to travel plans. You have a flight to San Francisco leaving Coeur d'Alene at three this afternoon, and a connecter to Port Silva where Svoboda will meet you."

"Thank you, ma'am."

"You'll get my bill. Now, as soon as Cass has finished, I'll gas up, buy provisions, that sort of thing. We'll go have lunch . . . in fact we'll bring lunch here, that's a better idea. And then about, oh, two P.M. we'll borrow a wheelchair and roll you out."

"No," he said, reinforcing the word with a shake of his head.

"No?"

"I'll get a cab."

"Vince, I want to take you to the airport."

"No ma'am. You'll be long gone by then, on the road, no hanging around here wasting time. Meg, I'll need you more at home than I do here. I'd like you to do most of your driving in daylight, and call me every night like you did when you drove to the conference. Check into a motel and fix a drink and call me."

"Shit. Gutierrez, I hate this," she muttered.

"Me too. Would you please come around to the left side of the bed and sit close to me for a few minutes, maybe hold hands? Not only is this a completely screwed-up vacation; I have to end it by getting on another fucking airplane.''

"Poor baby," she said, and eased herself onto the bed beside him.

MEG STEPPED OUT the back door of the hospital and stood for a moment blinking in the sunlight. There was a Shell station just down the road, with a supermarket next door. If they were on the road by noon, they could get in seven or eight hours of driving before dark. Maybe more.

"Oops! Pardon me." Dr. Wu had brushed against her as he came quickly out the door. A blush warming his ivory skin, he held up the cigarette he had just lighted. "Filthy habit, I'm trying to give it up."

"Good luck," she said, "and thanks for your help." She nodded a polite good-bye and set off past several crowded rows of cars toward the nearly empty far reaches of the parking lot. There was the van, but Cass was nowhere in sight. Perhaps she'd gone for a walk, taken her kitten out for some air. The van itself could use a good airing; Meg added kitty litter to her mental shopping list.

There was a vehicle parked to the left of the van now...parked unnecessarily close, thought Meg with mild irritation. It was an old no-color pickup truck with a hand-made camper in its bed. Tall for a camper, with a gently sloped roof, the structure was covered with brown shingles and had small round windows like portholes in a boat.

As she stepped into the narrow space between the two ve-hicles, the door of the truck opened and a man slid out, a man who must have been six and a half feet tall. He wore lug-soled boots, dirty jeans, and a blue-plaid flannel shirt under a stained sheepskin jacket. His face was gaunt, with patches of bunched and shiny skin along the left side; his shoulders looked bony even under the jacket, but very wide.

"I beg your pardon..."

"Mrs. Halloran?"

"What? Yes, I'm Mrs. Halloran." That's odd, noted a corner of her mind; everyone here had called her Mrs. Gu-tierrez, a mistake she hadn't bothered to correct.

"I'm sorry to bring bad news," he said softly, dark-brown eyes squinting down at her. "But it's your daughter."

"My...?" Meg felt her throat close. She put a hand over her mouth, then tried again. "My daughter? Katy?"

"Sorry, ma'am, but if you'd just come around here..."

He took her elbow and propelled her to the back of the vehicle, keeping his hold on her as he reached up to pull the door open.

"You've brought Katy here?" He must be from the horse camp, he looked like a horse person. But how had they found her, Meg?

The little camper was dark inside, as if the windows were covered. No light, and no movement... then a soft thump. "Katy?" Meg set her feet, turned and tried to pull her arm free. "What is this? What have you done to my daughter?"

He gripped both her elbows and lifted her up the two steps into the darkness. "Hey!" The door snicked shut, and she had her mouth open to yell again as something thick and woolly enveloped her head and shoulders.

He grabbed her wrists and pulled them together behind her back, to hold them in a single hard grip. "Just stay still now, hear? Or I'll have to hurt you, I got no reason to hurt you yet. Stay still!" He yanked her shirt loose from the waistband of her jeans and laid something cold against her skin. Took it away, and then there was a sharp point of pain, and a warm trickle of blood.

"Keep quiet or I'll stick you good. And your kid too, I'll cut her throat for her." He pushed Meg to her knees, shoved her flat, and whipped a cord of some kind around her wrists, then pushed her forward on her belly, grabbed her ankles and bound them. The blanket smelled foul and was greasy against her face. She twisted her head, trying to get her mouth clear of the woolly fabric, and there was another prick from the knife.

"I said stay quiet!" he snapped, and rolled her onto her back.

Don't struggle, she told herself silently, but her body disobeyed and tried to thrash itself free. His openhanded blow

knocked her head against something hard, and it was
through ringing ears that she heard him moving around
nearby. Then he was back, behind her, lifting her and
propping her against his legs, pulling the blanket away.
"Open your mouth." When she pressed her lips tight instead, he set a long hand across her lower face and squeezed.
"That's better. Got some little pills here, make you sleep."

The pills were dry, uncoated. She fumbled them with her
tongue and tried to push them out.

He brought the back of his hand up hard against her chin.
"Quit that. Now, here's water. Swallow nice, if you don't
want to drown."

She swallowed, gagged, got more water and had to swallow again. He held her mouth closed for a moment, strok-
ing her throat as if she were a dog he'd just medicated.

"Good, good girl." He let her drop and rolled her onto
her belly, enveloped her head and shoulders in the blanket
once again and shoved something up beside her, a chest or
box of some kind, wedging her in place. "Now you just lay
here and we'll get on the road. Be a little bumpy back here,
but that ain't gonna bother you for long." She felt him rise
and move away from her. "Door locks from the outside, all
the windows are covered. You yell, I'm the only one'll hear
you and I'll come back with the knife."

The truck creaked as he moved, rocked as he descended
the steps, lifted as his weight was gone. The door slammed,
and after a moment there were low voices in a quick exchange of words she was unable to make out. Another door
slammed, rocking the truck. Then a sliding door, the bastards were in her van. Engine sound, silky smooth with the
nice clean carburetor and new plugs she'd put in herself before leaving California. The camper shuddered as the truck's
engine fired, caught, and died. The starter rasped and
whined, and finally the engine caught again and settled into
a rattly wheeze.

The truck backed abruptly, swung wide, lurched forward; she concentrated all her strength on trying not to slide
around. Where was Katy? Was she here in this smelly, rattling darkness? Meg thought she had a sense of another

presence; now and then, when the truck changed notes for a gear shift, it seemed she heard breathing. Gagged, perhaps, and probably doped as well. "Katy, hang on," she whispered.

Sometime later a bump or a pothole sent her hard against the forward wall, where her head struck something smooth and yielding, familiar: her handbag. She pillowed her cheek on it gratefully. Bag. Keys. He hadn't...she was growing fuzzy, couldn't get her thoughts to track. He hadn't taken time to search her purse, to find the extra keys. But her van...keys...

She'd given the keys to Cass. Meg's surge of relief was so powerful it was nearly orgasmic. They didn't have Katy, they had Cass.

EIGHT

"HERE, WANT THE HEAD UP?" Hank Svoboda touched a button, and the bed said "hmmm" in a businesslike electric way.

"What the...goddammit, Hank, if I'd wanted to go to the fucking hospital...Sorry," Gutierrez muttered as he eased his aching shoulders back against two fat pillows. The hospital bed wasn't something brought in just for him, he had realized belatedly. Less than a year had passed since Svoboda's wife lost her long, mean battle with cancer.

"It's a good bed," Svoboda said, reading his thoughts. "Last bed we shared; Ellie and me used to crank it up like that and watch TV."

"Ah." Gutierrez took the steaming mug Svoboda was holding out to him. The roomy old Victorian house had been full of noisy life in the past: the three daughters and their boyfriends, then grandchildren, always a dog or two, and several cats. Now there was just a kind of dusty silence. It occurred to him that his last visit here was a long time ago; he'd been too deeply immersed in his own life with Meg and Katy. "Thanks, old buddy. For picking me up at the airport, for the bed." He took a cautious sip and grinned. "And for whatever this is."

"Rum toddy."

"Ah," Gutierrez said again, and had another sip. "Maybe I'll get a bottle and spend the next couple of days sitting on my porch. Drink some rum and watch the boats while I wait for Meg." He gave a thought to his nice little house on its hill overlooking the Pacific, and wondered why he'd wanted to go traveling in the first place. "So. What's been going on around here?"

"Nothing me and the boys can't handle," Svoboda replied as he settled into a characteristic pose: shoulder against

the doorframe, one booted foot propped across the other.
"Let's see. Four kids, tourists, took Daddy's shiny new
twenty-seven-foot cabin cruiser for a spin around the fishing boats, cut a full net off the *Me Two*. I had to lock up
Johnny Duarte and one of his cousins for the night, before
they put all four kids in the hospital. Damned hot-blooded
Portagees."

"Hard-working Portagees," murmured Gutierrez.

"Yeah, that too." Svoboda paused for a sip of his toddy.
"Then the mayor wants a couple officers at the city council
meeting next week. He won't say, but what I think, the
council's gonna overrule the planning commission and let
the new owners of River's End take out some live oaks and
put up a bunch of condos in that pasture the other side of
the highway."

"Well, shit," said Gutierrez. "Here we go again, cham-
ber of commerce in one trench and Earth First! in the other,
you and me in the middle. Speaking of middles, has there
been any more trouble with the vets and the old hippies?"

"Nope, that all petered out for kind of a sad reason.
Don't know if you ever heard of a antiwar activist named
Tannenbaum, that shot a cop in Berkeley some years
back?"

"Yeah, sure, Michael Tannenbaum. When I was at Cal
in '68-'69, he was one of the leaders of the antiwar pro-
tests. The shooting was late 1970, I think; I was back with
LAPD by then."

"Well, he turned himself in a while back and pleaded
guilty. Guy's got leukemia, one of the papers ran a big story
a few days ago that as much as said he was dying." Svoboda shifted his feet and took a big gulp from his coffee
mug. "So what happened here, the hippies got together a
caravan and went off with kids and dogs and everything to
join in a vigil for Tannenbaum, down at CliffHaven where
he's staying with his mama. Whole bunch of folks are
camping on some national forest land right across the road
from the place, probably got the private guards there real
nervous."

"Better them than us," Gutierrez muttered. "That's in the county, though; Sheriff Roncalli will probably want to borrow some people if things get hot." He shifted position, craning his neck to look at the bedside telephone. "Is that thing plugged in?"

"Surely is."

"It's past ten o'clock. Meg should have called by now. Anything else I need to know about?" he went on quickly.

"Val Kuisma got his heart broke again. He's moping around like an old hounddog, offering to pull guys' graveyard shifts since he's got nothing better to do nights. And Al Jenkel..."

"Well?" Jenkel was the only homosexual on the Port Silva force. Or the only one he knew of, Gutierrez corrected himself. "What about Al?"

"He's been taking a lot of sick leave. Some asshole started the story around that he's got AIDS." Svoboda's big weathered face took on a hard edge.

"Shit. Has he?"

"He says not. Says it's a persistent kidney infection. I believe him."

"Any idea who...no, never mind. I'll work on it. Say, Hank. Maybe we should call my house, just to make sure the answering machine is working."

"It was working fine an hour ago. Maybe we should have some more of this stuff." He took both cups away, and brought them back steaming.

"Whooee. I can smell the rum this time." Gutierrez cradled the mug in his hands and inhaled deeply. "Goddamn it, she knows I expect her to call."

"Does she now." Svoboda's voice was noncommittal.

"Sure she does. Practically the last thing I said to her was 'Call me every night.'"

"Might be Meg is tired of people named Gutierrez. Any daughter of Mary Louise could probably wear a person down real fast," added Svoboda, who had lived in Port Silva all his life. "You never made a dent in your sister, all those years. What makes you think you can straighten her kid out?"

"I don't," Gutierrez protested. "The idea was a change of scene, a chance for her to get out of the hole she's digging for herself. Unlike Mary Louise, Cass is smart. And she's only sixteen, for Christ's sake."

"Yeah," said Svoboda. "Well. How did Meg's conference go? That she went to Colorado for?"

"'A Week in Dickens' World,' I think it was," Gutierrez said, and frowned. "It was okay, I guess."

"You don't mind my saying so, Vince, you can sure be a self-centered son of a bitch."

"Look, buddy, we were...the day I got there we were just glad to see each other. Then I went to my sister's, and this thing with Cass came up."

"Sounds like a real nice vacation for Meg."

"Meg didn't..." mind, he was going to say, and then thought better of it.

"Lady's scared about to death when you get shot, I saw her that day. She takes care of you while you recover, probably about as much fun as sharing a cave with a grizzly. Then you off-load a messed-up kid on her. I tell you what, Vince." Svoboda straightened, stretched, and grinned. "When Meg gets back, I believe I'll let her know there's other lonesome single fellows around. Take me, I'm only five years older than you. Got all my own teeth, most of my hair. Plus I'm easy, real easy."

"Watch it, you old bastard. This is your boss you're talking to." Gutierrez returned his grin briefly, then turned again to look at the telephone. "You know, it would be easy enough to call the state police in, well, probably not Idaho. Probably Washington. Just to make sure she hasn't been in an accident."

"What it is, she drove as late as she could and then got to a motel and went right to sleep. Come on, Vince. She's a grownup lady been taking care of herself for a long time."

"Yeah, and I'll bet you were right the first time," Gutierrez muttered, and drained his mug. "She probably just doesn't feel like talking to me."

NINE

HARD MATTRESS. New foam, she remembered the man at U-Haul saying that. He lied, she thought now in sleepy irritation, and shrugged deeper beneath the blanket. Cold. Lonesome, Vince must have moved back to the other bed because his shoulder...

She pried her heavy lids open, peered into dimness, saw pale rays from somewhere high. No pillow under her cheek, just harsh taut fabric. The hand she edged forward found a solid rim and then emptiness. A cot, a canvas cot, and no sheets, just a rough thick blanket with a disagreeable smell.

She remembered the blanket, and the man, and the camper. On a whine of indrawn breath she pulled herself into a huddled ball, and was surprised to find that her limbs were free. A dream? No, there was the proof of her memory, in the chafed red line around her left wrist, around both wrists. She still wore the red-checked shirt she'd put on...yesterday? And jeans. Socks. Sneakers.

Meg pushed the blanket off and lifted her head to look around. She was in a small room, maybe ten by ten, with unfinished walls and ceiling. Wooden door, closed tight. No real windows, just a narrow screened vent near the ceiling of the adjacent wall and—she rolled to look over her shoulder—and another in the wall behind the cot she lay on. A corner room.

She squeezed her eyes tight shut and tried to remember. The camper, rough ride, sleep. She'd come half-awake, slowly, sick at her stomach and afraid she might vomit. Realized that the truck was no longer moving. Later, hours later, she'd begun to drum her feet and call out. Long, long after that came the sound of the door and then a man's voice.

She'd been desperate for a bathroom, begging him to free her. He'd pulled her roughly across the floor, untied her feet, lifted her out. When he took the blanket away, she'd nearly cried at the blackness, black dark. Night. A chilly building, with a toilet. Her hands useless, numb from hours under the weight of her body, he'd had to help her. Meg set her jaw against a lurch of nausea and then thought, well you silly bitch. Kidnapped, trussed up like a pig, maybe raped, and what bothers you is that some man peeled your pants down and sat you on a toilet.

No, not raped. She levered herself slowly to a sitting position and remembered his hands, cold and rough and making as little contact with her body as possible. She'd been able to get the pants back up by herself, and then he'd wrapped a long arm around her shoulders, an arm impersonal as an iron bar and just as unyielding. He'd half-carried her across hard-packed ground, through a door and another door, and dumped her on a cot, this cot. And left, to return a moment later with more pills and a glass of water.

And locked the door, that was the last thing she remembered. Now she blinked in the dim light, and rubbed gritty eyes. Another cot stood against the adjoining wall, Cass's big sleeping bag on it, unzipped and empty. Had Cass slept there? Where was she now? She must be terrified.

Meg pulled herself straight and set her feet squarely on the floor. Took a deep breath, and another. Her head felt as if someone had wrapped it in layers and layers of gauze, but her stomach was no longer churning, except from hunger. There was nothing in the room but the cots and her handbag there on the floor, he must have brought that in. She remembered stashing a chocolate bar in her bag, Dutch chocolate with nuts. Perhaps she'd sit here and eat that and try to work past the fuzziness. Just stay here in the quiet.

Not so quiet; there were voices out there suddenly. Or they might have been there all along, people talking to each other while she dithered around inside her own head. Low male rumble, then a light girlish tone: Cass's voice, sounding ordinary. The door opened; Meg caught her breath and looked up and up at the figure filling the doorway.

"Out," he said, and stood to one side. She lurched to her feet, steadied herself, then moved past him into brightness: a long, narrow kitchen, windows collecting morning sunshine.

Stove against the wall to her right. Refrigerator behind her, sink and counter along the left wall, under the windows. At the end of the room, before a pair of louvered folding doors, were a round table and four chairs. Cass sat there like a . . . a member of the family or something, a litter of dishes before her; her head was up, her face unmarked and showing no expression that Meg could read, certainly not terror. Beside her, poker-straight, stood a boy of sixteen or seventeen with a round pale face and short black hair more ruffled than curly. His eyes sent a beam of intense blue the length of the room.

"You probably need to go the latrine," said a husky voice behind her, and a big hand wrapped itself around her upper arm. "But first we need to get the rules straight."

Rules! Meg thought, in a burst of fury that burned her mind clean of thought. "You people have made a serious mistake, and I insist . . ."

The hand tightened and yanked back, and she was sure her arm would leave its socket. "Rules," he said again, and waited briefly before releasing her. She took a deep breath, and cradled her left arm in her right.

"Easy enough to keep you both locked in the storeroom," he went on, "but then I figured, what the hell, got one of you we've got you both. You," he said, and gave Meg a nudge, "go take a leak on your own this time. Right out the back door there and across the compound." Another nudge. "Just remember it's your daughter in here with us. You don't come back quick enough, we might start slicing little bits off her, like ears and fingers."

Cass's mouth fell open and her eyes grew round. The boy widened his stance and dropped his folded arms, and Meg noticed that his face was splattered with freckles.

"You too, little girl. You make any trouble, I'll carve my initials on your mama."

Cass fixed her stare on Meg, and drew breath to speak. No! thought Meg, and tried to say it with her eyes. Leave it alone! After a moment the girl lowered her gaze to the table and said softly, "No trouble."

IN SOME PECULIAR fashion her feet didn't quite fit the ground. Meg moved with slow steps from the back of the house toward the only other building in view, a low structure of concrete blocks with solar panels tilting up from its flat roof. The whole scene resembled a clearing in a forest: flat-packed earth in every direction and then, encircling like a distant fence, heavy brush and trees. Where on earth are we? she wondered, and looked at her watch. Ten A.M. Had to be the next day, twenty-plus hours after the Coeur d'Alene hospital parking lot. Saturday. But how many hours on the road? How many *miles*?

And why? The word zinged around in her head like a bumblebee, buzzing and bumping. Why why why?

She pushed the unlatched door halfway open and edged inside. Concrete floor, small high windows. Toilet, a couple of sinks, a water tank. In the far corner the floor sloped to a drain and long pipes climbed the wall to a shower head. Oh sweet Christ, a shower! she thought, and then saw herself standing naked in this cold room, no lock on the door, no curtain. She used the toilet quickly, washed her hands at the sink, then filled it with water and washed her face.

Outside again, she stood blinking in the morning sunlight, grateful for its warmth. From here she could see that there was a third building in what he'd called "the compound," a shed or a garage at the other side of the house. It had a rippled look, probably corrugated metal under the brown paint. The house was also brown, but made of wood. Board and batten siding, wood-framed windows, gable roof extending beyond the front wall to make a porch: it was a nice-looking little structure, handmade in an agreeable way and reminding her of cabins she'd seen in some of the older parks.

The back door opened, the angular figure framed there jerked its head in sharp command, and there was a shift of

focus, to a different and impossible reality that her mind
seemed intent on rejecting. What on earth is happening to
me? she wailed inwardly as she trudged back to her captor.
And where? No mechanical sound reached her ears, so there
could be no road nearby, or at least not a much-traveled
one. The air... she breathed deeply and considered... the
air didn't taste like that of the High Sierra; she didn't think
they were in real mountains. How far from Coeur d'Alene?

She was struggling with calculations as she climbed the
two steps to the back door. Driving time could have been
anything from an hour to, what, sixteen hours? Could she
have slept that long? They could be fifty miles from Coeur
d'Alene, or eight hundred, or in some other world entirely.
This was a dream, a nightmare and she would wake up any
minute.

The tall man was gone from the doorway, and only the
boy remained in the kitchen. "Hey, you want something to
eat?"

"No, I want..." She looked around the room and caught
her breath. "Where's Cass?" she demanded.

"Hey, be cool, no problem. They're out in the garage,
getting your stuff. There's bread and butter," he said, with
a gesture toward the table, "and jam. And milk and orange
juice," he added, turning from the refrigerator with a glass
jug in one hand and a plastic container in the other. "Ba-
con and eggs if you're real hungry, but I generally burn
stuff, you better fix it yourself." The tumbling spate of
words ended as he ran out of breath. He set his burdens on
the table and stepped quickly back, shooting a sideways
glance at her.

"Coffee?" She picked up a slice of bread and reached for
the butter dish.

"Oh sure, plenty of coffee. I better heat it up." He hurried to the stove, put a match to a burner and then set a blue-
speckled pot over the flame. "Cowboy coffee we call it,
might be kinda heavyduty for a lady."

Meg slathered jam over the butter and poured a glass full
of milk. Food for her stomach, energy; and coffee to clear
her head. Lots of coffee. "I'm sure it will be fine," she told

him. "Thank you, um...?" She looked inquiringly at him, and he said "Kev," and then sucked a disgusted gulf of air over clenched teeth.

"Thank you, Kev." Jon, Cass's blue-eyed Jon, had been her immediate thought as she viewed the sentinel-figure beside the girl's chair, but that "Kev" had come automatically. Besides, he looked younger and softer than the Jon of Cass's tales, with peach-down cheeks and the remnants of babyfat. So, Kev, tell me why? No, that's the complicated question, she decided, and instead took a sip of milk and swallowed and said, "Where are we, anyway?"

"Oh, we're just up in the..." He pressed his lips tight, frowned at her, then swung around to lift the lid of the cof-feepot, releasing a puff of steam. He turned off the burner, grabbed a cup from a shelf at the back of the stove and poured. "Here you go, nice and hot."

"Kev?"

"See, sometimes that's the way things go down; a guy has to do stuff whether he wants to or not." As if in response to his own words, the boy drew his body up straight and square and set his soft mouth in a firm line. "You just try to be cool, like a few days, maybe it will all work out."

"Maybe it will." The voice rattled against Meg's spine. The tall man had come in from the front of the cabin, car-rying blankets, pillows, and Meg's suitcase. He headed with his burden into the small room, the storeroom, he'd called it; and Cass trailed after him, lugging her own gear. Moving them in.

"Okay, Kev," the man said a moment later, "you go out with the girl, get the rest of the stuff."

"Sure, Jay, right," he replied eagerly, and Meg half expected him to salute. Cass trotted back from the store-room emptyhanded, shot a bright-eyed glance at Kev, then followed him out.

The tall man...Jay...stood silently a few feet away. Meg noted that her fingers were cramped from the force of her grip on the coffee mug, and willed them to loosen; she lifted the mug, inhaled the acrid steam and sucked up a great gulp of coffee.

Look at him. She did, for a moment. He was an angular, longboned shape, with limp dark-brown hair tucked behind his ears and muddy brown eyes set in cavernous sockets. His left shoulder and arm were held awkwardly, his left leg stiff-looking with the knee braced back. His scarred and weathered face held no expression at all.

Ugly. He was a vicious, ugly son of a bitch. "I don't know you," she said, pushing the words past a throat tight with fear and outrage. "I don't know you, I have done you no harm, and you have no right to interfere in my life. In our lives," she amended quickly.

The edges of his mouth curled upward briefly. "Rights— I got rights I ain't used yet. Wrongs, too."

"I demand to know..." she began, and stopped short as he shook his head without taking his eyes from her face.

"Don't do that, lady. Don't demand."

No. No, I won't, she decided, and looked down at the cup in her cold hands. She got slowly, carefully to her feet. "I'll get myself a little more coffee."

He made no reply, merely watched her walk to the stove inhale step step exhale step step inhale. Pour, what lovely steady hands. Remember to breathe, and turn around, and back to the table, and the chair. Victory. She blinked at him, focused her eyes once again, and saw that he held her handbag.

"Checked your van and your gear, but I almost forgot about this." He turned the flap back and upended the bag over the table. "Ah! Looky here." He displayed her Swiss army knife before putting it in his own pocket.

"That's just..."

"I know what it is." He stirred her belongings with one hand, spilling comb and lipstick and nailfile from their small plastic-lined bag. He lifted her wallet, opened it, slid credit cards out and back, palmed her driver's license. "Margaret Halloran. Must have been a Mr. Halloran one time?"

"He's... I'm a widow."

He returned his gaze to the license, frowning. The picture was four years old, but Meg didn't think she'd changed much: lean somber face, greenish eyes, heavy dark hair pulled back from a high forehead. More gray in the hair now.

"Five feet ten, hundred forty pounds," he muttered. "Real tall lady, what happened to your kid? Halloran must have been a shrimp."

"Genes can be complicated," she said in tart tones. His head camp up, and she added quickly, "My father's people were Welsh, and small." You've a mean, sharp tongue, Margaret, said a voice from her childhood, just like your father's and it will get you into trouble one day.

Her interrogator's face had flushed, except for the shiny patches along his left jaw. Burns? wondered Meg, and made herself relax as he scanned the license once more and dropped it on the table.

"I never heard of Port Silva. Where's it at?"

"It's a little town on the California coast, about two hundred miles north of San Francisco."

His lips curled back to expose long brownish teeth. "Letterman's in San Francisco. I don't like San Francisco."

Letterman... Letterman Hospital. The army hospital, in the Presidio. He was a wounded veteran, from his age a Vietnam veteran.

"You're a long way from home." He made the words an accusation.

"I...we, my daughter and I, attended a conference in Colorado Springs, for teachers. I teach high school." She took a sip of coffee, to drown the flow of words threatening to explode from her. Who was he? What could have made a pair of this damaged hulk and Kev the blue-eyed boy? Why?

"And you were headed back? To California?"

"Yes."

"Kinda long way around you took."

"We wanted to do some camping."

"Yeah? What happened to your trailer?"

Trailer. Her stomach lurched. He'd seen them before yesterday. Been watching them. Why? "We, um, we got tired," she stammered. "Decided to head straight home. So I turned the trailer in, it was just rented."

"And there's probably somebody waiting for you, out there in California?"

"A friend, yes." She let herself think about Vince for a moment. A second night without a call, and he'd be on her trail like a bloodhound. Be quiet, Margaret. "I've been calling him every few days."

"You're camping. Your friend will know you can't always find phones in the woods." He swept her belongings into a heap in the center of the table. "No keys. You travel without an extra key for that van?"

"There was one," she said quickly, "in a magnetic box under the left front fender. But it got lost." The box was still there, she thought. She hoped.

He nodded, picked up her handbag and shook it. He felt around inside, and her mouth went dry. Never tell a lie that can be proved against you. Not exactly a lie. More an omission. Don't, she begged silently, but his fingers opened the big zipped pocket, explored it, found the smaller pocket, pulled the zipper. She sat frozen, watching his hand, saw it come out. Empty. Where were the keys? she wondered for just a moment; then she cursed Cass for a thief and blessed her in the next breath.

He tossed the purse atop its contents and she reached both hands out to scoop everything toward her like a poker pot. He didn't move, didn't speak, and when she looked up it was to find him observing her with a kind of sad resignation. She'd seen a look like that on the face of one of her students, a boy who loved everything about his advanced biology class except for having, finally, to kill the nice white friendly lab rats.

"Jay," she said quickly. "Jay, you haven't hurt Cass or me, and we don't have any idea who you are, or where *we* are. Couldn't you please just put blindfolds on us again and take us back?"

He sighed and moved his head in slow negation as his right hand came up to cup and rub his left shoulder. "Where you are is in the woods, real deep in. You make it over the gate and onto the road, we'll catch you. Try to go through the woods and you'll find out the hard way, like maybe losing a leg, that the perimeter is secured. What's your kid's name?"

"What? It's K—Cass," Meg stammered, and felt sweat spring out on her forehead. Had something in her wallet caught his eye, a picture or a letter?

"How come yesterday it was something else?"

Yesterday. Yesterday, hospital, the parking lot. Her breath was quick and shallow as she remembered her terror when this gaunt stranger said, "It's your daughter." Remembered her gasped reply.

His eyes held hers, and chilly threads of moisture trickled down her temples, cold fingers tracing a path. "Ah, about a year ago my daughter decided to change her name, to Cassandra—Cass. Teenaged stuff, there's no point in fighting it. But I still forget sometimes, and call her by her old name. Katy."

TEN

"THE FIRE'S TOO HIGH."

"And what do you know about it," Meg snapped over her shoulder at Cass. She picked up the fork, gave the floury chunk of meat a nudge, found it sticking and decided that the girl was probably right. The Halloran/Gutierrez household subsisted on fresh fruits and salads, steamed vegetables, broiled meats and microwaved chicken; the only comfy-kitchen dish in Meg's repertoire was her mother's spaghetti sauce, and even for that she always had to dig out the recipe.

"My mom made pot roast all the time, before she turned into a chile-head," replied Cass. "Could you open the fridge? He told me to put these in to get cold." Meg pulled the refrigerator door wide, and Cass deposited half a dozen small bottles of Coke inside. "What you do after it's brown, you put in salt and pepper and bay leaf and some water and cover the pot. Then onions later, and carrots and potatoes for like the last hour."

"Cass, wait! Come here."

The girl hesitated, halfway to the back door. "Look, I'm supposed to be working, like helping split wood. *I* didn't get to sit around all morning drinking coffee."

"And *I* didn't decide on the division of labor," Meg told her. "I'd be more than happy to trade." As Cass frowned and shook her head, Meg spoke quickly, softly: "Cass, who are they? Who are Jay and Kev?"

"Huh?" Astonishment and then indignation marked the dirt-streaked face before her, and Meg sighed inwardly. She had not meant to be so direct, but this was her first moment alone with the girl since the day began. And one fact kept ringing in her brain like a tinny little bell: Cass slept in the van Thursday night, slept out there alone with her kitten, or so she said. Cass could have set this up.

"I thought Kev might have told you something while the two of you were working," said Meg, mending fences for the moment. "Are you all right? Did they drug you, the way they did me?"

Cass touched gingerly fingers to the edges of her mouth, and Meg felt a twinge of guilt as she noted faint bruise marks under the grime. "He tied this rag real tight across my mouth. After he shoved some pills down my throat. And he punched me in the stomach, it knocked my breath out so I couldn't yell. Dickhead," she added, and then sent a wary look in the direction of the back door.

"Did they say anything to you?"

She sighed and ran her hands through her hair, its spikes sadly flattened now. "Just hi, how are you, where you goin'? That was Kev," she added with a shrug and a rueful smile much too old for her small face. "So I said hi back, and stopped to talk, and that old... the other guy grabbed me." At a call from outside she stiffened and turned quickly. "I gotta go, he says we have to get it all stacked in the garage before it rains."

"Cass, be careful," said Meg automatically, uselessly.

"Yeah."

Maybe she has some sense after all, thought Meg, then groaned a moment later as the window over the sink framed two figures. In a flash Cass's posture changed from purposeful to seductive: hands in hip pockets, head to one side as she gazed up at Kev. Oh, Cass, you poor stupid little bitch.

POT ROAST. Meg found onions and potatoes in the pantry, and carrots in the fridge, which it turned out ran on propane. There *was* electricity, for lights and such; she'd learned only a few hours earlier that it came from a gas-powered generator out by the garage. The engine noise had been sudden, out of nowhere, and she'd thrummed with instant hope like a pointer catching quail-scent. She'd turned a moment later to find Jay watching her, his long face relaxed into a near-grin. She clenched her teeth now at the memory.

The "perimeter" was more than a hundred feet in any direction from the cabin as center. He'd have preferred mines, he told her, claymores or bouncing bettys, whatever those might be. But it wasn't easy to come by such devices in the day-to-day world, so he'd set out traps instead, the kind intended for foxes or raccoons or other varmints. In an irregular ring around the compound, concealed in the greenery. So he'd said, and Meg was inclined to believe him. She stood at the sink and peeled an onion, tears blurring her view from the window.

No electric lines out there, no telephone lines...no direct connection with civilization at all. If there was a radio, she hadn't seen it. The place might have been set up as a prison, she thought, and then reconsidered. The storeroom had not been intended as a jail cell; the hasp and staple for the padlock were of some weather-pitted grayish metal out of keeping with the handsome fittings throughout the kitchen, the hinges and knobs and drawer-pulls. Meg wiped her eyes with a napkin and went to inspect the door. Yes, newly done, there was still sawdust on the floor. So this was a home hastily modified to serve as a prison.

She set a lid on the Dutch oven, turned the flame as low as it would go, and returned to the sink and the window. Her body ached from hours on the camper floor, and something else ached, her heart or her spirit, as she made another survey of the setting. Might as well be the prison at Florence, Arizona, or San Quentin. Or the moon; even if she had the luck, and the nerve, to get to her van and its C.B. radio, where could she say she was? Assuming Jay hadn't removed or destroyed the radio.

So, a bolt for the van probably not worth the risk. But this version of San Quentin had no guard towers that she could see, and no guns so far.

Kev was on the other side of the cabin, busy. Suppose she were to reach the green edge, and then move carefully; she was a backpacker and hiker, with very good eyesight. And

Cass... would they really hurt Cass? Who was not her own daughter, after all. And besides, if she, Meg, brought help...

Jay's tall form was there suddenly, against the greenery; too far away to tell, but she'd bet he'd made no noise as he slipped through the brush. He was there for a minute, almost a stick figure at this distance, and then gone, back into the bushes. Step in a trap, you son of a bitch.

Round and round her mind went, until she was dizzy from the spinning. She and Cass were merely two females and captives for that reason, sexual victims-to-be in some weird mountain-man's fantasy. True, Jay had called her by name; but he could have learned that from the van's registration slip, in the glove compartment.

Or. She and Cass were hostages of some enemy, possibly an enemy of Vince Gutierrez's. The boy Vince killed two months ago had a big family, several much older brothers; perhaps they had arranged this and would appear soon to torment or to gloat.

Or. Jay and Kev were connected somehow with Cass's boyfriend, Jonathan Archer. Jon was angry with Cass and punishing her; or Jon had set this whole thing up with Cass's help and would soon come to claim her, leaving Meg...

The paring knife sliced through the last carrot and into the ball of her thumb. She stared at the line of red, then made a circle with thumb and middle finger and pressed, to watch blood well and drip in vivid splotches into the white sink. Pretty. So stand here and ask for answers and bleed to death. Or get your ass in gear.

There were Band-Aids in her suitcase. And an open pack of Trues in the side pocket of Cass's tote; a good jolt of nicotine might be just the thing for sluggish brain cells. Meg appropriated the whole pack, then paused to survey a room that was just as she had remembered it, unpromising. The door was solid wood, the ugly hasp held firmly by four screws. The high vents... with tools and time she could remove them, or cut out their screens, providing exit for Cass but not for her own larger frame. The walls, as she'd noted earlier, were just studs and siding, no insulation or wallboard. Be chilly in here at night; how fortunate it was summer. Hurray for good luck.

She lit a cigarette with a kitchen match, inhaled deeply and went across the kitchen to stand just inside the wide doorway and survey the front room, really about two-thirds of the cabin. A black iron woodstove on a platform of red bricks sat at more or less the center of the building, far enough forward of the inner wall to permit movement all round. Furniture was sparse: two cushioned wooden armchairs, two benches with seats padded but low backs bare, and a single tall stool with no back at all. Windows had no curtains, only dark green roller blinds. Four bullet lights pointed down from a cross-beam; a pair of kerosene lamps sat atop a bookcase along the left wall, a bookcase whose shelves were crammed with books.

A pair of sturdy bunk-beds occupied the wall to the right, butted into the corner against the storeroom; Meg noted that if she and Cass were to converse privately in their cell, it would have to be in very low voices.

There was a set of open shelves along that wall, piled with clothing, jeans and socks and underwear. From a row of wooden pegs hung a worn and dirty sheepskin jacket, a many-zippered jacket of black leather, a rain poncho, and a greasy Stetson.

If he had guns, and she'd bet he had, he probably kept them in the cupboard built into the right front corner of the room, a solid-looking piece of work with a flat wooden door set flush in its frame and a bronze lock. Locked of course. As she stepped quickly back from the cupboard, her gaze caught on a dark circle on the adjoining wall; target, she thought wildly, and pictured Jay standing here to practice, blowing neat, closely spaced holes in his very own wall. No no, Margaret, it's only a dartboard for Christ's sake and you'd better get out of here.

She tossed her cigarette into the stove and hurried out to check the pot, which was simmering nicely. The only ornamental touch in the whole cabin was here in the kitchen, a Sierra Club calendar hanging from a hook on the louvered pantry door. The picture, a coastal seascape with white spray creaming over jutting black rocks, reminded her so sharply of Port Silva that she inspected the lower half of the calendar through a haze of tears. The numbered spaces were blank, except for a penciled notation for Friday, yesterday: VA Hosp. 2 P.M. Yesterday afternoon. Somehow she didn't think he'd kept that appointment.

VA was Veterans Administration, of course. A man so damaged as Jay would need checkups, care. Medication.

Where would he keep his medicine? The same place everybody else did: in the cupboard nearest the sink she found a sparse collection of glasses and mugs, a bottle of vitamins and one of aspirin and one straight, small plastic bottle with no commercial label, just a strip of white paper curled inside, the word "sleep" printed in smeary ink. Tiny white uncoated tablets inside, lots of them. Meg bared her teeth at this last, considered tipping the vile things down the sink and reconsidered almost at once; in a pinch, Jay could probably devise other and nastier ways of keeping his captives comatose.

She set the pills back, reached deeper into the cupboard, and picked up one last container. It was square, plastic, with a big commercial label: aspirin and codeine. A smaller typed label was pasted crookedly across the bottom. Veterans Administration Hospital, Boise, Idaho: James Bennington Taylor, four times daily as needed for pain, by Dr. Brownlee.

"James Bennington Taylor. Boise." As she put everything back she whispered the words aloud, in a tingling elation which faded almost as soon as she closed the cupboard door. Identity, which would be useful to Gutierrez in trying to find them, was of little value to her; what could she do, intimidate the man by shouting his full name at him? And Boise was, what, some four hundred miles south of Coeur d'Alene. Two points on a map, not much of a trail.

At a sudden small sound she gulped breath and turned to face the open back door. Jay—James Bennington Taylor—leaned there, watching. The cupboard door behind her—had it swung open again? Words from the label were so clear and sharp in her mind that she thought they must be visible through her skull. After a long moment he nodded and came in. "Startin' to smell good in here."

It made no difference to him, she decided as he tromped past her into the front room. He'd left those goddamned pills right there, having given her free rein of the kitchen. There was a scrape of something, chair legs, from the front room, a grunt, and then a solid small "thunk." Another. Another. Longer pause, and then three more. He was throwing darts. She was a captive in fear of her life, humbly bowing and scraping and making dinner, and he was throwing darts.

ELEVEN

PERHAPS IT WAS THE DRUG, those little pills, in some kind of flashback. Or the nicotine...her brain was no longer accustomed to nicotine. Whatever the cause, she was having serious trouble with this present reality, with terror in a family setting; should one scream or pass the salt or both?

The four of them sat at the round kitchen table, Cass crowding a little closer to Kev than was really necessary. The girl was in her teen-temptress role, body inclined in the boy's direction, hand brushing his forearm as she reached for salt or butter. Her remarks to him were low-voiced, except for an occasional giggle.

Kev...ugly syllable, "Kevin" easier to say...was apparently Catholic, crossing himself matter-of-factly before picking up his fork. Neathanded and mannerly, he was practically a parody of a well-brought-up young man doing his best to be tolerant of a silly girl. Any mother's pride and joy, thought Meg. Bright eyes, no pimples, terrific posture, might be the student body president of some smalltown high school. So why did she keep thinking of the Ayatollah and his baby troops?

Jay made no attempt at conversation but tucked into his meal, head bent and fork scooping. Meg glanced at his profile from the undamaged side, the right side, and decided that he'd probably been a nice-looking youth, one of the skinny, awkward kind who always get tangled up in their own feet. There was still something boyishly unfinished about his face, although he had to be in his mid-thirties. He shifted in his chair and shot a sharp sideways glance at her, and she hastily lowered her gaze.

The food was an American-cookbook illustration: big shiny chunk of meat, white and yellow vegetables heaped in a bowl, brown gravy. The youngsters ate with enthusiasm,

Kevin offering Meg a grin and a "Hey, terrific!" (To which she responded, instantly but silently, Choke on it, sonny.) She herself took small bites, chewing thoroughly and swallowing with effort foods that to her did not differ in taste, only in texture. Finally Jay pushed his plate back, looked directly at her, and said, "Make some coffee."

"Not for me. Excuse me," said Kevin. He got to his feet and headed for the back door. Cass stood up quickly to follow him and Meg said, "Cass, wait."

The girl paused with a hiss of impatience, and Meg said quietly, "Please help me clear the table."

"Hey, fuck that! Come on, I worked outside all . . ."

Jay was on his feet, his left arm a blur as he delivered a backhand blow that knocked Cass into her chair and sent the chair skidding. "Don't you talk dirty to your mama!" He leaned across the table, long jaw thrust out, eyes narrowed. "Just get your ass over there and help like she asked you."

Meg heard Cass's wail, indrawn and bitten off; saw droplets of spittle fly from Jay's tight-stretched lips; watched a thread of blood trail from a corner of Cass's mouth before the girl got her hands to her face. Held her own breath. Noted, as Jay straightened and rolled his shoulders loose, that his damaged arm could not be counted much of a handicap.

"I'm gonna build a fire," he said to Meg. "Bring me a mug of coffee in the front room. And you and your kid get things cleaned up, including yourselves. I gotta go out in a while, which means you go to bed."

"It's your fault he hit me." Cass spoke in a fierce whisper as Meg followed her back to the stove. "I bet you were even glad it happened!"

"Not in the sense that you mean." She set plates on the sinkboard and leaned past the girl to turn on the hot water faucet.

"You're not even my *mother*."

"That's true. Would you like to go in there and tell him we've been lying?"

"*I* didn't..." Cass closed her mouth and sniffed loudly, her eyes filling with tears.

"Hold still a minute, there's blood on your face." Meg cupped the girl's chin, tipped her face to the light, and touched a damp napkin gently to the corner of her mouth. "If that slap reminded you that we're in serious trouble here, then I think it was a good thing." She stepped back. "Keep your mouth shut, your eyes open, and don't do anything, not anything, to set that man off. You stay here and I'll clear the table."

NO. OH NO, she wasn't going in there. Meg was reaching for the doorframe with both hands when Cass caromed into her, jostling her forward into the dark little room. "Bedtime," said Jay from behind them.

"Dickhead," muttered Cass, too softly to be heard. Meg drew a deep breath, exhaled slowly, repeated the exercise. Stupid...she'd known they were to be shut in. Same room she'd been in and out of all day, no more scary than anything else around here. Nine o'clock, she thought it was, fully dark out. Breathe, and breathe.

She heard a door opening and closing; movement, rustling and banging, in the front room. Footsteps; she turned and Jay was standing in the doorway. "I guess you can have this," he said to Meg, and thrust her lamp at her, the little standing battery lamp she'd bought for campground use. In his other hand, his right, he held a long, heavy-looking rifle with a wooden stock and a bolt action. "Now I'm gonna padlock your door here, and the other doors are locked, too. But if you should manage some way to get out, Kev will be waiting for you with this." He hefted the gun in demonstration, and pulled their door tight.

"I know Kev seems like a kid, kind of a friendly kid," he said through the door, and they heard the slap of the hasp, a scrape, then the click of the padlock. "But he's a good shot, I been teaching him. And it's no big deal to shoot somebody from a distance. Hardly even feels like killing."

"He wouldn't!" whispered Cass. As Meg turned the lantern on and set it on the floor, Cass shed her shoes, jeans, shirt, and ribbed tank-top, and settled onto her cot wearing only a pair of white bikini panties. "Kev wouldn't, he's . . . he's a Catholic!"

"Cass, why don't you keep at least a shirt on?" Meg had stripped, showered, and put on clean clothes in record time. She had no intention of removing them again, here.

"What are you, some kind of virgin? My mom says clothes are hypocritical, she says in a really honest world everybody would go naked. At least, that's what she used to say."

"Never mind the politics, just remember which side of that door the lock is on."

"Oh. Okay." Cass pulled the tank top back on and slid into her sleeping bag. "Listen, I don't see how Kev can be a bad person, he goes to church every Sunday. He's even thinking about being a priest. He says his mother started out to be a nun but couldn't finish, and she'd really like it if he got to be a priest."

"He'll need to find an order that accepts kidnappers."

"No, but you know what I think this is? I think it's maybe some kind of war game, where guys divide up into armies and hide from each other and take prisoners and like that." Cass slid lower in her bag. "We're the prisoners, and pretty soon they'll shoot us with red paint or something and let us go. Or the other side will find us. There's this camp I heard about, that Jon . . ."

Cass fell abruptly silent, and after a moment Meg said, "Jon what?"

"Nothing. It wasn't Jon, I remember now, it was somebody else."

"Who?" When Cass made no answer, Meg settled onto her own cot and crossed her legs tailor-fashion. "You know, when I saw Kev I thought at first he must be Jon."

"Kev's just a boy. Jon's a man. He'll be eighteen in three, no, two days. On Monday."

"Oh. And then what?"

"Then nothing."

Silence stretched, and Meg settled her back against the wall. Here in this little room, breathing hard to contain a claustrophobia she'd never before experienced, she had no belief in Kevin, the nice boy. Kevin a captive also, Jay's captive? Sexual victim? Didn't feel right. Not father and son, and she didn't think they were brothers. Uncle and nephew, perhaps? No, she was letting the family image of earlier in the evening blur her thinking; there was between the two men none of the affectionate/irritable byplay of male relationship. Two soldiers in somebody's army, that was the way they felt to her. Not the kind of war-games army Cass had dreamed up either. She would, by God, be happy to shoot the pair of them with real bullets if she could get her hands on a gun. Which reminded her.

"Cass. Have you seen my keys? The extra set of keys to the van?"

"I told you before, I'm not a thief." Cass's back was turned, her voice directed to the wall. "They must have fallen out again, I don't think you close that zipper tight. Or that man took them, Jay."

"I don't think so." No keys. But the van was old and not complex, and she could start it without keys, given time. Time and freedom. There was a well equipped toolbox in the van, hidden in a not-very-secret compartment in the rear. Maybe Jay hadn't found that, or hadn't bothered with it. Otherwise, what she had was one tiny screwdriver and a small set of snips, tools for changing strings on Katy's guitar. She'd forgotten they were in her makeup bag, and Jay had missed them or ignored them in his search. Pretty light armament there, Maggie.

"Cass?" There was no answer, but Meg could feel the girl listening. "Cass, we need to know where we are. Do you think that tomorrow you could get into the van and take a look at the odometer?"

"That's what shows the miles it's gone? I know that already: 98,999. Kev saw that when we were getting stuff out; he said that van runs pretty good for something close to turning 100,000."

"Oookay." Meg leaned her head back and stared up into the darkness. Her last gas purchase had been in Butte, and the mileage then was...98,555. She juggled cities and numbers for a few moments. ''Ah.''

''Is it good, or bad?'' Cass's voice was small and woeful.

''I think good. It seems we're maybe a hundred twenty-five miles from Coeur d'Alene. If your uncle starts looking for us there at the hospital, which he surely will...a hundred twenty-five miles is practically local. He'll have a good chance of picking up some kind of trail.''

''Or Jon will.''

Jon? Oookay, Meg said again, but silently. If Jon was part of the plot, Cass was clearly not going to admit it. If she simply had reason to believe he was following, Meg could only say cheers, all volunteers welcome.

''I wish I had Fred here.'' Cass's voice was the tiniest whisper now. ''I don't see why that dickhead wouldn't let me bring him in.''

''Jay doesn't like animals, at least not in his house,'' Meg reminded her. Fred the kitten had played himself into exhaustion outdoors before supper. He'd seemed happy enough to return to his home in the van.

''He's the animal,'' Cass said, pulling her sleeping bag higher.

The heat from the iron stove didn't reach this room. Meg dug her down jacket from her bag, settled it around her shoulders, and realized at once that it was larger and shabbier than her own and smelled of Vince. Hoo boy. She caught her lower lip in her teeth, bit down, and concentrated on the sharp bright pain. Start to cry in this goddamned black hole and you'll never stop.

She stared at the lamp until her eyes were safely dry, nice lamp like a little private golden sun. Wasting its battery; she sighed, reached down to turn it out and settled back onto the cot, pulling her legs close and wrapping her arms tightly around them. Iron cords seemed to run across her shoulders and up the back of her neck, where they knotted themselves harder and throbbed.

Easy. Head up, legs folded, hands on knees. Inhale long. Exhale...six, seven, eight. Abou Ben Adhem, may his tribe increase...led all the rest. Good for Abou. Have you heard of the wonderful one-horse shay that was built in such a logical way it ran a hundred years to a day and then, of a sudden, it—ah, but stay...Terence, this is stupid stuff; you eat your victuals fast enough...

Forty years of listening and reading, tucked away in the corners of a rag-bag mind. Here a missed rhyme, there a beat not quite right, how does it go? Much later, dark outside but the barest hint of light, stars or moon. Cass's breathing slow and steady, her own the same, muscles not iron now just muscle. She shrugged Vince's jacket off, straightened her legs. If she balanced carefully, she could stand on the frame of the cot and inspect the vents.

The metal frame of the vent was nailed in place from the outside, proof against anything but noisy battering with a heavy tool. She tested the screen with her fingers and was wondering whether she should try her little snips when she heard an engine, and caught the gleam of headlights.

Meg teetered for a moment, while hope swelled to fill her chest and press at her throat. Please, God. A moment later, tears made warm tracks down her cheeks as her brain registered what she was hearing: the wheezy, rattling old engine of the camper truck. Jay was back.

She wiped her face on her sleeve, braced her feet, and put her ear close to the screen. The garage was right out there, perhaps ten feet from the cabin. She heard the truck brake, heard its door open and slam, heard what had to be the garage door, heavy rumble and screech of metal.

"Jay." Kevin's voice, low and quavery; relief? or fear?

"Yo, kid."

"You were so long I was getting worried."

"I decided to go up on the ridge, smoke a little grass and look at the moon. That's what I used to do in Nam."

"So what did they say?"

"Well, Willie...I think he must have forgot how good I was at my job."

"But everything's okay?"

"Everything's never okay."

TWELVE

GUTIERREZ PERCHED beside the counter like a crippled bird of prey and glared around the two-story living room. Late sun poured through open deck doors, gilding the shaggy wool carpet and the pale oak floorboards, warming the muted colors in the Wide Ruins rug that hung on the end wall. He took no pleasure in the display; the flat, shadow-casting rays were a reminder that Saturday was almost over.

His own house hadn't turned out to be much of an improvement over Hank Svoboda's place; it was equally dusty and quiet and even more empty. Katy's music stand splayed its metal legs in a corner, her guitarist's footrest on the floor beside it. Meg's old moccasins waited by the deck door, and just outside was Grendel's steel water bowl, dry. Maybe he should go rescue the big dog from the kennel...no, just have to take him back, probably tomorrow.

Gutierrez reached for his glass and his elbow struck the telephone, bringing a hollow "bong." His resulting glare should have melted the instrument. God*damn* but he hated telephones, a pain in the ass when you didn't need them and only half useful when you did. A distant metallic whirr brought his head up: the old pendulum clock on the fireplace mantel. One, two, and slowly on to eight.

Enough, he thought, and took a sip of whisky. He knew Meg Halloran better than he'd ever known anyone in his life, knew she had a short fuse and a hot temper but was incapable of sulking. She might be angry with him because of Cass, but she'd call as she'd promised; she wouldn't leave him here sweating and swearing and rapidly going crazy. Something had happened to her.

As a new sound suddenly overrode the faint hum of traffic on the highway below his hill, Gutierrez spun the stool around and lurched to his feet. A separate engine, gearing down for the climb: Meg's van?

No, of course not. Svoboda's truck. He braced his good shoulder against the doorframe and watched the old truck crawl up the driveway, recently surfaced with asphalt because Meg had insisted. The truck pulled onto the parking area in front of the house, and a door slammed—no, two doors. And two sets of footsteps on the steep open staircase leading to the deck. A moment later Svoboda paused at the rail opening to catch his breath. "Goddamn, Vince, now I remember why I don't visit you more. You planning to move downstairs? That what all the work's about down there, excavating and plumbing and such?"

Gutierrez shook his head. "That's for Katy, a big room and her own bath. We're turning the sleeping loft into a master bedroom for Meg and me, and we'll use the little room on this level for a study." He turned and walked stiffly across the floor to perch again on his stool. "That's what we had in mind, anyway. How are you, Val?" he added, with a nod to the young man who had stepped out from behind Svoboda's big frame.

"Hi, Chief. I'm good," replied Val Kuisma with a shrug and a grin more woebegone than cheerful. Just under six feet tall and whip-lean, he still looked like the high school cross-country runner he'd been some years earlier.

"Ran into Val at Johnny Wing's place; he decided to come along, help out, maybe run errands." Svoboda moved to the counter to set down several paper bags. "Look, I got some supper here, pot stickers and lemon chicken, hot and sour soup. I figured I'd put the soup in a mug, and you could manage the rest of it left-handed."

"I'm not hungry." Gutierrez poured another two inches of Wild Turkey into his glass and added icewater from the pitcher he'd prepared earlier.

"Ah. Well, I got a couple of bottles of chardonnay, too; Bernie's calling this one 'Angie's Choice.'" Svoboda's son-in-law owned a small but beginning-to-prosper winery in the Anderson Valley. "Why don't I pour a couple glasses, for me and Val, and you can tell us what you got working here."

"What I've got working is the fucking telephone, more or less." Gutierrez drained half his glass in one gulp. "I've talked with highway cops in California and in Oregon and in Washington and in Idaho. There have been no reported accidents involving a blue Chevy van, no injuries to anyone resembling Meg and Cass. Nothing wild seems to be going on anywhere right now: no prison escapes or civil disturbances, no floods, no big forest fires."

"Hey, that sounds like good news," offered Val, and then flushed as both men looked at him. "Sort of, anyway."

"Then I called the hospital in Coeur d'Alene," Gutierrez went on. "So far as anyone could tell me, Meg has not been back there. No one remembers seeing her or Cass leave on Friday. Dr. Wu, he's the one who treated me, is off duty until Monday night. They wouldn't give me his home number, but they finally agreed to call his house for me. He's gone fishing, probably won't come back until the last minute."

"You talk to Mary Louise?" asked Svoboda.

Gutierrez nodded, his face grim. "Mary Louise has heard nothing and is sure nothing could be wrong. She *says*. I figure she believes Jonathan Archer is involved, and she's scared of the family."

"So she won't officially declare her kid missing," Svoboda noted.

"You got it," said Gutierrez. "I could probably browbeat her into acting, but I'd have to go to Colorado Springs to do it. So I called Archer Senior. He told me his son is away visiting friends and then he hung up. Then I called that ranch camp in Plumas County to see whether Meg had been in touch with Katy; but since I'm not a parent, no one there will tell me anything."

"That the rocking R, the Reardons' place?" At Gutierrez's nod, Svoboda reached for the telephone. "I've known Roy and Betty for twenty years, they'll talk to me. You got an extension?"

Gutierrez pulled his feet close to his stool as if to rise, then thought better of it. "In the loft, but there's a jack right over there. Val?" he asked, and Kuisma leapt for the stairs.

Betty Reardon was happy to hear from her old friend Hank Svoboda. Betty could say for sure that Mrs. Halloran had last called her daughter three days ago, Wednesday, although it had previously been her habit to call every other day. Betty was confident that nothing could be wrong, and she would surely not say a word to Katy.

Gutierrez gave the woman his phone number and a polite thank-you. "Bullshit!" he snarled as he shoved the phone aside and picked up the bourbon bottle, to tip it over his glass with a shaking hand. "There is no way, no way in hell, she would not have talked to Katy by now. Oh Jesus, Hank, what am I going to say to Katy?"

"Nothing at all just yet." Svoboda pulled a cardboard container from a paper sack, doused the contents with soy sauce and vinegar, and got forks from the kitchen. He speared a pot sticker, bit into it, chewed absently. "Okay, what's the next thing?"

"I call the Coeur d'Alene police again. They were not impressed this afternoon; the sergeant I spoke with told me very politely that forty-eight hours wasn't really what you'd call missing for a grown woman. Goddamn it!" he snapped. "I've been telling Meg for the past year that we ought to get married. If I was her husband, maybe those bastards would move off their dead asses."

Another sergeant in Coeur d'Alene was equally polite. They had prepared the missing person report and started it through channels. They would appreciate it if Mr....excuse it, if *Chief* Gutierrez could send pictures of Mrs. Halloran and her traveling companion.

Gutierrez would indeed do that. He repeated his own certainty that Mrs. Halloran was the victim of someone or something beyond her control. He gave them the van's license number again. "And one more thing. She usually buys Shell gas, and charges it. When she left me at the hospital, she planned to stop at a big Shell station on Interstate 90 just west of your town. Thank you," he added after a pause, "I'd appreciate that. I'll be in touch."

He hung up the phone with exaggerated care. "Fuck Pacific Bell and AT&T and all the rest of them. Hank, that friend of yours with the air charter business. Do you think he'd fly me to Idaho? Or maybe," he added thoughtfully, "to Colorado. Colorado Springs and then Idaho."

"Hell yes, Jake Delucca'll short-hop you around the world long as you pay him for it. But Vince, you and airplanes . . . you ever fly on a *little* plane?"

"Nope. But I might be a whole lot better without any other passengers to see how chickenshit scared I get."

"Want me to come along? See," he went on as Gutierrez raised his eyebrows, "you're not exactly in shape to drive once you get there. Might be you'll even need a little help with leg work, no offense intended."

Gutierrez sighed, and straightened under his shoulder brace. "You want to offend me, you'll have to get in line. But you, old buddy, are supposed to be acting chief here in my absence."

"Hey, Chief Gutierrez, how about me, could I help?" Val Kuisma's voice was eager. "I've got lots of comp time coming, and I'd be real happy to get out of town."

Gutierrez turned a speculative gaze on Val Kuisma, young and strong and useful. With his Finnish father's green eyes and his Portuguese mother's black hair and olive skin, the boy was as handsome as he was sweet-tempered; his love life was a perpetual roller-coaster ride. "Maybe Port Silva could get along without one of its patrol officers for a few days. How about it, Hank?"

"Oh, I reckon we can manage."

THIRTEEN

THE THOUGHT OF TRYING to go to sleep brushed Meg's mind and was promptly dismissed; every hair on her head was separate and alert, her very skin wide awake. With a sigh she stretched out on her cot, covering herself first with Vince's jacket and then with a blanket. Vince was at home in the hillside house, a gray cube of cedar set on stilts above the Pacific. Built, he'd told her, by a friend of his, a novelist who wanted to escape from his screenwriter's life amid the noise and fury of Los Angeles to a simple, natural setting where he could produce his magnum opus, his novel. He'd lasted less than a year, and had sold the house cheaply to Vince . . . glad to escape, he said, before he sank completely into solitary alcoholism.

She couldn't remember the man's name, so apparently the big novel never happened. But he'd made a good house, no mean accomplishment. She and Vince would live there until they were too old to climb all those steps . . .

Katy! she thought suddenly, and pulled the jacket up under her chin. What would happen to Katy if Meg never came home? She'd lived in Port Silva for two years, loved it and her school and her friends. Loved Vince. But Meg's mother would be sure to want to take her only granddaughter home to Tucson.

Listen, Katy, listen to me. There's nothing for you to worry about, you have a good time with your horse, Sam, the Morgan that you told me about when I talked to you about a million years ago, I guess it was Wednesday night. Grow another two inches because you're going to be a tall person, how could you help it with what you had for parents? I know you're working on that damned dive, but I didn't tell you not to, did I? And this will be a surprise, I'm going to get you the electric guitar as soon as the downstairs is finished and you can play down there. God, electronic music...why do you want to do that?...

One scrap, one little corner of her mind, stayed apart to listen. Both men were inside now. Moved around in the kitchen, the front room. Spoke a word, two words. Kitchen light out. Creak from the bunk-bed, so *close* not more than four feet away. Footsteps. After a while, a faint drift of something sweet in the air, marijuana.

A chair scraped, and footsteps sounded again, soft, not quite even. And the bed. Dark grew even darker, perhaps the moon had set. No sound at all from the others; then a rustle and a soft whimper: Cass. Meg felt a surge of gratitude to Cass, that she was there instead of Katy, gratitude and pity and finally guilt. Shh, shh, sleep, Cass. A snore from beyond the wall.

Later, it felt much later, there was a new sound, first the barest whisper and then almost a rustle: rain, a gentle rain blown against the little house by an easy wind. Small rain. Western wind, when wilt thou blow, that the small rain down may rain? She squeezed her eyes shut and blanked her mind against the rest of that verse.

Later. Meg rose quietly from the cot, felt for the lantern and then set it aside; it would send light through the vents or under the door. Working in the dark, with the occasional help of a pocket flash from her suitcase, she wielded her tiny snips against the screen above her cot and slowly, carefully snipped every wire along the bottom edge. Bolt hole for Cass, at least, she thought with a sense of accomplishment.

Okay, but suppose the cut edges show, glisten silver in the sun. What a nasty possibility, do something about it. She shoved Cass's bigger and very heavy bag aside, set the girl's tote atop the bag and opened it to find a makeup bag like her own but larger, stuffed with a collection of pencils and bottles and tubes. Mascara there, of course, the kind with the spiral wand. Stand up here now, lady, and dab that shiny screen with the cute little brush, best to keep busy it certainly beats thinking. Makes for a truly unusual Saturday

night, no, Sunday morning, and if you get silly and fall
down there won't be any Sunday afternoon at all.

She put the mascara back in Cass's tote, closed it. Shoved
the bigger bag with the side of her foot and thought, What
on earth is that? Rocks?

Cass turned, moaned, settled. Meg released her breath
and knelt beside the bag. Zipper, good luck it wasn't noisy
Velcro. She wrapped her hand around the tab and eased it
back, all the way, until the bag gaped open. Slid her hand
inside. Soft fabric. Woolly ball, socks? Something slick and
quilted: a robe. Sweater. A pair of solid, pointy things:
heels, on shoes. Weapons-quality, those, she noted. Something round and flat and hard, wrapped in toweling. She
pulled the object halfway out and turned her pocket flash on
it: a skillet. *The* skillet, by God, that she'd paid the trailer
people for.

Skillet, and lid. Small saucepan, with lid. Spatula, and big
spoon. Two metal plates; a packet of flatware. The little drip
coffee-maker. Meg put everything away again and sat back
on her heels. Either Cass was simply a magpie, unable to
keep her fingers off anything not tied down; or she
was…what? She was preparing to set up a household, that's
what! thought Meg indignantly. She was getting ready for
Jon: pots and pans, plates. Even a cat, for Jon who liked
cats. Christ on a crutch!

After a moment she subdued her anger and returned to
that bag, and then to the smaller one, and finally to the tote.
A few more household items, like a salt and pepper set, but
no keys. Perhaps the sneaky little bitch wasn't planning to
take the van. Or perhaps she was simply too smart for Meg
and had hidden the keys elsewhere.

Nearly three. She thought she could sleep now. Or she
could wake Cass, she needed to do that sometime before
morning. No. Two hours' sleep, she'd wake at five and wake
the girl. She settled Cass's bags to look untouched, opened
her own case and fished out the bottle of gin; how nice they
hadn't confiscated that, her jailers. One little nip, using the
nice big red cap Bombay bottles had; and then a nap. A nip

and a nap; she was light-headed already. Five o'clock, she told her mind firmly. Two hours. Wake up at five.

MEG'S EYES snapped open in a room still dark, a faint gray beginning to show at the vents. The rain had stopped, but the air was moist and cool. She closed her eyes again and stilled her own breathing; no sound of movement from beyond the wall, only a steady rumbling snore.

She pushed her covers aside, eased her legs over the edge of the cot, slowly pushed herself upright. Stood up. Cass was silent and unmoving, only a frill of hair showing over the top of her sleeping bag. Meg knelt beside the cot, put a hand lightly on the girl's shoulder, and leaned close. "Cass?"

Cass made a wordless mumble and tried to shrug lower in the bag.

"Cass. I need to talk to you. Before the men wake up."

The shoulder under Meg's hand was suddenly stiff, transmitting returning consciousness like electricity.

"Please. Turn over so you can see me, and be very quiet." The girl obeyed, and Meg found herself looking at a pair of huge eyes in a pinched face, a small animal peering out of its cave. Sneaky, untrustworthy animal...no no, defensive, Meg told herself. Defensive, thieving little wretch.

"It's all right." She put a finger to her lips and nodded toward the wall. "They're still asleep. I wanted to tell you that I cut the screen last night, there." This was one of the decisions she'd made, to tell Cass about the cut screen lest she discover it and inadvertently call attention to it. "It's an emergency escape hatch, for you. Too small for me. In case we don't think of anything better."

"Oh," breathed Cass, and stuck her head out to look up at the vent. "Yeah. Great."

"And there are some things I need to ask you." Now, Meg thought grimly, while you're still half asleep and maybe even grateful. "Where is Jon?"

"Where...? I don't *know*, I told you that. I don't know where he is and I wish I did!" The last words broke from whisper to low wail, followed by a convincing sniff.

"Was Jon involved in anything seriously illegal or dangerous? Something to make enemies?"

The girl sat up suddenly. "Wait a minute," she said, and Meg put a quick shushing finger to her own lips.

"You think these guys," Cass went on in a fierce whisper, "that faggot motherfucker Jay, you think he's Jon's fault? No way!"

"There has to be some reason," Meg began, but Cass clutched the sleeping bag with both hands and thrust her head forward. "Probably those guys are after Uncle Vince! Probably we're in this shit because we're related to a cop!"

"That's certainly a possibility," said Meg quietly, and Cass bit back whatever she'd been ready to say, her eyes widening.

"And a third is that friends of Jon's are trying to help him."

Cass shot a look at her duffel bag, but Meg did not follow the glance. Another decision made in the night: the subject of a few stolen pots and pans could be dealt with in better times, should any come along.

"Jon doesn't have friends, just me. And he wouldn't let anybody else . . . Jon wouldn't let anybody hit me," Cass finished in a soft rush of words. "He wouldn't let that crazy guy *touch* me."

Meg sat back on her heels, no wiser than when she'd started. "One thing I am sure of," she said evenly, "is that Jon is not here to protect you. So it's up to you to remember that Jay is dangerous. For instance, if he sees you being too friendly with Kevin, he might . . ."

"Don't you tell me what he might do, I *know* what men do!" Cass spat the words out in a fierce whisper and then rolled onto her belly to bury her face between her arms. "That stuff is nothing new to me, I learned all about it from my mom's boyfriend when I was fourteen."

"Oh, Cass." Meg put an arm across the rigid shoulders. "I'm sorry."

"He was just like this creep, lying around the house all day smoking dope while my mom worked and I went to school. He said it was my fault, I asked for it."

"And what did your mother say?"

"Oh, well, my mom...there wasn't any point in telling her, my mom can't handle shit like that. Anyway, the guy split right after."

Meg tightened her grip, and laid her cheek for a moment against the girl's hair. "It wasn't your fault. Hear that? It was not your fault."

After a moment Cass shrugged herself free and sat up. "But this time it would be, is that what you're saying?"

"I'm saying that we are captives, and helplessness itself is a turn-on to somebody who is sick to start with." Meg took a deep breath; keep your voice low, lady. And keep it simple. "I'm saying that if Jay breaks loose, he may not stop at rape. I'm saying I'd like for both of us to get out of here alive."

Cass opened her mouth, closed it, and nodded.

"Fine." Meg got to her feet as someone groaned and then swore in the front room; it was much lighter now, her watch said almost six. Sunday morning, maybe they'd all go to church.

"The jailers will be here any minute. Would you like to be first at the washhouse?"

"Yeah," said Cass, and began to scramble into her clothes.

Meg went back to her own cot, lay down, and pulled the blanket up. Soon there were footsteps, the rattle of key and padlock, then a widening shaft of light from the door and Jay's gruff voice: "One of you come on, hurry it up."

Meg waited perhaps a minute after the door had closed on Cass before rolling to her feet and hurrying to the other cot. She shook clothes, punched the pillow, lifted the sleeping bag to look under it. She unzipped the bag and began a careful inspection, the top edge and then the near side and the bottom. At the far corner of the bottom her fingers met something hard; she pulled the bag closer and found a gap in the stitching. She slid her fingers inside, worked them over to the corner, grasped the object hidden there, and pulled it out. Key case.

Decision time again. She could simply leave the keys there, in a good hiding place. But suppose Cass decided to operate on her own, to flee through the cut screen and take the van and roar off to meet Jon somewhere? Leaving Meg to whatever fate Jay decided upon.

Or she could keep the keys and tell Cass she had found them, say without anger that she felt they were better in her keeping.

In the end, she removed the keys, snapped the hard case shut, and put it back in the sleeping bag. She was wearing her newest Levi's, their stiffness giving her a sense of protective armor. One key went in the watch pocket, the other in a hip pocket, and she was quite sure neither showed.

FOURTEEN

ELIZABETH'S LONG LEGS made the room small: six strides from door to draped window, a stiff-bodied turn that set the open robe flaring behind her, six strides back. Window and door and window again, and then she paused beside the dark dressing alcove, crossed her arms beneath her breasts and leaned inside. After a moment she straightened, shook back long pale hair and resumed her pacing, forward, back, forward, bare feet making a faint rasp on beige tweed carpet. From outside came a low, steady hum: eighteen-wheelers trucking on south past Eugene, Oregon, on Interstate Five.

A gentle tap-tap on the door; she spun around, grimaced and slid her left hand gingerly under the right strap of her nightgown. The band of discolored flesh beginning there ran diagonally across her chest, dark imprint of the shoulder belt that had saved her from worse injury two days earlier. There was the rattle of a key, and the door swung inward. Ben Taylor had a plastic ice-bucket in his left hand, a bottle under that arm.

"Where have you been?" Elizabeth made each word a separate entity.

Ben came in and eased the door shut. "Waiting, in the bar and then the coffee shop, and trying the phone every fifteen minutes. SallyAnne obviously had a late date tonight; I just got through to her." He squinted at the glass-topped desk beside the door and sidled close enough to set the ice-bucket down without dropping the bottle. "How's the kid?"

Elizabeth closed her robe and yanked the belt tight. "She's been asleep for the past hour. And you're drunk."

"I am not *drunk*, I'm merely relaxed. Did you spend some time in the tub with the Jacuzzi?"

She shook her head. "I was afraid it would make too much noise."

"We could go down to the sauna if you'd like, probably be good for both of us."

"And if she woke frightened and made a fuss? And someone complained?"

"Elizabeth, you have a veritable pharmacy in your nurse's bag. Why not give the poor little kid something to help her sleep, and help us poor old folks in the bargain?"

"Small children can respond unpredictably to sedatives," she snapped.

He shrugged and opened the brandy bottle, poured an inch into a small glass and then glanced at her with raised eyebrows.

"No, thank you. One of us should stay sober." Elizabeth lowered herself stiffly to the edge of the bed. "What did she say? Sally whoever, Michael's nurse?"

"She told Michael just this morning that we were coming, or that you and Tessa were coming. She says it perked him up so much that his mother noticed and called it to the doctor's attention."

"Oh, Christ," she whispered.

"I've nothing at all against prayer, but I don't believe it's necessary in this instance," he said, and took a quick sip of brandy. "Michael won't give us away. He was a little worried that the Demerol he's been taking might make him careless, so he's cut back on it until we're safely there."

"I can't do this. Ben, I can't. I'm going back to Idaho."

"I'll take you back, of course; you have only to say the word." He set his glass down and moved close, to cup her face in his hands, stroke her temples and trace the line of her jaw. "But you're the toughest lady I know; you can do whatever you have to, always could." After a moment he let go of her and said in more ordinary tones, "This was *your* decision, remember? Worth some risk to make Michael's dying easier, that's what you said."

She took a long, shaky breath without raising her head; in her lap, her interlaced fingers tightened, twisted. "Did Sweet make contact?"

Ben emptied his glass in a gulp. "No. Must be no problems."

"Well. That's something. That's good."

Ben turned to the desk, dropped ice into a water glass and poured in a good measure of brandy. He fished a small bottle from a paper bag, filled the glass with fizzy soda and held it out until she reached for it. "Want to flip a coin?" he asked after she had taken a mouthful.

"No. We'll go on."

"Good girl." She looked up sharply, and he added, "Sorry. That sounded patronizing. But I think you've made the best decision. Let's see, it's three A.M. Sunday morning, and both of us, all three of us, need sleep. If we leave here around noon and drive 250 miles today and 350 tomorrow, the last fifty or so very slowly over narrow country roads, we could arrive at CliffHaven without fanfare that evening, Monday evening."

"That sounds manageable, if we can keep the baby amused." Elizabeth's eyes were a piercing blue even in the dim room. "You're being sweet and helpful, Ben. The absolute altruist, which as I remember it is not your native role. Suppose Michael slips up and talks to his mother? Or SallyAnne, suppose you haven't paid her well enough?"

"One possibility is that Mother T. says Oh joy, here comes my grandbaby. Second is that she calls the police, which means we're screwed, temporarily at least."

"You mean I'm screwed. Transporting a fugitive is probably a much lesser charge than what I'll face." Elizabeth pushed herself to her feet and went to the desk to set her glass down, drop in more ice, pour soda, add a liberal slosh of brandy. "What about third?"

"Third, fourth, fifth, infinity; didn't your mother ever tell you not to borrow trouble? What you'd better do is drink that fast and get to bed," he advised. "You look like death."

"Thank you, Ben. That's a particularly sensitive remark."

"Sorry. Although," he said, looking hard at her, "it's probably all to the good. You don't want to arrive at

CliffHaven looking anything less than a distraught widow-to-be."

She flew at him with both fists; his brandy glass hit the carpet and rolled as he caught her wrists, yanked them down and pushed them behind her in a parody of an embrace.

"Right, let's just clear the air here." He gave her a push as he released her; the backs of her knees hit the edge of the bed and she sat down abruptly. "We both—*both*," he repeated, "want to do right by Michael. And after that, *you* want to do good with Michael's money, and I figure some of the good you can do is to me, in gratitude for my support both physical and moral. Okay?"

"So he did inherit!"

"I'll accept the fact that you didn't know. Yes, contrary to good sense and probably the advice of a whole raft of lawyers, when Marcus Tannenbaum died in January he left his many millions, or most of them, to his terminally ill son. But don't start planning to expand Shelter nation-wide just yet."

"It's not community property." The words trailed down like a soft four-note scale.

"Correct, you've been doing your homework. Beyond the trust fund the old man set up when Tessa was born...if we keep you out of jail you may possibly get control of that...beyond that, the money is Michael's to leave as he wishes, to charities, or to you, or most likely to his daughter."

"Couldn't you find out about it?"

"A will is not public record, my dear, so long as its maker is alive. I'm fairly sure Michael has made his, but I couldn't get him to talk about it. Maybe he was too tired and my questions too subtle; maybe he was just jerking me around a little, he was always good at that. In either case, I think we'd be wise to get there while he's still able to make changes."

FIFTEEN

"THIS IS ONE beautiful machine," sighed Val Kuisma, pink-cheeked with pleasure; he'd spent most of an hour watching Jake Delucca pilot the twin-engined Beechcraft. "Jake told me all about it. And he gives flying lessons; he says he'll make me a special price. Hey, Chief," he added as he sat down beside his boss, "you look a little better. Not quite so green."

Gutierrez, who'd been deep in a maze of thoughts and plans, immediately felt a surge of nausea. "Kuisma, why don't you go back up there and count clouds or something. And ask Delucca how long till we land."

The word "land" brought another flip-flop from his unhappy stomach. Gutierrez closed his eyes and heard Kuisma's "about forty-five minutes" as if from a great distance. This was not, after all, the worst airplane ride he'd ever taken. The weather had been smooth so far, nobody was smoking, nobody was shoving predigested-looking food in his face. The trip was not even quite as expensive as he'd anticipated, because Delucca had a load of mining equipment waiting in Colorado Springs for transport to California.

Besides, flying did him a great service in keeping his mind away from the pictures in his head. He'd been a cop for half his life, and cops see too many unhappy endings.

GUTIERREZ DECIDED not to call ahead, and was lucky enough to find his sister at home; but things went rapidly downhill from there. Mary Louise thought it was too soon to worry. Mary Louise was late for work. Mary Louise did not need the kind of trouble Mr. Archer could make for her.

"And what about your daughter?" He ground the words out through clenched teeth.

"Well, Cass. If she *has* gone off someplace with Jon Archer, it's her choice, not mine, her responsibility. Eddie ... my *novio*, Eddie Morales ... Eddie thinks I've been too easy with Cass, spoiled her. He says none of the women in his family would get away with talking and acting the way she does."

"And this Eddie, he's the man Cass mentioned the other day?"

"See, that's what I mean! She called him a greaser! Eddie is a fine, hardworking man even if he does look tough, and he's been good to me. Of course, he's had some trouble, and the police make him nervous, so he wishes I wouldn't ... get involved with them. Unnecessarily involved, that is."

Gutierrez's shoulder hurt, his gut hurt, and anger was tightening around his head like pincers. Life as Mary Louise had always lived it: find a man and do what he tells you and everything will be just fine. Maybe, he thought now—as he always did—if Papa hadn't died before she was a year old ... if Mama had been more loving and less demanding with her tag-end baby ... or maybe nothing would have made Mary Louise anything but what she was.

"He doesn't think Jon Archer has anything to do with this," Mary Louise added, "and neither do I. I think they're on the road to California, Cass and your Margaret; that's a long drive."

"Margaret Halloran is a grownup lady with a daughter of her own." With some effort Gutierrez kept his words flat and measured. "She loves me, she'd know I'd worry, she would not do this to me."

"*I* would. Vincente, you're always so intimidating, so pushy. You never do just what people ask you, you always have to take over. Margaret, Meg, expected to have a nice vacation with you, and then you stuck her with somebody's spoiled brat of a daughter. If I were her, I wouldn't call either."

Mary Louise's face was white and set, a combination of fear and stubbornness; behind him he could hear, or feel, Kuisma holding his breath. "Well, that's fine, Mary Louise.

With that attitude, you sure as hell wouldn't be much use to me at the police station. Val, let's get out of here."

SOME TWO HOURS LATER a silent Kuisma drove the rented Toyota through moderate Sunday afternoon traffic. Gutierrez, stiffly upright in the passenger seat, stared out the side window at the same scene he'd looked at exactly one week before. Bright clean sunny town. Chilly, hard-surfaced.

"What? No, don't get on the freeway. Just a few blocks, you'll come to, uh, Colorado, that's it. Colorado to Manitou. The Archers live in a rich-folks colony called Pinewood Estates; it's actually on the outer edge of Manitou Springs."

"Okay. Say, the police department here looks pretty good, don't you think? Neat layout, new equipment... you should see their computer room, Chief. And I thought the guys were, unh, pretty helpful."

Gutierrez had spent an uncomfortable time with two local cops, trying to convey his sense of urgency without too-frequent reference to such terms as "experience" and "gut feeling." The crisply uniformed officers, their combined ages less than his, were straightbacked and respectful to a visiting police chief, although they clearly believed that Meg would roll up to her own front door any minute.

"Tolerant is what you mean," he snapped now in reply to Kuisma, no doubt another secret skeptic. "Of California lunatics who can't keep track of their womenfolk."

"No sir, that's not what I mean." Kuisma was hurt. "I know Mrs. Halloran too; she was my sister Betsy's English teacher last year. My whole family thinks Mrs. Halloran about walks on water. And anyway I respect your judgment. Sir."

"Okay. Fine." Gutierrez wished bleakly for the stolid, comfortable presence of Svoboda. Kuisma was a lifelong hunter and backpacker; he had worked on forestry fire-fighting crews to put himself through college. But he was still more puppy-dog than cop. "Here's Colorado coming up."

The road angled northwest, past small businesses and trailer parks and gas stations. Red rock formations loomed against the skyline to the right, and after a few moments Gutierrez closed his eyes and tried to concentrate on the hot floorboard beneath his boots, the poorly sprung seat under his butt, the dull ache along his collarbone. The high-pitched rattle of the engine. Meg would hate that; she believed machines deserved the respect of proper mainte-nance.

Those particular red rocks were called the Garden of the Gods. A week ago...no, a week and a day, Saturday, he and Meg had stayed in a campground facing the Garden across several miles that might have been no distance at all. Just the two of them, with Cass not yet in their lives or even their thoughts; they'd relaxed with drinks and a small campfire and then they'd gone to bed in their trailer.

"Well shit," said Kuisma in disgust as he missed one bump in the rocky road only to hit another. "Sorry, Chief. You'd think people who live in places with big brick walls and double iron gates would at least have their road paved."

"Rich people are funny about things like that," mut-tered Gutierrez. "Besides, this way they can hear us com-ing. And see us," he added, grimacing at the cloud of red dust rising behind them. "Archer's place should be...yeah, 172, there with the white wall."

The Archer property had no gate, just an arch flowing up from the wall across a broad driveway. They drove past red rocks and cactus and other desert vegetation to a house that was low, broad, and southwestern, built of adobe bricks with protruding beams and deepset windows. The driveway fanned out into a parking area; Gutierrez climbed stiffly from the small car and stalked to the carved, tile-framed door, Kuisma on his heels.

The man who pulled the door open was not more than five and a half feet tall, holding himself to make the most of every inch. In knit shirt and khaki shorts he displayed the trimly muscular body of a tennis player; his tan included even the top of his head, framed by a thick horseshoe of very curly graying hair. He regarded them for a moment from hard brown eyes; then he nodded and stepped back.

"You might as well come in; but I'm leaving for an appointment in ten minutes."

"Nice to know we've been announced," murmured Gutierrez, remembering the efficient policemen downtown. "I am Vincent Gutierrez; we've spoken by telephone. And this is my colleague, Officer Val Kuisma."

"Lawrence Archer." The smaller man closed the door and led his visitors across a tiled floor into a room that was obviously a combination study and office, with floor to ceiling bookshelves, a broad desk, several leather armchairs. Val, bringing up the rear, paused to glance toward the far wall of the entry area, where glass doors were open to a flower-filled patio with a splashing fountain.

"Boy, this is sure a pretty house," he murmured. "Excuse me, Mr. Archer."

"Quite all right, I'm proud of the place. I assisted in its design." He sat down behind the desk and gestured them to chairs. "Mr. Gutierrez, I have nothing to say to you beyond what I said when you called yesterday. My son can be of no concern to you, or to your sister, or to your niece. I'm sorry that you have . . . ah, lost track of the girl. But my son knows nothing of her present whereabouts."

"I'd like to hear that from the boy himself."

Archer tipped his chair back and folded his arms across his chest, tucking his hands under his biceps. "That won't be possible. Jon is visiting a friend whose parents have a place in the mountains northwest of here. The cabin is secluded, with no telephone."

"So you can't know for sure that he's there."

Archer's chair came forward with a thump. "I know he's there because he told me that was where he was going. He'll be back in another week; if the young woman hasn't turned up by then, by all means come to speak with him."

Gutierrez drew a deep breath. "Mr. Archer, my sister believes Cass and Jon were in love; Cass told her they were going to get married."

Archer shrugged. "I've met your sister, and to be frank, I found her a silly woman, the kind a young girl might well run away from."

"Maybe," said Gutierrez, aware that his face was reddening. "But my fiancée, Mrs. Halloran, isn't silly, and she's missing, too."

"You saw them midday Friday, I believe. And this is Sunday. You obviously keep a tighter rein on your women than I do on mine, Gutierrez. My wife went to Europe six weeks ago, and I've had two postcards." Archer glanced toward the corner of his desk, where a silver frame displayed a professional photograph of a woman with hollow cheeks and a lion's mane of blond hair; he picked up a Lucite picture-cube that stood beside the frame, looked at it, and pushed it across the polished wood to Gutierrez. "This is my son, Jonathan.

"His I.Q. is over 150," Archer proclaimed. Gutierrez mentally added a trumpet fanfare as he looked at the first photo: a figure on a steep ski slope, bent in classic form. "He's going to Exeter for an extra prep year this fall, and then to Harvard or, preferably, Yale," Archer went on. Gutierrez gave the cube a quarter turn and saw blue water and a viciously sleek speedboat at a sharp angle, white wake splashing. "The boy's an incredible competitor. If he can just…when he learns to channel his talents he'll be the best trial lawyer of his time," said Archer. Another quarter turn, to show a long-legged youth in a white suit marked on the breast by a red heart; the mask was up, the foil held erect.

"So I'm sure you can understand that the notion of Jon's marrying anyone at this point in his life is ludicrous. I'm not surprised that your little niece is crazy about him, but the rest of it is just schoolgirl romanticizing."

On the fourth side of the cube the boy and his father stood on either side of a gleaming black motorcycle. Archer, the shorter by probably eight inches, looked straight at the camera, his face creased in a broad grin. Jon stood easy, big right hand resting possessively on the frame of the bike. His face, almost in profile, was handsome in an old-fashioned movie star way: high forehead under combed-black dark hair, straight nose, square jaw. He seemed to be looking not at his father but past him, over his head.

"Possibly," said Gutierrez. He held the photo up to scrutinize it more closely. "Would you mind giving me the name of the person your son is staying with?"

"Yes, I would mind," snapped Archer. "The people are family friends, and I won't have them bothered. You'll simply have to accept my word for the fact that Jon has had absolutely no contact with your niece for the past week."

They all jumped at a dull explosion from the hall outside the open door; Kuisma leaped to his feet and dashed out. "Oh shit. Here, Ma'am, you better step around that real careful or you'll cut yourself."

She was tall for a woman, perhaps five feet eight; and her broad shoulders and long arms suggested that she'd had a rawboned strength before fat overtook her. Now she looked Kuisma up and down, and finally grinned widely as she took his outstretched hand to let him guide her bare feet around a splattery mess of damp earth and pottery shards.

"Doris, what the hell is going on here?"

She released Kuisma, with obvious reluctance. "I was just taking this here portulaca out to the patio, and I tripped."

"Well if you'd wear *shoes* for Christ's sake."

The woman shook her curly gray head at the mess, then looked again toward the study door. She caught Gutierrez's gaze and held it, pale blue eyes narrowed.

"Just get this cleaned up," said Archer. Doris tossed a glance at him, and Gutierrez read irritation in her face and no subservience at all.

"Val," he said, "why don't you help Doris, while I have a last word with Mr. Archer. He has an appointment, and I think we should probably make one, too."

Kuisma gaped for a brief moment before composing his face. "Sure, Chief. Ma'am, if you'll just show me where to find the broom and dustpan..."

"You're correct, Chief Gutierrez," snapped Archer, "and I'm late already. So if you'll excuse me."

Gutierrez reined in his temper and reached into his pocket. "I'm not trying to make trouble for you, Archer; I just want to find my family. Here's my card. I'd appreciate a call if you learn anything that might help me."

A SHORT TIME LATER Gutierrez and Kuisma sat well back in the driveway of a house with a FOR SALE sign on its gate and watched Archer whisk by in a Mercedes sports convertible. "Give it a couple of minutes, Val," said Gutierrez. "We don't want him to look back and see more dust than he could have raised."

"I don't think he's looking back, Chief," said Val, but he sat with his hands resting loosely on the Toyota's steering wheel until Gutierrez said, "Let's go."

"She has this little cottage off in a grove of pine trees behind the house," Kuisma said. While wielding a broom for Doris, he had explained their mission, the little she hadn't already gathered from eavesdropping. "See, she's some kind of cousin of Mrs. Archer's mother. She was married once, right after World War II, and she had a baby boy, he died. Then a long time after that she came here to work. She says Archer's a prick, but he pays good, and she likes having her own place. I guess she likes the kid, too, this Jon."

"Isn't she worried about losing her job, talking to us?" It was asked casually; Gutierrez wanted information and would get it if it cost a whole flock of housekeepers their jobs.

Kuisma shook his head as he turned once more into the Archer driveway. "She says she's the best private cook in the county, that's how she got so fat. Archer likes to entertain, impress people; he thinks it makes him a big deal that everybody tries to hire her away and she won't go."

"DORIS, I THINK I'VE heard Cass mention your name," Gutierrez lied a few minutes later.

"Yeah, I guess she might've." Doris had changed from her denim skirt and white shirt into a flowered muu-muu which reached nearly to her ankles. "She used to help me in the kitchen sometimes while Jonny was fooling around with his exercise gear, that Nautilus stuff his dad bought him.

Good little worker, she is. Look, you two fellas sit down, and I'll bring you some coffee and cake.''

"Hey, let me help." Kuisma sprang to his feet and trotted after Doris toward her kitchen. Good boy, thought Gutierrez, staying where he was and inspecting his surroundings. Nice solid little cottage, thick walls and big windows. Overstuffed couch and chairs covered in shiny fabric with big roses on it, wall to wall carpet, lots of pictures. Horses, mostly, he discovered, and dogs. And Jon Archer. At least he assumed the little boy was Jon; the older one definitely was.

"I see you've known Jonathan most of his life," Gutierrez said to Doris when she returned with a tray.

"All of it." She set the tray down, poured big mugs full of coffee, stood back and gestured. "Help yourselves. Sour cream chocolate cake, my own recipe.

"I love Jonny," she said when they were all seated. "You can see from the pictures how cute he was, and I always been putty in the hands of a good-looking male, story of my life. But that don't make me stupid, I could still tell good from bad. Fact is, Jonny's not a real good person."

Gutierrez set his fork down quietly on his cake plate.

"Well, the poor kid," she said defensively, "he's got this mama and daddy can hardly stand each other, both of 'em screw around a lot. Basically mean-hearted, selfish folks that don't care about anything except money and showing off; if they'd had a dumb ugly kid they'd likely have adopted him out. Anyway, Jonny don't like anybody much. Enjoys making fools of people, sometimes hurts 'em. That's one reason I like that little Cass; Jonny is nicer with her."

"Nicer?"

"Yeah. I guess it's because he knows she's had a rotten time, no father and a dingbat for a mother. And young as she is, she was messing around with some real no-good guys when Jon met her. You might say he kind of rescued her."

"I suppose you might."

"Me, I always hoped he'd someday, oh, maybe get religion or somethin'. When he found this poor little girl and at least tried to treat her good, it made me real happy."

"So you helped them," suggested Gutierrez.

Doris hunched her shoulders in a shrug of apology. "Over this last week I passed messages. Cass, she'd call and talk to me like friends which we were, kind of—what she was doing, where she was, where she was going. And she'd ask if maybe I could tell Jonny if he called. And he called, and I told him."

Cass had called Doris, in her cottage on her own phone, Monday night, Tuesday night, Wednesday night. She had relayed the details of her trip, the route and proposed stopping places. She had told Doris about the van and the trailer, with descriptions and license numbers. And Jonny had called the same nights, late.

There had been no calls Thursday night. As Jon and Cass both knew, Doris played canasta with another lady and two gentlemen every Thursday evening, and often as not she stayed the night with her particular gentleman. "But then Cass, she didn't call on Friday. Jonny was real angry, swore a lot at her and at me. He figured it was your fault," she said to Gutierrez, "that you'd found out and stopped her calls. When he ran out of swear words, he hung up. I ain't heard nothing since, since Friday, from either of 'em."

Gutierrez absently cut off a bite of cake and put it in his mouth and then set the plate aside. Cass had managed to make a phone call every night they were on the road; he had not been aware of these calls, nor so far as he knew had Meg. No call Friday meant Meg had found her out and stopped her. Or Cass had been too tired and had forgotten. Or something or someone else had prevented her from calling. Prevented both of them.

Muscles were making random jerky twitches in his legs and across his shoulders; he got to his feet, accepted a coffee refill from Kuisma, moved to stand before a window. "Could you tell where Jon was calling from?"

She gave her head a slow, doleful shake. "First night, I heard him say something, sideways like, to some Dave. I figured that was David Guillaume, the boy he was supposed to be staying with. If I'd thought about it, I'd have guessed they was in Colossus; that's the town closest to the Guillaume place."

"The other nights?"

"No idea. Well, Friday night he was calling from some bar, with country music."

And how many of those between here and California? "Doris, what did you think he had in mind?"

"Now look, how would I know..." She settled deeper into her chair, shoulders slumping. "I figured he was gonna catch up with this girl, and then the two of them would run off. Shit, I run off with a guy when I was sixteen...and one or two more, later."

"There's something here I don't get," said Kuisma. "The two of them were right here in the same town, and I guess Cass's mom wasn't going to put up a serious fuss." He cast an apologetic look at Gutierrez. "So why wait? Why did he wait to chase down the road after her?"

"Well, his birthday, of course." When Doris drew only blank looks from the two men, she sighed. "Jonny's gonna be eighteen years old tomorrow, and out from under his father's control...what control there was, because Larry Archer's half scared of his own kid and that's a fact. He'll have a chunk of money, too, Jonny will, that his grandmother left him. Them kids can go where they want, and do what they want," she finished, with a kind of forlorn satisfaction.

And this big rich kid who frightened his own father...what would he do to a woman who seemed to stand in his way? Meg had agreed not to interfere if Jon turned up, and she was wise in the ways of adolescents. But she was also short-tempered and sharp of tongue.

Gutierrez's narrowed eyes had remained on Doris while his thoughts raced. Now she began to squirm, color flooding her round cheeks. "I guess I better tell Larry...Mr. Archer," she muttered. "About the calls, I mean."

"Yes, I think you should." Gutierrez finished his coffee and set the mug on the tray. "He'll want to find out where Jonathan is; I wouldn't be surprised if he's working on that already."

"Which he won't tell us, probably," said Kuisma. He ran his fork over his cake plate to collect a few last crumbs.

"What he finds out, I find out. And *I'll* tell you," said Doris grimly. She stood up, shaking her dress loose. "I don't want Jonny hurt...you promise you'll not look to hurt him? But I don't want him to hurt nobody else, neither."

"Thank you," said Gutierrez with a small formal nod. "We'll do our best to see that no one is hurt. May I ask one more favor? Could you get us the registration number for Jonathan Archer's bike?"

She could. She strode off to the main house, to return in short order with a slip of paper. "That BMW bike cost as much as a small house. There's the number, and there's my phone number, too. I'm always home here between noon and two, and most nights after eight."

As the two policemen left the cottage, Gutierrez looked at his watch. Almost four-thirty. He wouldn't call Port Silva for a few hours yet. Give her the full two and a half days. One thousand miles, in a van which was in good shape, over good roads...more than enough time. If Meg had not reached home, or called, by eight o'clock tonight, there could no longer be any doubt that she was in trouble. In that case, and given all the possibilities that had crossed his mind, he half hoped the trouble *was* Jonathan Archer.

SIXTEEN

"FORGET IT! Goddamn stuff tastes like rat piss." Jay glared at the coffee mug and Meg thought he meant to knock it from her grip; then he grunted and let his raised hand fall to his denim-clad thigh.

"Shall I make another fresh pot?" She'd been running coffee to him all morning, wondering at his ability to just sit there drinking; the man must have a bladder to rival that of an elephant.

He gazed in her direction, his eyes so deep in their sockets that they reflected no light. After several long seconds, he said again, "Rat piss."

Meg cradled the mug in her hands and watched him lever himself to his feet; he shook his head once and then a second time, reached across to grip and squeeze his bad shoulder, dropped his jaw to release a rumbling belch. "Gotta go to the latrine. *You* don't put a foot outside the hootch while I'm gone."

He clomped through the kitchen and out the back door, leaving it ajar; she took the coffee to the sink and poured it down, watching him through the window. She thought he was different today; responses a beat late, movements and speech a little slower. He was like a toy, a robot, whose batteries were beginning to fail.

When he was halfway to the washhouse she turned and hurried back to the living room. The corner cupboard was still locked, no real surprise; she stared at its smooth wooden surface for a moment and envisioned herself attacking it with an axe, splintering her way to the guns she was sure were inside. Axe, right, the kitchen axe.

Or the poker. Made of black iron with a point and a small hook, it was some two feet long and probably weighed no more than two pounds. No suitable tool for breaking in the

cupboard. And no suitable weapon against Jay, either...
unless she put it in the stove first and heated the point to a
glowing red. Thrust it at those sunken eyes. She dropped the
thing with a clatter. God help her but she knew she couldn't
do that.

Kerosene lanterns on the bookcase became Molotov
cocktails right before her eyes. Perfectly possible and perfectly ridiculous, Margaret; self-immolation will not be
helpful.

She poked her hands under the clothes on the shelves, to
find just clothes, no magic weapon that could stun from a
great distance without drawing blood. The bunks were twin
tangles of grayish sheets, with dark blankets hanging askew.
Catching a glint of metal from beneath, she pushed the
blankets aside and saw not space but drawers, four of them.
A photo album and a shoebox of loose pictures filled the top
drawer on the right; she riffled through a few photos and
saw a grim-faced man against a rail fence, a small boy on the
shoulders of a taller boy, the small boy on a horse with the
taller one holding the reins. The three males in a row, stair-
steps. No woman in this family?

He must have stumbled on the back step; it was the thud
and his muttered "son of a bitch!" that gave her time.
When he came into the room she was standing before the
bookcase with her head tilted as if to read titles. Her shoulder muscles tingled with the desire to turn around and look
at the bunk, the drawer; had her hurried push closed it?

"Willie gets those for me." He was looking past her at the
books. "I been trying for fifteen years to understand all
that. So Willie sends whatever he comes across. He's the one
with the education."

They were books about war, mostly about the Vietnam
war: books by Fall and Fitzgerald and Webb, by Michael
Herr and Philip Caputo. A couple of oral histories, one or
two novels. And some older books, dealing with other wars.
Red Badge of Courage, *Andersonville*, *All Quiet on the
Western Front*. Xenophon's *Anabasis*, for heaven's sake. A
broken-backed Penguin edition of *The Iliad*.

"If you've read all those, you have quite an education yourself. Who is Willie?" The last three words hung there naked in the air and she thought, Oh shit! She hadn't meant to do that; her jaw still ached from the open-handed blow he'd dealt her earlier when she asked how long he meant to keep them, her and Cass.

This time he treated her question like a rude noise best politely ignored. "I got an education in killing," he said in the flat everyday voice one would use to say that he had finished high school. Not a warning, just a statement of fact. He lowered his butt wearily to the stoveside bench and slumped forward, arms braced on spread thighs. "Bring me a couple three Cokes."

Yessir, thought Meg. When she returned from the kitchen with three bottles, the curved and ribbed old-fashioned kind, he gestured toward the stove platform and watched her set her burdens on the bricks. "And a bottle of rum," he said, and paused, "from under my bunk."

Miming a search, she pulled open the photo drawer, peered in, closed it. As she reached for the drawer beneath, she kept in her mind's eye that "family" of three males and wondered: might those boys be Jay and his Willie?

Bottles lay in the lower drawer, three of dark rum, one of a paler Mexican rum, one of tequila. She lifted out a flat-tish bottle, Myers's dark rum. Eighty proof; too bad it wasn't a hundred. Or maybe not. Slow and morose now, this lunatic who was her keeper might go off like a rocket if he got drunk.

She took the rum to him, and at his nod set the bottle beside the Cokes. Good little goddamn servant. Right, good little alive and breathing servant and mind your manners. He picked up an old-fashioned bottle opener from the bricks, the kind that used to be called a church key. Meg eyed the sharp little point . . . her freshman year in college, a girl in her dormitory had tried to commit suicide with one of those. Unsuccessfully, as she recalled.

"Drink this, down to the line."

"What?" Her back came straight and her shoulders square as she looked at the Coke bottle he held out to her.

"Down to the line," he repeated. "I hate the taste of this shit by itself. Drink it down to make room for the rum."

Meg looked down, away from him, demurely and obediently down. Reached for the bottle, put it to her lips, took two swallows. A third. "There. Is that satisfactory?"

He tipped his head back, slowly, until light touched the muddy brown eyes. "Satisfactory. Yeah, I guess that's satisfactory. Till the next one, so you better hang around."

She perched in one of the padded chairs until he told her to fetch his cassette player from beneath the bunk. "And the tapes in the carrier," he added. Her carrier, it turned out, and her tapes; the bastard had appropriated them from her van. She brought him the tapes, sat down once more and listened to her music with him, listened to the Dead. He stared past her, moving his head just slightly behind the beat. "Truckin." "Ramble On Rose." "Sugar Magnolia." If the odd little song called "Ripple" was on this tape she would surely cry, just throw back her head and howl.

When Kev burst through the front door, it was as if a glass bell had shattered to let air and the world in. "Hey, I thought it was about time..." The boy scanned the room with a stern blue gaze that narrowed as he saw the bottle on the bricks. "You know, Jay, booze can really mess a guy up, specially somebody who's got this real important stuff happening and needs to be careful. My uncle says..."

Jay straightened his back, raised his head, slowly lifted his Coke and took a long drink. Kev shut his mouth and drew his feet together with a movement that would have produced a click had he worn boots. "I always got my job done without any complaints," Jay said, and wiped his mouth with the back of his hand. "How about you, you got the trenches dug?"

"About half, yessir," said Kev, with a salute that didn't quite look like a jest. Chicken-coop, that's what Jay had said was needed, and two strong kids to do some digging. Bunker or stockade was what a glance at the layout had suggested to Meg's mind; people-pen. Maybe this was after all some kind of insane war game, and there would be other prisoners.

"If that wire ain't a good foot and a half down," Jay reminded the boy, "the coyotes and foxes will eat a lot more chicken than we do."

"Well, we did like one side and most of another one. Isn't it lunch time?"

Jay looked at his watch. "What it is, is time to patrol." He pulled his feet closer to the bench, put one hand flat as an aid to rising, then shook his head. "I'm the CO, think I'll stay easy right here. Leave the patrol up to the grunts, like you."

"Hey, sure." Kev's blue eyes flashed. "Can I take the carbine?"

"Nope." This time Jay got all the way up, dug into his jeans pocket and limped toward the corner cupboard. "You blast off with a .30/30 this time of year, fuckin' game wardens'll be on our ass in about five seconds. You just stick with the Mossberg."

"Well, shit. Okay, okay." Kev followed Jay to the cupboard, to stand waiting with his hands in his hip pockets. Keys clattered faintly on their metal ring as Jay inserted one, turned it smoothly, pulled the door open. Meg, watching silently, intently, saw a dark interior, two handguns clipped to the right wall, two or perhaps three long narrow shapes propped to the left. Jay reached in to grip what looked to her like the rifle he'd brandished the night before, long barrel and wooden stock and bolt action.

She blinked and saw that the enormous thing was only a .22, the kind she'd gone after rabbits with millions of years ago in her childhood. Only. Not so *only* to the rabbit, she remembered. A .22 in the hands of a good shot... Now Jay handed the weapon to Kev, reached back into the cupboard with a scooping motion, then pushed the door shut and locked it.

"Okay," repeated the boy, shouldering the rifle in military fashion. "Ammo?"

The older man held out a closed fist, Kev extended a palms-up right hand and two slim shells fell into it with a slight clink. Right, .22 longs. With those you shot rabbits or squirrels or perhaps fleeing women. Apparently one of the other weapons in that cupboard was a .30/30. Meg's brother, Neil, in his man-of-the-woods days, had blown large holes in a number of deer with a rifle of that caliber.

"Hey, shit, man. Give me a clip, okay?"

"Two shells'll be plenty for starters. We used to say Charlie never carried more than six."

"HOW'S THE COKE holding up?" asked Jay, as Meg set three fresh bottles on the brick hearth. He didn't turn to look at her, merely settled his rump more solidly on the tall stool and tossed another dart, this time with his left hand. And a second. And a third.

"I just put the last eight bottles in the refrigerator," she told him. The level of dark liquid in the rum bottle had fallen to the halfway mark. Jay had drunk slowly, steadily, through lunch while eating almost nothing; had continued to drink as the afternoon crawled past. So far as she could tell, the liquor was having no effect.

"Guess I'll have to pick up a couple cases tonight," he muttered, and sighed and threw, with his right hand this time. And another. And the third. "Eighteen, four, and triple six, right," he said after peering at the board. "Left is fourteen, five, and fuckin' zip. What's that make it?"

Meg looked at twin columns of figures in a notebook and broke the lead in the mechanical pencil as she scribbled two more. "Left, ninety-two. Right, thirty-six."

"Looks like right wins again; double fifteen and six is a cinch." He leaned sideways, made a long right-armed reach for his Coke, sipped and put it back, all the while watching Meg as she gathered the darts from the board.

She put the darts, red feathers for left and blue for right, in his outstretched hand, intent on getting them flat and safe into that palm without touching it herself. Then she stepped to one side, brushed hair from her sweaty forehead, and said, "Could I work outside for a while?"

"What?" He turned only his head to blink at her like a gaunt gray reptile, some kind of desert lizard.

"I...I'm stronger than my daughter, I could get more work done." Out in the air and the sunshine, where I could breathe, she thought. Give Cass a turn at this, fetch and carry and wonder whether, just for amusement, he might turn and toss a dart at a moving target. "And I'd like to be outdoors for a while."

"You'd like. I bet you'd like. I bet you think, give you half an hour or so, you could outfox poor old Kev some way." An ugly grin stretched his mouth wide.

"No, that's not...I just..." It's what she should have been thinking, dumb spineless shit. "I'd just like to move around a bit," she said lamely.

"You probably could, too," he went on, as if she hadn't spoken. "The boy ain't quite what he looks like, but he ain't real smart, either." He looked down at the darts, separated them by their colors, stroked the feathered flights with a long forefinger.

"Or maybe you're worried about your kid," he suggested, eyes still on the bright feathers. "If that's it, you can forget it, Kev won't try to get in her pants. What he did, he made a vow of abstinence to some priest. No dope, no booze, no cunt, not till he's twenty-one.

"So for right now she's safe as a church. But you won't be, not unless you get out of my sight in a hurry." His face twisted in sudden fury, and the backswing of his right arm caught her high across the chest, nearly knocking her off her feet.

"Women, goddamned women," he snarled, breathing heavily. "I never should've let...get out! Get your ass in the storeroom and keep it there till I call you."

MEG PULLED THE DOOR shut behind her and stood very still, listening for the sound of steps, breathing in great gasps that hurt her chest and made her head spin. Vince my love, good old cop Vince, Gutierrez you bastard, you had better come *soon*. That man...I am a big strong woman I thought I could take care of myself and now I think, I think that man could kill me just with his hands. With one hand.

All her muscles, in her arms and legs, her shoulders, even her face...all were twitching and quivering. If she didn't manage some kind of cooldown from hours of total tension, she was going to find herself whizzing around the ceiling like a deflating balloon. She inhaled deeply, stretched tall, then let her head and shoulders roll slowly forward and down, limp as a rag doll.

Sun salutation: focus inward, then arch and bend and reach and arch again...to end with palms together. Like praying, which wasn't such a bad idea. Dear God, I realize mine is a very unfamiliar voice, but I'd certainly appreciate it if you could show me how to get us out of this. Please?

The prayer might be a waste, but the movement wasn't; she repeated the series rapidly, and a third time, while sweat dampened her hair and made chilly trails down her ribs. Sunday afternoon, more than forty-eight hours since the parking lot and we're still alive; what does that mean?

She dropped to her belly to stretch and arch: cobra, bow. Forty-eight hours, and we haven't been raped or mistreated. Well, not mistreated much. What does *that* mean? Jay, self-admitted killer, doesn't go in for sex? Gets his kicks by giving his victims-to-be plenty of time to imagine their own fate? The man certainly had her number there; waiting, waiting, she could barely keep herself from screaming at him to go on and get it over with.

She sat up, bent herself slowly forward over an extended leg. We have some value, something making it worthwhile not only to keep us but to keep us in good condition. Ransom? Ho ho, sure.

A shoulder-stand, and then a plough, which compressed her breathing but somehow cleared her head. They're waiting for *something*, some connected event. Or for instructions. Jay is, he went out last night and he's going again tonight, looks like some kind of schedule. And he's anticipating something grim and final; there's doom all around him, thick as sea fog. Who is Willie?

For the moment all this was distant, an intellectual exercise. The body, spent and easy now, managed to ignore the mind. Meg lay flat on her back with her eyes closed, in the position called Savasana. Don't do, just be, be loose and heavy and still. Empty airy space, no movement and no sound. All right, sound, but don't hear it, don't let those voices work on the nerve ends. Voices from outside, soft and confidential...Cass, and Kev. Nearby, nearer than the work site: perhaps they'd come to the shade of the cabin for a break. Probably relaxing with a Coke. Yuck.

There was a thump and some rustling, as if one or both of them had settled against the wall. "...taller than you and really strong; of all the guys with bikes, he's the only one who's never laid it down. My mother hates him, but she..." A pause; had Cass remembered she had at the moment two mothers? "She's not the one who should be making rules," the girl went on in prim tones. "*She* lives with this guy she's not married to."

"*My* mother is, well I guess you'd say a hero." The boy's voice, low rumble with an occasional squeak.

"Wow, really?"

"Maybe even a saint. See, she couldn't let on who she really was. She called me Buddy and pretended I was just her little brother. So I was raised by this old lady who was supposed to be my mother, but I know she's really my grandmother."

"What about your father?"

"I didn't have a father," said the boy in low tones, and Meg thought, Well shit, a bond, that's terrific. "See, my real mother was like a soldier," he went on. "She marched and fought, and if the cops tried to mess with her she blew 'em away. That's why she couldn't come home very much."

"Blew them... Listen here, my uncle..."

Shut up, Cass! Meg tried to send the unspoken words through the wall like bullets.

"And she worked with poor people like, you know, Mother Teresa. That's what I'll do when I'm a priest. Or maybe I'll just join the Provos, like our Dennis. That's my...my uncle. He went to the old country to bring the money we'd collected, and he stayed, to fight."

"What old country are you talking about?"

"Ireland, what do you think? We're descended from the warrior kings of Ireland. Didn't you ever hear of Brian Boru? And listen, there's even a St. Kevin."

Heavenly days, St. Kevin! thought Meg, bemused. Someone, perhaps her father, had told her of that pure young man; at the tender age of twelve he had taken a bunch of nettles to a wench bent on seduction, and had beaten her severely.

"Hey!" Jay's voice brought Meg bolt upright, and it was a moment before she realized he was outside. "You two better get off your asses and on your feet," he growled. "Chances are it'll rain all day tomorrow."

Tomorrow. Sounded like tomorrow was just another day, everybody still alive and working if it didn't rain. Meg wrapped her arms around her bent legs and laid her cheek on her knees. Rain, all of us inside together while the rain comes down. Will we all live through that?

THUNDER MUTTERED and grumbled in the distance, while heavy-bellied clouds lumbered across a darkening sky. The kitchen felt cozy, something to do with lights on in the daytime and the smell of cooking. Frying chicken, in fact; she'd dipped the pieces in milk and egg and rolled them in seasoned flour and now they were sizzling and browning in hot oil. Lots of oil, and all that fat in the skin that was crisping and browning so nicely; she never did this to chicken at home, but Jay...

As Meg poked a fork into a drumstick and turned it, a spurt of hot fat struck her inner wrist; she said "Shit!" and dropped the fork, then tossed a quick glance over her shoulder. Jay, in the doorway, paid no attention, probably hadn't even heard.

She moved quietly to the sink, turned on the cold water to let it run over the burn. Maybe she should stick her head under that chill stream. Or just go out to stand in the rain, once it began. Somehow, she had settled into a role in a play she'd seen many times: mute and harried woman trying to feed a man and clean up after him and keep out of the way of his fists. As the water cooled her burn, the rest of her body prickled with shame.

She turned the faucet off and stared at the reddening splotch. Good, let it blister and hurt, and remind her what was real in this pinched little world of the compound. Jay still slouched against the doorframe with Coke bottle in hand, directing a blank-faced stare at nothing she could see, at the distant trees or perhaps at something inside his own head. Another thunder roll, closer and sharper; Jay's shoulders jerked, and his dangling left hand clenched spasmodically, but his face changed not at all.

Just like Neil: that was the thought that had been hanging at the edge of her consciousness. Six years ago—no, seven—Meg had spent a whole month, a hot miserable July, in a Manhattan apartment trying to help her older brother survive a severe bout of depression. He had looked the way Jay looked and behaved in the same manner: lethargic, unresponsive, locked into a cold gray world of his own, surfacing occasionally in a brief burst of fury and then sinking back. Neil had spent twenty hours of every twenty-four in a high-backed wooden rocker, creaking back and forward and back with his eyes fixed on a hanging spider plant. He told her later that he had decided on suicide but couldn't find the energy to accomplish it.

The rum bottle, there on the kitchen table, was nearly empty. But maybe he wouldn't stop with that; he had plenty of backup. Neil's doctor, she remembered, had forbidden alcohol completely. So, what would it do? Hasten Jay's slide to the depths? There was a thing to pray for, a Jay semicomatose as Neil had been, someone even a middle-aged woman could overcome. She turned the chicken one last time, then lowered the flame and wiped her hands on her Levi's.

"I'd like to get a breath of air, before it rains?" she said to Jay, who made no reply but moved aside slightly. As she stepped carefully past him, a jagged bolt lit the sky, followed a moment later by a bone-jarring clap of thunder. Cass squealed as the gray kitten squirted out of her arms and streaked for the woods. "Fred, come back! Get him!" she yelled to Kev, who did. "Come on, Fred, don't be scared of a little lightning," she cooed.

Cass was dirty, suntanned, and seemingly cheerful. Somebody who has lived her kind of life should be more aware of danger, thought Meg. Or maybe, if you've been mistreated and disappointed often enough, you decide that nothing you do is going to make any difference anyway. Kev held the kitten over his head and Cass reached for it. "Come on," she wheedled, "give him to me."

Kev, unlike Cass, did not tan. His face was pink, his nose beginning to peel. He had shed his shirt early in the day, and now his bare shoulders were so red they seemed to give off waves of heat.

"What do you want with this dumb little cat anyhow?" he asked. "Ought to let him go, see if he can make it out there with the real animals." He pretended to set the cat down, and Cass shrieked and swooped to reach for her pet.

"Give him here!"

"Come and get him." Kev swung the kitten high again. Fred yowled, squirmed free of the gripping hand and dropped to Kev's bare shoulders.

"Ow! You fucking bastard!" he roared, and peeled the little cat away. Thin dark lines gleamed wet against red skin, blue eyes widened and narrowed in a blaze that seemed to shoot sparks. The boy set his feet and brought his arm across and back and around in a whippy sidearm motion. Meg saw the twisting flight, saw the animal splayed across Jay's face. Saw big hands flash up, seize, twist and toss the gray scrap away. Thought she heard the snap of the spine.

"No no no no-o-oh!" Cass flew at Jay through the air almost the way the kitten had. Meg launched herself, caught the girl with a shoulder in her belly, knocked her breathless, brought her flat, and fell on top of her. Seeing, in her head like a fast-running film, Cass fly and hit and twist snap fall.

SEVENTEEN

"KATY CALLED? GODDAMN. Goddamnit to *hell*!" The snarled words hurt Gutierrez's throat, and probably Svoboda's ear as well. "Sorry, Hank. But I practically *begged* that damned woman at the camp not to say anything to Katy."

"I don't believe Betty or anybody else said a word." Svoboda's voice was firm. "Katy wasn't real worried, Vince; mostly she's just having a good time and wanting to tell her mother about it. Like she learned to do a perfect back dive off the highboard."

He could see it, see a narrow tanned body leap and arch and descend like an arrow. Then surface, with a toss of dark hair, a flash of blue eyes. He had watched Katy trying that dive at the university pool in the spring; Meg, sitting next to him in the bleachers, had groaned aloud. The image of Katy was suddenly replaced by one of Meg, eyes closed in a remote face.

Gutierrez held the receiver away from his ear while he wiped his sweaty forehead against his shirt sleeve. "Yeah, I'm here. What did you tell her?"

"Well, mostly I lied," Svoboda admitted. "I told her that she shouldn't worry. That I'd heard from you on Friday and everything was fine. That you'd planned to head deep into the woods, probably out where there weren't any telephones."

"Shit. Maybe I should send her a postcard, sign it from the both of us."

"I wouldn't do that. One person lying is enough."

"Yeah," agreed Gutierrez on a long sigh. "Okay, it's been two and a half days now; I'll give it two more. If I haven't made some progress . . . if I haven't found Meg by

Tuesday night…then I'll call Katy. No by God I won't, I'll fly over and *get* Katy.

"But I'm leaving for Coeur d'Alene," he went on quickly. "Tomorrow morning as soon as Delucca and his plane are ready. Mary Louise is…well, just the same old Mary Louise. Lawrence Archer knows less than I do and anything he finds out he's sure to cover up. And the chief of police here is good buddies with Archer, besides which he's very tight-assed about people with names like Gutierrez."

"You know yet where you'll be staying in Coeur d'Alene?"

"Call the police station; I'll be there or they'll know where I am. The chief's name is Brownell."

"I'm staying in touch with the highway patrol here, and the state police in Oregon and Washington," Svoboda said. "Only unusual thing so far is there's some fires working up in the Klamath and the Shasta-Trinity. Everything's real dry, and then they had lightning. Say Meg maybe took a side trip, she could've got stuck in one of those little mountain towns, where phone lines are down. Anyway, that's a possibility," he added when Gutierrez made no response. "I'll keep on it. Val working out, is he?"

"More or less," said Gutierrez shortly. "He's out doing some digging about the Archer kid. While I sit here at the motel grinding my teeth to bloody stubs." The motel was new, and this room had been decorated in colors ranging from a pinkish gray to a dark tone somewhere between blue and purple. Padded and fuzzy, everything but the walls; the place made him itch. "Any big problems in Port Silva?" he asked as an afterthought.

"Possible arson at the high school with minor damage. Little run of household burglaries probably being pulled by a bunch of kids…. Nothing you should worry about. And like you figured, Sheriff Roncalli wants to borrow a couple of men to help him out down by CliffHaven, the deathwatch for that Michael Tannenbaum fellow; piece of woods there is starting to look like a city park before a Grateful Dead concert."

"It will probably be on television tonight," muttered Gutierrez. "Hank, I think I hear Kuisma coming. I'll be here until maybe five A.M. Then Coeur d'Alene."

As he hung up the phone, someone rapped on his door; not Kuisma, unless he'd forgotten his key. "Just a minute," Gutierrez barked and climbed stiffly out of the low soft chair. He adjusted the figure-eight brace that immobilized his shoulders, then strode to the door and pulled it wide. Mary Louise gave him a bright smile which was not repeated on the round dark face of the man standing behind her.

"Vincente, I brought you some supper, and some news. And this is Eddie Morales, my boss and my, um, friend."

Gutierrez nodded to Morales and stepped aside to let the pair of them in. Mary Louise wore four-inch heels, a short black skirt and a ruffly, low-necked white blouse, presumably her working costume. Morales had on a black tee shirt, black jeans, and black biker's boots, with a black headband restraining bushy graying hair. He was shorter than Gutierrez but wider, with a thick neck and a high, hard belly.

"*What* news?" Gutierrez asked as he closed the door.

Mary Louise looked around for a place to put the covered containers she held. "Oh, this is a nice place. Two double beds and a big TV and *two* armchairs. And a desk," she added, and set the food down on its plastic surface. "I brought you tamales, Vincente, beef tamales, and some green chile pork, and a bean burro. The cook at La Perla is excellent, muy bueno."

"Thank you, Mary Louise," said Gutierrez through clenched teeth. "What news?"

"Cass is all right, I'm sure of it, because she took my rings."

"Rings."

"The kid robbed her mama's jewelry," said Morales, crossing his arms over his chest. "I think we ought report it to the cops."

"Don't be silly, Eddie." Mary Louise lifted an edge of aluminum foil and inhaled the pungent aroma of the steaming pork. "Eat, Vincente, while it's hot. Fresh tortillas in that packet, there."

She gestured toward another plate; Gutierrez eyed the small hand with its long bright-red nails and considered slapping it. "WHAT RINGS?"

Morales dropped his arms, caught Gutierrez's glance, and took a hasty step back. "The wedding rings," Mary Louise said quickly. "Mine from when I was married to Fred. And Fred's, he gave it back to me; I don't know why, and I don't know why I kept it. But today I was looking for something else, and there they were, gone!"

"I see. Mary Louise, how long has it been since you last saw the rings?"

"Oh, I don't know. Not long, I don't think; that was the only wedding ring I ever had, so I looked at it now and then. But you see what it means?"

"Tell me."

"It means she was getting *married*. Why else would she take wedding rings, especially Fred's that was way too big for her? They were just gold with some little flowers worked in the surface, no stones. Not worth much money. So she's with Jon, and it's all right."

Gutierrez drew a deep breath and released it in a sound that was almost a growl; his temples were pounding and his head seemed to be contracting and expanding with his pulse. Morales shifted his feet uneasily and said, "Hey, buddy, take it easy, okay?"

"You take it easy, *buddy*. In fact, you wait outside. My sister will call you if she needs you."

"Yes, Eddie, go on; I'll just be a few minutes. My brother has felt like hitting me lots of times, but he never actually does it. You go sit in the truck and have a beer."

Morales stared at Gutierrez, who stared back. The shorter man shrugged, turned on his heel, and stomped out.

"You know, Vince, she loves him. Cass does love Jon." Mary Louise stood straight and clasped her hands loosely before her at waist level; it was the pose her high school choir director had insisted upon for his young ladies twenty-five years ago. "Maybe they should have their chance."

"Jonathan Archer hit you, Mary Louise. What makes you think he won't hit Cass?"

"He didn't really hit me. He pushed me, and I bumped my head," she said earnestly. "I think maybe Jon isn't really a bad person, Vince. Just young and determined to get his way. Lots of men are like that; if Cass loves him, she'll learn how to handle him."

"Jesus Christ, Mary Louise! She's not even sixteen years old!" His sister's face took on a too familiar look of pure mulish stubbornness, and Gutierrez thought, just for a moment, that he understood why a man might hit a woman. "And what about Meg?"

"Meg?"

"Margaret Halloran. My *novia*," he said through clenched teeth. "If Jon and Cass have gone off happily to play house, what do you suppose they've done with Meg?"

"Oh." She touched her fingertips to her lips, thinking. "Maybe Meg agreed to give them a head start? I don't believe Jon would hurt her, Vince. Even if he wanted to, I don't think Cass would let him."

She watched him for a moment more. "I'll stop by church on the way back to work, I promise. I'll say a prayer for Meg. And tomorrow," she added with a sigh, "tomorrow I'll go the police and report that my daughter is missing."

He jerked his head in a nod; she started for the door and turned back.

"I love my kids, but I've never claimed I was a very good mother. And while I was worrying about Cass...I really did worry...underneath the worry, I kept thinking how much easier my life will be if she stays away. I mean if she's married to Jon or at least with him, and happy." She met his eyes and looked quickly away. "Cass is so hard, Vince; she hates my friends and she thinks I'm a slut. It doesn't seem right that your own child should disapprove of you. Mama was very strange, to me anyway, but I never disapproved of her."

"I know, Mary Louise." He put his good arm across her shoulders, gave a brief squeeze, and led her to the door. "You'd better get back to work. I'll be leaving for Idaho early tomorrow; I'll let you know if anything turns up." He released her and pulled the door open. "Thanks for the food."

ABOUT TO REACH FOR the telephone again, Gutierrez paused next to the desk and inhaled. He'd forgotten about supper, and the chile pork smelled wonderful. He fetched a beer from the cooler chest in the dressing room and finally succeeded in twisting the cap off while gripping the bottle with his knees. Goddamned cripple. He managed a half-dozen bites of the pork, scooping with a tortilla and spilling globs of the fragrant mess down the front of his shirt. Finally he covered that dish and settled for a tamale, which he could at least hold in his hand. His wristwatch . . . he rubbed it against his shirt; how had he managed to get chile on his watch? Quarter of nine, Lawrence fucking Archer should be at home.

"Nope, he ain't here." Doris's voice was low, as if she were worn out or maybe drunk. "He's on a tear, spent the last few hours calling everybody he could think of. Nobody has seen Jonny."

"Where is he now?"

"Out at the airstrip getting his plane ready. He's got this little Cessna he flies himself."

"Doris, do you know where he's going?"

"Yeah, I think Idaho. He had the cops go connect with the Guillaumes, found out Jonny left there Thursday at the latest. Dave Guillaume spent Wednesday and Wednesday night at *his* girl's, and when he got back home, Jonny and his bike were gone. Nobody's heard anything from him since, except for that call to me Friday night."

Gutierrez mulled this over. Colorado Springs to Coeur d'Alene was just under twelve hundred miles; he and Meg had worked that out at home, maps spread all over the table. The three of them, he and Meg and Cass—pulling a trailer, stopping to sight-see—had taken four days to cover the distance. But if Jon had left early Wednesday, strong kid on a good bike, he could have made Coeur d'Alene by

Thursday night or Friday morning. Perhaps he and Cass had planned all along to connect there.

"I spoke with my sister just a few minutes ago," he said to Doris, and went on to tell her of Mary Louise's missing rings.

"Sweet Jesus, that'll send Larry a mile straight up without no plane at all." There was a certain grim satisfaction in Doris's voice. "What he kept saying, be *goddamn* if my boy's going to wind up tied to some little spic bimbo. Don't see what he can do about it, though. Not after Jonny's birthday tomorrow."

Maybe, thought Gutierrez, it was the birthday that was significant to everyone. Maybe after he was officially and legally of age, Jonathan Archer would release Meg and go on his way with his girlfriend or wife. Whether Meg was still in condition to be released probably depended on how much she had tried to interfere. He had his mouth open to ask Doris what she thought her Jonny capable of, then decided it was a pointless question. Doris's loyalty was clear.

"I'll be in Coeur d'Alene tomorrow, early," he told her. "You can tell Archer that. And Doris . . . if you need to get in touch with me, you can reach me through the Coeur d'Alene police. Remember, I have no wish to harm Jonny; I just want to find Mrs. Halloran, and Cass." His interest in Cass was more vengeful than avuncular, but that was another thing he probably shouldn't say to Doris.

VAL KUISMA swept a hopeful gaze around the combination beer garden and dancehall called Sherwood Forest. Located on the outskirts of Colorado Springs, the Forest was known as a place where minors could get served. It was the fourth stop of the evening for Kuisma and his companion, and Officer Jim Jacobs was sure they'd connect here.

A voice from behind him said, "You grab the mugs, I'll take the pitcher," and Kuisma turned to obey. Under a floppy forelock the color of straw, Jim Jacobs had a snub nose, freckles, and round hazel eyes. It was a face that had made him a natural for undercover drug work on several high school campuses, among them the private school from which Jon Archer had graduated the past spring.

"Barlow's sure to be here; nobody, *nobody* but Harry drives that Targa." Jacobs had spotted a familiar silver Porsche in the parking lot. "Harrison Barlow the Fourth, age probably nineteen. Fat little bastard with zip for brains but lots of money. Except he never does have small change, so we'll get hit on for our beer." He led the way past mostly empty tables toward the back of the building, where a big section of wall had been rolled up like a garage door. Just outside, on a concrete patio, bodies gyrated to music blasting from banks of overhead speakers; beyond the patio was a forest of spindly pines, every tree with a table or two beneath.

"Back this way, Val, where the trees cut the noise some. Ah. How's it going, Harry B?"

At nineteen Barlow looked an out-of-shape thirty-five, with tight black hair slipping back from a sharp widow's peak, a pudgy pale face and a long nose ending in a bulbous droop. Now he looked up from his empty beer mug, blinked, and pulled his lips wide in a grin that exposed big, perfect teeth. "Well hey, Jake. I got a whole table here, man, so sit."

Jacobs introduced his "cousin from California," poured beer all around, settled onto the empty bench and motioned for Kuisma to sit beside him. The baby-faced cop congratulated Barlow on his admittance to some small private college Kuisma had never heard of; and Barlow said he was sorry Jacobs had failed to graduate.

"Oh, if I get a couple of papers in before the end of the month, they'll give me a diploma. Hey, Val, our school... College Prep... has this terrific old Korean teaching martial arts. Harry was on the team, and they won judo matches all over the state. Val here," he added brightly, with a jerk of his head in Kuisma's direction, "is into judo too, brown belt and working toward a black."

Val arranged his face in what he hoped was a confident grin as he tried to remember some of the moves he'd been taught in his police training course four years ago. All that came to mind was how to fall safely. Barlow kept his eyes on his beer mug as he pushed it forward for a refill. "Tell you the truth," he said, "I wasn't very good. I only took it up because a friend talked me into it. When he quit, I did, too."

"Jon Archer, right? I remember somebody told me you and Archer were buddies from way back."

"Just kid stuff," Barlow said with a shrug. "Same neighborhood, same schools, his old man and my old man played tennis."

"I didn't see the match he quit over, but I heard it was a personal thing and he got tossed around pretty good by...shit, I don't remember who." Jacob's round eyes managed to look sad as he gazed across the table at Barlow.

"By a fuckin' scholarship kid named Yoder!" snapped Barlow. "Fees my folks paid, you'd think they could keep the downtown sleaze out. Anyway, Yoder didn't beat Jon. Kim was referee, and the old bastard practically let Yoder get away with murder."

"Yeah, I heard that, too," said Jacobs. "Val, we oughta look Jon Archer up, see if maybe he'd give *you* a match."

"Hey, that's a hell of an idea," stammered Kuisma, and took a long gulp of beer.

"What do you think, will Archer be here tonight?" Jacobs asked Barlow. "I haven't seen him around since the end of school."

"I haven't seen *you* around." Hard little black eyes beside the long nose, a twist to the mouth: it was a ratty-mean face that Barlow buried in his beer mug as a boy and his girl paused under their tree, the cops' tree, to exchange greetings with Jacobs. A friendly and cheerful pair they were, Kuisma noted, and clearly not aware that it *was* a cops' tree. Their classmate, however, their real classmate...what was the matter with him?

"Ever do any deer hunting?" he asked Barlow quietly, for no particular reason except that he was eager for the coming season and being in the mountains always made him think of hunting.

"No!" replied Barlow so sharply that his blue-shadowed jowls quivered.

Jacobs had been listening. Now he turned on his grin again and said "Hi, Jules," to a tall sunbleached blonde who was breathing hard as she wiped sweat from her brow. "Like you to meet my cousin, Valentine Kuisma. Val, Julie Tremaine. And her friend Becky Smith."

A small dark girl smiled and ducked her head as Julie reached out to relieve Kuisma of his beer mug. "Hi. Dancing is thirsty work, do you mind?"

Kuisma unfolded from the bench, looselimbed and topping six feet one in his good old cowboy boots. "No, ma'am," he told her with an admiring grin.

"Hey, you're tall for a Valentine, and cute. Wanna dance?"

"I'd really like to," he said, and meant it. "But I think I'm supposed to be saving myself for judo, if we can find some guy named Jon Archer."

Julie gave an exaggerated sigh and shook her head. "First of all, he's probably out in the woods somewhere. And besides, you don't want to play hard games with Jonny; he'll break your arms and legs just for fun."

"Julie!" The dark girl's face had reddened. "That's not fair."

"Out in the woods?" Jacob's voice held mild curiosity.

"Oh, hunting or something. Hunting people, probably," said Julie with a slanted look at Harry Barlow.

"You shut up," said Barlow in a near-whisper. He splashed beer into his mug, drained it in three gulps, and stood up. "Gotta go."

"MAN, I AM REALLY out of shape," panted Kuisma some fifteen minutes later as he and Jacobs crossed the parking lot. Julie had not wanted to talk about Jon Archer or anything else, Julie had wanted to dance.

"It's the altitude," said Jacobs.

"Nope, it's old age. Twenty-six and I'm over the hill. What was it in there with Barlow?"

Jacobs shook his head. "Nobody had anything to say about it, or about Archer. We've got one more stop to make; climb in and hold on."

Kuisma obeyed, and Jacobs whipped his Jeep Cherokee toward the lights of town, then more slowly along streets that were a mix of residences and small businesses. "Hey! This is a funeral parlor!" said Kuisma as they pulled into a dimly lighted parking lot before a low stucco building.

"Right. Jamesons' Mortuary. They keep a night watchman, to discourage weirdos. And they pay okay, so it's a good job if you're not squeamish. Yeah, there's the Harley. And here he comes."

A tall figure padded around the corner of the building and stopped twenty feet from them, to shine a flashlight in their direction.

"Hey, Yoder," said Jacobs softly.

"Hey," replied the boy, as he switched off the flash and came forward to slap right hands with Jacobs.

"Got many tenants tonight?"

"Three, but they're in bed already." A dark silhouette against the white building, Yoder lifted broad shoulders in a shrug.

"Can you spare me a few minutes?" Without waiting for an answer, Jacobs gestured in Kuisma's direction. "This is a friend of mine from out of state, and he's looking for Jon Archer. Have you seen him?"

"Nope."

"It was you who dumped him on his ass in a judo match?"

"Right."

"Why?"

Yoder leaned against the building and crossed his arms. "Is this an official inquiry?"

"Not yet," said Jacobs; and Kuisma thought, Okay, we're cops again.

"Bastard came by my house a few times, like we were friends, and then I found out he tried to mess with my sister." Yoder's voice came from deeper in his chest now, without its former college-boy crispness. "She was only fourteen, but Archer's the kind of guy who thinks that on the wrong side of town, big enough's old enough. In a judo contest, I figured to hurt him some without going to jail for it."

"Harry Barlow says you and Kim cheated," said Kuisma.

Yoder shook his head, and his teeth glinted in a grin. "No need. Archer *thinks* he's good, but he's lazy, he just likes the flashy stuff. I'm not half the natural athlete he is, but I'm one hell of a worker."

"Didn't he try to get even?" asked Kuisma. "I'd have thought somebody like that, he'd get a bunch of buddies together and catch you alone some night."

"I watched my back pretty good for a while," admitted Yoder. "But I think the guys who used to play his games with him got tired, or grew up. When he went off to that Bill Williams wilderness camp in June, Harry Barlow was the only guy who'd go along."

"Bill Williams?" snapped Jacobs. "Is that redneck bastard still running his goddamned private kill-kill school down in Pueblo?"

Yoder was clearly startled. "I don't know where...kill-kill? I thought it was one of those survival game places, where you run around in the woods and shoot paint bags at each other."

"With Williams they use real guns, real knives, real clubs and fists," Jacobs said, and turned to spit into the dust of the parking lot. "On real people. For my money the man's a fucking sadist."

"My boss will sure be interested in this," said Kuisma softly to his fellow cop. "Thing is, I'd like to find out a little more about it before I report."

"Sure. Right, we'll go downtown and..." Jacobs paused. "No. We'll go to my place. We'll just make a couple phone calls to a couple friends of mine in Pueblo. And Yoder, it's no big deal, but I'd just as soon you didn't tell anybody we talked to you."

"No problem."

EIGHTEEN

MEG REACHED ACROSS to lower the flame under the coffee-pot, her ears alert for sounds from the front room. He had built a fire in the stove right after supper, and had settled there in silence to absorb heat, and rum; any minute now he'd call her to refill his mug.

And she'd like to fill it with something useful, like rat poison. Her spine prickled, tiny hairs lifting along its length as she knelt to explore the curtained-off area beneath sink and counter. Detergent and cleanser, ammonia, plastic buckets, sponges and a scrub brush, a can of mechanics' hand cleaner. Mink oil. No tools, he must keep those in the garage. No rat poison either, just a spray can of Raid. Like mace, that might be useful as a temporary stopper, but you'd better by God have somewhere to go right after using it.

She used the sink edge to pull herself upright, stifling a groan as she did so. She'd banged her knees and elbows and wrenched a shoulder in tackling Cass, had taken blows in the softer portions of her body as she carried the twisting, kicking, screaming girl to the storeroom. By tomorrow she'd be very sore indeed.

Cass. Meg turned the coffee off and moved quietly across the room to the locked storeroom door. Cass had yelled and sobbed and even beat on the door for a time; when she finally fell silent, Meg assumed that she had literally howled herself to sleep. But that was hours ago. She pressed an ear flat to the door panel and heard nothing.

"Rain." The word came like a low groan from the living room. Meg turned so quickly she nearly fell over her own feet; her hands, she noted with disgust, were trembling, and her face was suddenly bathed in chilly sweat. You son of a bitch, you can't do this to me. Rat poison, Drano, I'll find something. As soon as I can breathe again.

"Rain, goddamn rain just never stops. Even if there's not drops falling, the air's so wet a fish could live in it. Your clothes rot, your shoes rot, your skin rots.

"And leeches. You ever seen a leech?" She jumped at a sharp sound and then realized that he must have spat against the hot metal of the stove. "Of all the shit that gets you in the jungle, rot or mosquitoes or snakes or rats, leeches are what I hate the worst. Look like big lumps of snot. Get down your collar and up your sleeves. Gotta tie your pants legs shut to keep 'em out. I used to have this dream that one of 'em got up my ass, ate his way straight through and came out my mouth."

Another sizzle. "No reason. No reason in hell," he drawled, "for a white man. To spend his time. His blood. Someplace like that. Willie was ab-so-fuckin'-lutely correct."

There was a clap of thunder, and then a quickening in the rattle of raindrops against the cabin. Still no sound from within the storeroom prison where Cass slept; very odd, thought Meg.

"But"—he sighed and she heard him gulp liquid—"but this is cool rain, mountain rain. You, come in here and open the front door, so's I can remember what good rain smells like."

Meg obeyed, made slow measured steps past Jay to the door and pulled it open. She stood there for a long moment inhaling: wet earth, and the wet wood of the cabin, and smoke, and the scent of pines. Freedom. If Cass had wakened and smelled this, would she have pushed the screen from the vent and fled? Possibly. And where was Kev? He'd gone out right after supper, with the .22. Where was he now?

"Okay, lady, you get back to the kitchen. Finish cleaning up."

As she was returning to her assigned place, the calendar caught her eye, with its VA notation. Medicine, all medicine, was poison in the wrong—or maybe she meant the right—amount. The little vial of sleeping pills was gone from the cupboard by the sink; but maybe she could find where he'd hidden it. In the pantry, or the living room drawers? The pantry was in Jay's view should he turn, the drawers right in front of his face. God.

She carried a flour cannister to the pantry, pulled the door open to set the cannister in its place and left the door wide. Box of salt to be put away. It belonged on the second shelf with the cornmeal, flour, baking powder and such. Some mothy little bugs fluttered at her and she caught herself just before slapping one.

Iron skillet and big saucepan: a space awaited them on a middle shelf. He had quite a few pans, including a big blue speckled roaster and a stock pot, for heaven's sake. Toward the rear she found muffin tins, six and then six more empty little hiding places. There was a sharp crack different from thunder, and Meg said, "Aah!" in a kind of indrawn wail and banged her elbow on the doorframe as she spun around.

"That's ol' Kev." Jay lurched up from his bench and moved toward the open door, to lean against the frame and stare out into the rainy end of the day. "Christ knows what he might have started in this weather... maybe raccoon."

Or Cass? Meg hooked clawed fingers together in front of her chest and pulled until her shoulder muscles quivered. Would the boy shoot Cass? Surely he could simply catch her if he wanted to. If she was out there. Tell Jay! she thought suddenly, and was trying to find the words when he spoke again.

"I kind of liked that part," Jay said without turning. "Scouting and sniping, it's a whole lot like deer hunting, and I got my first buck when I was eleven. Those VC dudes were good. Trail one of those and catch up to him, you know you're good, too. Everybody knows."

And you taught Kev to shoot. To shoot people? Meg dropped her hands and squared her shoulders. Nothing she could do about it. She collected the plastic bag of potatoes from the counter by the sink, carried it across the room to the pantry. On the floor under the bottom shelf, that was where she'd found it. She knelt, set it down, reached behind it and felt other bags, a big can. Something furry brushed across her hand and fled with a faint dry scrabble; she bit her tongue so hard that she tasted blood. Apparently Jay did not use rat poison.

She hadn't heard him move so probably he was still watching the rain. She pushed the potatoes into their place, reached with both hands to explore the shelf above them. Nothing: plastic containers, more cans, boxes. Bare gritty boards.

"Hey. My coffee mug is empty."

Rum is poison, but probably too slow, she thought as she levered herself to her feet. What if it occurred to him to ask about Cass? To wonder why she'd been silent for so long? She took his coffee mug, filled it, brought it quietly back, handed it to him.

He sniffed it. "You wouldn't be getting too heavy with the rum, would you? Trying to wipe me out?"

"Shall I bring you the bottle to inspect?" She heard the sharp edge in her voice halfway through the sentence, and clasped her hands together to conceal their trembling. *Stupid.*

"Yeah. Yeah, why don't you do that?"

Back to the kitchen, lift the bottle and carry it in. What's one more little humiliation? Keep your head down and your mouth shut and finish searching that pantry before he shuts you in for the night. Before he decides it's time to let Cass out, and unlocks the door and finds she's gone. No, she's not gone, she's not out there. She's sleeping.

He was leaning against the doorframe in the other direction now, staring into the room at the fire, or at her. She held the bottle up, he gestured to her to bring it closer and she obeyed. "Hunting. That was okay," he muttered. "Little yellow bastard is gonna kill you, you kill him first. You and him." She took a step back; he hissed at her and she stood still.

"What was bad was wiping out a whole ville." His words were slow, and so soft that she tipped her head to hear.

"Grandmas right down through the babies. Some guys got used to that, but I never could."

Another shot sounded from outside. Meg fumbled the bottle and caught it against her body.

"Dumb kid," he said in mild irritation, and for an instant she thought he meant Cass. "Anything he shoots, he better finish off," Jay added, and did a half-turn against the axis of the doorframe to look out again into the rain. Swallowing hard against rising bile, Meg backed one step toward the kitchen, then another and a third before she turned.

There was no noise in the kitchen. And none from the living room, except the crackle of the fire and the soft rustle of rain. She chanced a look around the edge of the pantry door and saw his back, slumped shoulders, head lifted to the darkening sky. Top shelf, she still hadn't searched there. Do the top shelf, she told herself, and then go listen at the door.

She was not tall enough to see, only to feel. Cans, small ones soups and chili, several big ones of tomato—no, grapefruit juice. Fat bottle: pickles? Pickled cabbage, she discovered; big jug of dills behind that. The bastard had a veritable grocery store. Mustard, felt like. Something there!...no, stuffed olives in a tall narrow jar, for martinis and God knew she could use one. Dusty shelf. Then at the back, her exploring fingers found the little plastic vial, and another beside it and a third. Way back there as if hidden. She set her middle finger delicately on a flat caplike surface and flicked gently forward and a cool cylinder fell against her palm.

She curled her fingers around and pulled her hand out and down in one smooth motion. Don't look at it now just let the hand slide under the shirttail and into the front Levi's pocket and there it is, not big enough to make much of a bulge and the shirt hangs over. At the sound of movement from the next room she began to push pans aside on that middle shelf, noisily making room for the skillet that was already there. She lifted the skillet lid, let it drop back into place.

"I'm going outside," said Jay. She turned to find a gray-winged specter, blinked and realized that he had put on a rain poncho.

"What you better do," he added, "is take some food to your kid before Kev comes in and cleans out the fridge."

JAY LIFTED THE PADLOCK from its hasp and pushed the door open. He put a hand flat against Meg's back and pushed her much as he had the door, and she stumbled into the room, her heart pounding and all her flesh tightening against what might be coming.

The light beam from his lantern shot past her and touched Cass's sleeping bag, its foot and its rumpled length, and then the pale disk of her outraged face; the girl gave a little whinny of fear or perhaps fury as she dropped flat again and pulled the bag over her head. Meg felt her own muscles go slack and thought, for a moment, that she was going to wet her pants.

Jay reminded them that he would be close by; moments later Meg heard the back door opening and closing. "Cass?" Meg said, and paused to try to draw some moisture into her dry mouth. "Cass, I have some supper for you. Would you turn the lantern on, please?"

"I'm not hungry," Cass said hoarsely, but she got up from her cot to scrabble about on the floor. "I can't...okay, here it is."

Light bloomed, and Meg saw a dirty tear-streaked face, puffy of eye and sullen of mouth. "I shouldn't even eat his rotten food," Cass said, and the corners of her mouth jerked down. "I want to *kill* him, that's what I want." Meg kept silent, and after a long moment Cass sat down on the edge of her cot and reached for the plate and the glass of milk.

Meg took several slow steps backwards, until she felt the other cot against the back of her legs. She lowered herself to the taut canvas, pulled her legs up and crossed them tailor-fashion. Cass hunched over her plate, tearing at a chicken leg with quick bites. The ungrateful little wretch wasn't even sorry for the trouble and pain...come *on*, Margaret! The child cried herself to sleep and she's hardly responsible for your fevered imaginings. She's been asleep, the window screen... Meg peered up into the corner, to see no sign of any tampering...the screen is there and she's here and whatever Kev was shooting at is no concern of yours. Unless it should be Vince.

Her legs began to shake; she set the heels of her hands on her knees and pressed down. Stop that. Vince Gutierrez was no man to walk into a trap, to make himself an easy target for a gun-happy adolescent. Oh no? mocked a small voice from deep inside her head. Isn't that just what he did two months ago? Deep breath; that was different, a calculated risk, not a trap. Maybe, but won't he take a risk for you? For his niece? And how much can even a cop calculate?

Shut up! He won't come alone, and Kev is just a baby playing war; he'll never in the world take Gutierrez by surprise. But what about Jay? Meg blinked hard several times and focused her gaze on Cass, watched as the girl's sharp white teeth stripped the last shred of meat from the bone; the grubby hands like quick little paws and the face pinched by fear made her resemble a small cornered animal.

It might have been better if she had attempted escape, successfully or not, because she was not going to be any help. You are a burden, my girl, thought Meg wearily, a burden and an enigma. Does your boy Jon really want you, I wonder? And if so, for what, beyond the obvious?

"What does Jon want?" she said aloud; and Cass's hands jerked, sloshing milk onto her jeans.

"Oh shit, look at that. Shit."

"Well? What?"

Cass sniffed, took several gulps from the glass and set it down. "I don't know." She picked up the second piece of chicken. "He wants just what he wants, that's all. He wanted a cat, and he's going to be *so mad* that I didn't take better care of Fred, that I let that dickhead kill Fred."

"What could you possibly have done about it?" asked Meg in astonishment.

"Something. I don't know what, but he'll think I should have done something." Cass took a single bite and set the chicken thigh back on the plate. "He's gonna be really pissed that this happened too, all this," she added with a vague wave around her. She pulled her knees up under her chin, hunched her shoulders and did not quite control a shiver.

"Cass, you don't have to let Jon mistreat you."

"What do you know about it," muttered the girl without raising her head. "Anyway he doesn't mean to, he loves me. It's just that he has this bad temper when somebody does something stupid."

Jon didn't sound like much of an improvement over their present companions. "Was it Jon who gave you the kitten," she asked, "in, wherever it was, Billings?"

"No way! I told you, I bought Fred from this guy in the flea market. I haven't seen Jon," Cass said vehemently, "not since that Friday before Uncle Vince came to town. My mom wouldn't let me."

"I can't believe he'll blame you for getting kidnapped," Meg said firmly. "And he'll never know about Fred unless you tell him."

"He knows..." Cass cleared her throat and began again. "He'll find out some way."

Meg thought back over their trip, light-years in the past. Cass had been on her own each evening, not long but long enough to meet Jon. But then why hadn't he turned up here? And she'd insisted that she hadn't seen him...*seen*. Telephone calls, of course. Dummy.

"Were you planning to meet him somewhere? Somewhere in Idaho, for instance?" With all those stolen pots and pans that were weighting down her bag like a traveling hope chest. And the cat, the cat.

"Don't be dumb! I was going to California with you guys. And then you got me into this mess, with that motherfucker killer."

"*I* got you into..." Meg snapped her teeth shut. How did she know she hadn't, or Vince hadn't, some way? Cassandra had a well-developed skill with the quick counter-punch; no wonder her mother had been eager to ship her off.

"I bet I'd like the part of California where you and Uncle Vince live," said Cass in sorrowful tones. "My mom used to talk about it. I bet I'd like my grandmother that I'm named for. I could live with her and go to school, a different school where nobody would know anything about me." She laid her cheek against her knees and sighed. "Meg? What do you think, am I going to get to Port Silva?"

"By God, we both are. I'm just trying to work out how," said Meg, pressing her forearm against the small bulge the medicine bottle made in her pocket.

"What I'd like to do is kill that motherfucker. Get the keys to his gun cupboard and load all those guns and just shoot him and shoot him." She sniffed, and wiped her eyes against her shirtsleeve. "What did he do with him? With Fred?"

"Kev said he was taking him into the woods to bury him."

"Oh. Well, when I get out of here tomorrow I'm going to make Kev show me where," said Cass. "Then I can put a flower or something, on his grave."

Good old friendly Kev, who was out there now murdering raccoons. "Cass," she said carefully, "I understand why you hate Jay, I hate him myself." Understatement. Or perhaps just inadequate statement. "But I don't think it was his intention to kill your kitten."

"He's a crazy, ugly man and he hates cats!"

"He was just standing there when Fred landed on his face. He said later…" The words had been so soft Meg was not absolutely sure she'd heard them. "He said he thought it was a rat."

"Bullshit!"

"Just remember that it was Kev who threw the kitten. He was being rough with it, it scratched him, and he threw it."

"Bullshit," said Cass again, but with less fervor. She picked up her glass of milk and drained it. "What it is, you like Jay. He's big and you probably think he's good-looking.

He's this poor guy who got hurt in a war or can't speak English right, or does too much dope or booze. Or his wife ran out on him. You're just like my mother, you get hot for losers.''

Meg's spine went stiff with outrage: You miserable little slut, you've been twitching your ass at Kev ever since we got here. But she clenched her teeth and kept the words unsaid. Had she just heard the back door open?

"You may have a point, Cass,'' she said quietly. "It's a natural defense, to try to understand someone who's controlling you, try to make a friend of him so he won't hurt you. It's what you're doing with Kev.''

"No it's not! Kev is a . . . he's just a kid, he wouldn't hurt me. Anyway, he likes me, I'm being really nice to him.''

"Jay is coming, I think. You sit there, and listen to a story. Pay attention!'' Meg snapped in a near whisper, and then continued in the same low tone.

"In my daughter's nursery school there were many animals, small animals in cages. And we had a glass cage, an aquarium really, in which we kept a big king snake.''

Cass hugged herself convulsively and opened her mouth, but Meg waved her to silence.

"The bad thing about the snake was not that he was mean, which he wasn't, or slimy, which he definitely wasn't. It was that he had to have live food. Live mice.''

"Ooh. Gross.''

"Right. It made everybody so uneasy that we fed him on weekends, when the kids weren't around. But let me tell you about the mouse.''

"I don't want to hear!'' Cass's voice was a harsh whisper.

"You listen. One day I put a mouse in the cage, and he went crazy with fear and squeaked and ran around and I left to do something, clean the bathroom or something. I forgot about it, and when I came back an hour later, guess what?''

"Gross. Don't *tell* me.''

"The mouse was just walking around that cage as if he owned it, as if the snake were a piece of furniture. The snake wasn't ready to eat yet, so he hadn't attacked; and the mouse had become used to him. Remember that, Cass. Because when I came back to school next day, that snake was all alone in his cage, with a mouse-sized lump in his middle."

NINETEEN

"I'D GO OUT OF MY MIND if I lived here." Knife and fork squeaked against china as Elizabeth reduced a slice of chicken breast to near-mince. She set the plate on the high-chair tray and said, "Eat now, darlin', there's a love," in absent, soft-edged words from some other time and place. The little girl dug her spoon into a mound of mashed potatoes; Elizabeth settled back into her own chair, shifting its position so that she would not be facing the window.

Ben looked up from his steak, eyebrows high, and she gestured toward the wide expanse of plate glass. "That damned mountain, looming there like some white-domed...conscience. Judge. God the father."

Ben glanced out and shrugged. "Lots of people drive long distances to see Mt. Shasta."

"I'd drive long distances to get away from it."

"Now, how'er we doing here? Why, look at you, honey, cleaning your plate like a little lady." The waitress put her hands in the pockets of her denim pinafore and beamed down at the child, who stared back solemn-faced from round gray eyes. "Just as good as gold," the woman crooned. "How old is she?"

"Tessa is twenty-eight months old," Elizabeth replied.

"Well she *is* a tiny little thing. But she'll grow, eating like that. Oh dear," she murmured, eyeing Elizabeth's plate. "Might be it's a wee bit underdone for some folks. Could I bring you something else?"

Elizabeth too looked down at her plate: slices of roast chicken breast, potatoes, green peas. With a sigh she picked up her knife again, and her fork. "It's good; I'm just not very hungry."

"You do look kinda peaked," said the woman. "If you want, I'll package that up and you can take it along, eat it when you feel better."

"Yes. Yes, thank you," Elizabeth said. She put the utensils down, pushed her chair back and stood up. "Ben, will you take care of it? And give me the room key; I think I'll take Tessa up and get her ready for bed."

When the door opened to his knock some thirty minutes later, he stepped into a room with drapes drawn, the only light that from a bedside lamp. Elizabeth wore a robe, her face shadowy in the pale frame of her loose hair; the little girl, in fuzzy sleepers, sat in the center of one of the big beds sucking her thumb.

"Christ, Elizabeth, the place feels like a cave." He set a paper bag on the low dresser-desk. "Here's the rest of your supper, plus a pint of milk. And the nice waitress sent along a treat for Tessa. Hey, Tessa Tessa," he chirped. "Tessa like doughnuts? Nice sticky sugary doughnuts?"

She stared at him and made no reply except for a moist sucking noise. "Ben, she's already had her bath," Elizabeth protested.

"Right, right. But couldn't she *say* something? Come on, Tessa." He approached the bed, leaned over and gave the mattress a hearty bounce; then he grabbed the child, swung her high and carried her toward the window. "Come on, let's take a look at that big old mountain out there."

She twisted in his grip and cried "Lis'bet!" on a long wail that broke into sobs.

"Ben, don't be stupid! Give her here." She plucked the little girl from his arms and cradled her close, cupping the smooth blond head against her shoulder.

"Well, shit." Ben leaned against the windowframe and pushed one of the drapes back; the mountain seemed almost within arm's reach, snowy peak gilded by the last rays of the setting sun. He held the curtain wide and stared out silently; Elizabeth carried the child off to the dressing room, to lay her in her crib and sing softly to her until the sobs had become only an occasional hiccough.

"You know, Elizabeth," he began as she came back into the room.

"Please close the curtains."

He let the heavy fabric fall and settled his rump on the sill, arms crossed on his chest. "Elizabeth, we may have a problem here. That kid has so far demonstrated a vocabulary of about nine words, none of them strung together in anything resembling a sentence. Michael was probably talking in the womb. I think he may be disappointed."

"That's just too bad," she snapped. "Shelter is not your average middle-class nursery school, with museum visits and flashcards. Our babies spend their days with other babies, and the women watching them are tired-out, worried people who think nurture means trying to provide enough food."

"I take your point, but mine is still valid," he said. "And one other thing. Either this little girl has taken a firm and I think irrational dislike to yours truly, or she simply does not like men. This too may make instant father-daughter rapport difficult."

"Michael left me with a three-month-old baby. He couldn't help it, but that didn't change the result: I was just another single mother with no support and no resources except that old farm." Elizabeth jammed her fists into the pockets of her robe. "The children at Shelter get food and a place to be safe, and I think they get love. But nobody has the time or the inclination to feed them fairy tales about daddies."

"Okay. Okay," he muttered. "I guess Michael will understand that, if he's strong enough." He stood up, stretched, and headed for the dresser. "I'm going to have a little brandy. Why don't you try to finish your chicken?"

He poured himself a tot of brandy. Elizabeth took the foil cover from a paper plate and sat down in an arm chair. She ate silently, doggedly, for a minute or two; then she rose, set the plate on the dresser, and fled to the bathroom. The toilet's flush nearly drowned out the noise of her retching.

"There must have been something wrong with that chicken," she told him when she returned. "I hope the baby doesn't get sick, too."

"You haven't kept a meal down in two days," he said, and snapped on the overhead light. "Look at yourself," he commanded, gripping her shoulders and turning her to face the mirror. "Just look."

Her face was as pale as her hair, with deep grooves from nose to mouth, blue shadows like thumbprints under each eye. Sweat beaded her temples, and her lips trembled until she pressed them tight.

"Grieving widow-to-be is one thing," he said softly, "but Michael will take one look at you and think you're Death itself come for him."

"I'm sorry, I can't help it." She tried to pull away, but he held her.

"Elizabeth." Their eyes met in the mirror. "You're not doing anything wrong." Her head moved in the smallest of nods. "Trust me, things are going to work out. Unless..." He frowned at their reflections, then turned her to face him. "Elizabeth, you led me to believe you hadn't been... Jesus Christ, you're not pregnant? Now there is one thing that would really screw up the works."

"Don't be ridiculous!" she snapped, and pulled free of his grip. "I had my tubes tied right after I delivered Tessa; *no one* will do that to me again. I simply have a nervous stomach."

"Whew," he said on a long breathy sigh. "I suddenly had this vision, you and me in court three or four months from now trying to get old charges dismissed. And here's the sad widow, belly out to here, guess what she was doing while her poor husband...Jesus. Here, maybe a little brandy and soda will settle your stomach, relax you."

She shook her head and moved away from him, to turn down the covers of the nearest of two double beds. "Liquor doesn't relax me." She dropped her robe and turned to face him, crossed arms lifting her breasts as she hugged herself and shivered. "I need *you* to relax me."

HE WOKE IN THE DARK, peered at his watch, pushed the covers back and began to ease his long body from the bed.

"What's the matter?" Elizabeth's voice was sleepy, and her reaching hand too slow. "Where are you going?"

"I think I'll try to call. I'll go downstairs; don't want to wake the kid."

She groaned as she came up on one elbow. "What time...? Ben, it's not even ten o'clock. Too early for that nurse."

"Sometimes she comes in early. If I get through to her now, I can still get a good night's sleep."

"Oh." She settled back into her pillow and drew the blankets high.

"Tomorrow is Monday, a three-hundred-plus mile day," he reminded her softly.

"Yes. I wish..." She turned to lie on her back. "I wish we could just *call* Sweet, without setting it up in advance."

Ben, who was standing with his back to her tucking in his shirt, did not turn. "Why would you want to call Sweet?"

"Because I'm feeling it was wrong to involve him in our, *my* troubles; he's too fragile. And Buddy... Buddy has an emotional age of about twelve and thinks he's meant to be a saint or a warrior or both. He nearly drove my mother crazy, and I certainly never meant Sweet to be fully responsible for him."

"Ol' Sweet is tougher than you'd think."

"I hope so," she murmured sleepily. "Ben?"

He was bent forward putting on his shoes, and his "What?" was a soft grunt.

"You wouldn't sell his land, would you? To a developer?"

"It's his land. In his name."

"Yes, but you're his big brother, the only person in the world he cares about. He'd give it to you in a minute if you asked."

"I won't. I won't need to." He turned and leaned across the bed to kiss her, and to slide a caressing hand under the blankets. "You just lie here and keep the bed warm. I won't be long."

TWENTY

ON THE THIRD TRY Jay got his left arm into the sheepskin sleeve. He found the other sleeve, shrugged the jacket up over his shoulders, and reached to pluck the worn and greasy Stetson from its wall hook. His movements were slow and deliberate, like those of a man underwater; Meg thought this was not surprising, since he'd been consuming rum steadily throughout the day.

"Gotta go. Little late tonight, gotta hurry."

Maybe he'd crash his truck. Or get arrested; did cops in Idaho, if that's where they were, pick up the locals for DUI? She played with that mental picture for a moment: big solid men in uniforms gathering Jay up, making him walk a line or breathe into a balloon, taking him away. Or even better, nice local cops, bringing him home. Bringing him in here. Sure, and he'd shoot the cops or have Kev do it.

Jay stepped carefully from the wall to the stove, to stand with his hands in his jacket pockets and stare at the fire. Meg caught a whiff of rank body odor; she didn't think he'd had a shower since their arrival. Nor changed clothes; on the top shelf by the bunk, the stacks of plain gray-white underwear were just as high as they'd been yesterday morning. All that underwear must mean he did usually change.

"Your kid is sure taking her time," he muttered. "I gotta get going, what the hell's she doing?"

"She's still upset about her kitten," said Meg.

"Tough shit," he said, without intonation. "She takes much longer, means *you* won't get to the latrine tonight."

"Don't be ridiculous," she snapped, and caught her breath as he swung around. About to lower her glance, even apologize, she changed her mind. She'd been docile as a cow all day, until she was sick of herself. And she wondered...
"*You* may not be interested in bathing, but I am."

Even though he used his right hand, it was a slow and awkward blow; she was able to slip most of it, taking a rasp of knuckles along her turning jaw. Keep it up with the rum, friend, she told him silently as she straightened and stepped back.

"I need a shower," she said in softer tones, "after working in the kitchen all day. Please?"

The door opened and Cass sidled in, face scrubbed and hair damp. She looked at the two of them and bolted for the storeroom. Jay hunched his shoulders and shoved his hands back into his pockets.

"You can lock that door and leave; I'll go have a shower and come back and just sit here by the fire," Meg promised. "I won't make trouble, not with my daughter locked in and you carrying the keys."

A silence several breaths long. Then he shrugged. "Okay by me. I'll tell Kev, he'll be outside watching. You go to the washhouse, then get back here and stay. Otherwise, you're a target. He's got hawk's eyes, Kev has, and besides that he's getting a little itchy."

Meg went to get her things from the storeroom and to say good night for the moment to Cass, who was already buried in her sleeping bag. Then Jay snapped the padlock shut, gave Meg a brief stare, and shambled out the door. She stood in the doorway, listening, and thought she heard voices; presumably he was telling Kev that she was on a longer tether tonight. She certainly hoped he was telling Kev.

The old truck was not eager to start; finally it settled into a one-cylinder-short rhythm and rattled away. Meg rolled up her pants legs and draped herself in her blue nylon rain poncho. She stepped outside and headed for the lights of the washhouse, walking as firmly as was possible in her rubber flip-flops; if Kev was nearby, the gray veil of rain concealed him.

Business first. She'd snatched a single brief look at her booty, just enough to learn that what she had found in the pantry was not the vial of anonymous "for sleep" pills she'd seen earlier. Now she fished the plastic bottle from the pocket of her jeans, and took it to the strongest light, the one over the sink, for inspection.

The prescription label was typed. James Bennington Taylor, for depression. 1 tablet daily at bedtime. Do not exceed dosage. One hundred tablets, each 100 mg. Amitriptyline hydrochloride. No further refills, said the label; and it was dated three months ago. The bottle was full, in fact looked unopened. Clearly Jay was supposed to be taking these pills; just as clearly, he was not doing so.

Her brother had hated his antidepression medicine because it sometimes had side effects: a palsylike shaking of his hands, or a slurring of his speech. She couldn't remember the name of Neil's medicine; it was shorter than this, probably a brand name. Meg unscrewed the cap and pulled out the wad of white cotton. Round tablets, coated some color between pink and lavender, letters and numerals stamped into the surface. She looked at the tablet in her hand, rolled it around in her palm, dropped it back in the bottle.

Well. Think about it. She set the medicine bottle on the sink, stripped her dirty clothes off and dropped them on the floor. Hot water, blessed stuff, and soap. She scrubbed hard all over, as if to wash away despair as well as grime, and tried to think. Neil's medicine had been a tricyclic antidepressant, that's what his doctor had said; she hadn't known what that meant and still did not. But he'd taken it at bedtime, she remembered that. Less than one hundred milligrams, perhaps seventy-five?

She kept that label in her mind's eye as she rubbed shampoo into hair greasy from sweat and cooking, working the last of the lather out of the heavy mass just as the water began to cool. Do not exceed dosage, surely that was important, surely the label on Neil's medicine had said that, too. His doctor certainly had; he'd made a big fuss about it and had insisted that Meg count the tablets each day. He'd said that overdose could bring on convulsions or...

Or what? She turned off the shower and bent to wring water from her hair before wrapping a towel around her body. She didn't remember what else, only that it was clearly

life-threatening. It didn't matter, really, in what way these
little tablets were lethal, just so long as they were. She stared
at herself in the mirror over the sink and saw not her face
but Coke bottles. Then coffee mugs, get it into his coffee.

She was concentrating so hard that she heard no noise of
approach, no footsteps, not even the sound of the squeaky
doorknob. Suddenly the washhouse door was wide, Kev
framed there with one hand on the door and the other cradling his rifle.

On a harsh indrawn breath she jerked her shoulders back
and let the towel fall to her feet. The rain-cooled night blew
its chilly breath on her damp skin, and Kev's face flamed.
Meg swept her left hand up to cover her breasts, closed her
right hand around the plastic vial, and then in one swift
movement crouched to gather the towel around her.

"Oh shit." He jumped backwards and pulled the door
closed. "I'm real sorry, ma'am," he called. "You were out
here a long time, and Jay made me promise I'd watch you
real close. But not *that* close, I didn't ... hey, I really apologize."

THE CABIN WAS WARM, its close air smelling of human bodies, fried food, smoke, and perhaps fear. She opened the
back door to freshen the place, but this unorthodoxy so
clearly made Kev nervous that she gave up and closed it. She
prowled the two rooms for fifteen minutes, pausing here to
survey the bookcase, there to twitch bed covers straight,
beside the stove to add a small log. Kev, circling the building like a wary cat, would eventually realize she was just
puttering, well away from either door.

The other pill bottles were still in the pantry, right where
she'd left them. They proved to contain the same medicine,
with the same dosage recommended by the same doctor, A.
Achenberg. One was full, still topped with cotton, the other
half-empty. She put them back and took a tea bag from a
red Lipton's box.

She puzzled over the significance of the bottles as she
made a cup of tea. No sensible doctor would have pre-
scribed all those pills at once. Maybe Jay had decided to stop

taking the stuff for whatever reason, but hadn't wanted his doctor to know lest he interfere. Or Jay had been saving the pills in case he decided to kill himself. And had forgotten he had them? Don't count on it.

Meg stood at the kitchen sink to drink her tea, and to crush a tablet. Pill in the bowl of a soup spoon, crush it with the back of a teaspoon; it was a technique she remembered using with baby aspirin. The pill was whitish inside, crushed into a crystalline powder, and dissolved readily in water.

After flushing the sink out, she stood there and drank more tea and crushed another pill, and another, and another. Ten or eleven, fifteen, twenty-five or so and then the tea ran out and the tension began to get to her, tightening her muscles and causing her heart to pound.

Live free or die, wasn't that some state's official motto? Kill or die? Kill or be killed. She poured more hot water over the same tea bag, stirred in lots of sugar and went on with her work.

Finally she crushed the last pill, poured the powder into the vial and capped it, shoved the vial into her pocket. She washed spoons, and washed down the counter top where she'd spilled lots of powder, probably a tenth of the total. But ninety times the normal dosage should do it.

One mouthful of tea left in the cup; she swallowed the cold sweet stuff, stretched to ease her shoulder muscles and found herself looking out the kitchen window. Nothing to see out there except her own reflection, smeared by a sudden wash of raindrops against the glass. The face of a murderer, that's what she was looking at. If you poisoned someone who was holding you captive, could you call it self-defense? Picky picky and who cares.

She did. She didn't want to kill anyone. Perhaps the pills would merely make him sick, incapacitate him. Sophistry, Margaret. Point a gun and pull the trigger, and you're choosing to kill. It's no simple thing to shoot to wound, Gutierrez had pointed out grimly one night as they watched a cop show on television. Nor to poison for specific manageable results, unless you were a doctor. Where was Kev? she wondered suddenly, and stood very still to listen. Jay

had been gone now for more than an hour, Kev on guard out
in the chilly rain the whole time. Perhaps he'd taken shelter
somewhere like the washhouse. Or he might have gone off
on the track of some animal, playing deerstalker in the
woods. And she was here diddling around with exotic
pharmaceuticals while she might be escaping.

She turned off the light in the kitchen, moved into the
living room and hesitated briefly before switching off the
bullet lights. She'd just sit here for a moment in the glow
that flickered from the transparent door of the iron stove.
Nice, friendly. Anybody might choose to sit here in the
semidark and enjoy the warmth.

Count, she told herself. Sixty. And sixty. And again. And
a fourth time, or was it fifth? No sound at either door. She
took a deep breath and rose from the bench. Not the front
door, the gleam of the fire would show if she opened that.
She pulled on her still-damp poncho, slid her small flashlight into a rear pocket of her Levi's and stepped gently toward the kitchen, cringing at the faint squeak of her
sneakers on the floor.

She pulled the door open and slid out and eased it shut.
The rain was falling straight down with a steady thrum-
ming sound. One light on in the washhouse. None in the
garage, she didn't even know whether the garage had lights.
No sound except the rain. No movement.

She stepped down two steps and was on the dirt, so hard-
packed here that it wasn't even very muddy. Garage on the
other side of the cabin, very close but in the opposite direction from the washhouse; she wouldn't be able to claim she
was going for a pee.

One foot after another, close against the cabin for the
protection of its eaves—or for its reassuring bulk. She
neared the corner of the building and thought of Cass, right
in there asleep. Maybe not, maybe watching from the vent
with its torn screen; what would she do? Yell?

What would he do to Cass, Jay? When he returned and
found Meg gone? Nothing more than he planned to do
anyway, to both of them. They were dead, she and Cass, if
things went on according to Jay's scenario . . . or whosoever,

somebody's. So the best thing would be for her to get away and bring help.

Now she had to cross the opening between cabin and garage, and anyone, Kev, looking into that gap might see the movement. I'm doing this for both of us, Cass. As the words formed in her mind she knew them for lies; she was doing this for Katy, for herself and Katy. She leaped across the gap and leaned against the ridged metal surface of the garage. No sound from there, either.

She crept along toward the front, the garage door. Paused to touch her pocket for perhaps the third time; keys, yes. Stopped at the corner, and stepped carefully around. Her rain-darkened poncho should not be eye-catching against the brown paint.

There were twin roll-up doors, the nearest high on its tracks as Jay had left it. Which meant that her van was in there in the dark behind the closed door, and she'd have to open the noisy thing to get out. Never mind... the van. It had been standing idle for two days, but it was a dependable old workhorse and would start at a touch, if there was gas. She crept through the open door and found herself momentarily disoriented by the rattle of the rain on the building's metal roof. Like being inside a waterfall.

Gas. She had planned to fill the tanks as she left town Friday. One had been empty, the other low; if whoever drove the one-hundred-plus miles here didn't stop at a gas station on the way, she'd be attempting her escape on little more than fumes.

Her outstretched hand found the back of the van; she gave the vehicle a pat and then guided herself around to the driver's side. She was about to ease the door open when she remembered the interior light. Okay, the window was down; she hauled herself up and in, pulled off the light cover and removed the bulb. Breathing hard, she settled into the driver's seat, gripped the wheel and froze there, transfixed by familiar contours and textures and smells.

"Gas!" she said aloud. She got her flashlight from her pocket and directed a sheltered beam at the dashboard. Empty metal bracket: Jay must have taken the C.B., but keys in the ignition imagine that! Turn the key and check the gas gauge, and guess what, empty. She reached down and flipped the switch to the other tank and the needle jiggled and came to rest just a hair above the E.

The gauges were accurate; she had probably enough gas to get the engine running and move the vehicle out the gate. To meet Jay, or be caught by Kev. Gas.

Gas generator. It chugged along every day for several hours; there had to be fuel. She slid from the van, crept around its front, turned her flash against the back wall and could not believe what she saw. Luck, finally and by God about time. A five-gallon can with a long spigot—no, two of them. One sloshed disappointingly, but the other was clearly full. And it was gasoline, oh yes.

Five gallons would get her out. Careful don't clatter, don't make a noise, and for heaven's sake don't make sparks. She emptied the can and set it back in place, thought about taking what there was in its mate and decided not to push her luck. Gas cap. Back in the driver's seat and leave the door ajar. Gas gauge: quarter full you sweet thing and pump the pedal once, twice. She had decided while she worked that her best bet was to start the engine and then open the garage door, the real noise-maker; then leap in and back out full throttle over anything in the way.

The sudden blaze of light shocked her nearly senseless; she heard her own whinny of terror, tasted blood from a bitten lip, gripped the steering wheel harder to keep herself from falling. Heard a shot, thought fuck it go ahead.

"Get out here or I'll blow you full of holes."

Kev. And if he shot into this fume-filled building he'd probably blow her up, her and the van. She pried her fingers loose from the wheel, nudged the door open and clambered wearily out. "I'm coming."

He stood perhaps ten feet away in a rain-hazed wash of light from the door, watching her over his left shoulder. As she stepped through the doorway he began to bring his arms level, and she saw the rifle barrel his poncho had shielded.

"Would you really shoot a woman?" she called. "An unarmed woman? Even the Provos don't do that."

"Stop right there!" His voice was high with strain, but he dropped his rifleman's pose to face her fully. "You got no business out here."

"And you have no right to keep me here. Why not let me go, Kev?" she said softly. "You know, when I found the keys in the ignition I thought maybe you'd left them there on purpose, for me to find and use."

"No! I forgot them. What about your kid?" he demanded suddenly. "Were you going to drive off and leave her?"

"No, no. You could get her out for me, there must be another key to that padlock. It would be so simple, Kev." She brushed rain from her face and then reached out to him, spread her hands in earnest plea. "If you let us go, we'd just drive away in the dark and we'd never be able to find our way back even if we wanted to."

"Oh no. Hunh-unh. No way."

"I would promise absolutely never to tell anyone."

"See, it's like I told you the first day, sometimes honorable men have to do things they don't like. If there's a good reason." A heavier sound overrode his earnest voice and the drumming of the rain; Meg let her hands fall and her shoulders slump, turning her head away from the glare as the old pickup lumbered down on them. It splashed to a stop, and Jay shut the engine off but left the lights burning as he tumbled out.

"The fuck's going on here?"

"She was gonna run, Jay," said Kev. Meg said nothing at all, just stared into the darkness and let the rain fall on her head.

"I thought she was okay, asleep or something, everything quiet," the boy said breathlessly. "Then I was making a patrol, and I saw this little light in the garage."

Meg said nothing.

"I don't need this, I don't need any of this," said Jay. He gripped her shoulder, flung her against the wall of the garage and began to hit her. First openhanded, a back-and-forth full-arm swing. Then again, faster and harder, slamming her head against the metal wall. She saw fists coming, covered her breasts and took fast hard punches on her forearms and then on her ribs.

"Hey, Jay, take it easy!" Kev, alarmed.

Jay grunted and hit her once in the belly, a blow that doubled her over and sent her, gagging, to her knees in the mud.

"Now. You won't feel much like running for a day or two, or even walking." He yanked her to her feet and half-dragged, half-carried her to the cabin.

TWENTY-ONE

GUTIERREZ'S HEELS hit the wet tarmac of the Coeur d'Alene airport with a jolt that brought his teeth together hard. He grimaced, pressed a hand to his collarbone, then shook his head as Val Kuisma moved to offer support. Jake Delucca was last down the ladder, muttering curses as he peered up at the sky.

"Sonuvabitch. Fuckin' window is damn near shut already, and I'll be here for... Goddamn. No hangar space either, I'll just have to tie her down."

"I'll pay for your lost time," Gutierrez told him.

"Sonuvabitch. No you fuckin' won't, I agreed to bring you." Delucca, a sparely built man of medium height who moved as if he had nervous springs in his boots, bounded ahead of the other two in the direction of the airport building. "If I'm still here when you're ready to head for home, you can pay me to take you."

Kuisma strode along beside his boss, clearly trying to keep an eye on the other's face without actually walking backwards. Gutierrez knew he looked like a green-tinged Death's head; he'd had several recent glimpses of himself in the mirror in the toilet. "Knock it off, Val!" he snapped now. "I'm not going to fall down, and there's nothing left in my stomach to lose."

"Yessir."

Gusts of wind stirred their hair and snatched at their clothing; the sky, which had shown a few hand-sized pieces of blue as they landed, was indeed closing back in, a sullen canopy of gray. The thunderstorms that had drenched the Idaho panhandle Sunday and Sunday night weren't through yet.

Kuisma shouldered the door open, and Gutierrez stepped inside and looked around. "I'll arrange for the rental car," he said to his companion. "You locate the airport manager and find out whether Lawrence Archer ever got here."

Archer had not landed in Coeur d'Alene, Kuisma told his boss ten minutes later as he slid into the driver's seat of another Toyota. "The manager says they've had only two single-engine aircraft land here in the last twenty-four hours. He says the nearest airports for a sensible pilot would be Missoula or Boise."

"Maybe he didn't need to come. Maybe he's found his kid," said Gutierrez. "Never mind. Let's go call on Chief Brownell."

By the time they found the police station rain was falling again, a steady determined downpour as if the sky had decided to become one with the lake and obliterate the town altogether. Kuisma had managed to promote a big black umbrella from somebody at the car rental desk, and he held it over the two of them as they sloshed across the parking lot toward glass double doors.

Inside, Kuisma folded the umbrella as Gutierrez strode toward the information counter on the right. A young woman in a light-blue uniform stood in the enclosure, directing words over her shoulder to a uniformed man. She turned her neat dark head as Gutierrez advanced, scanned his face, met his gaze, and smoothed her expression into one of wary attention. "Yes?"

"I am Vincent Gutierrez, chief of police in Port Silva, California. I spoke with Chief Brownell yesterday."

"Chief Gutierrez. He's been expecting you."

"My men were to get in touch with me here if anything came up. Have there been any calls?"

"No, sir, not so far. I'm Officer Mardian," she added as she opened the counter gate and stepped through. "Chief Brownell's office is this way. I hope we can help, sir."

"So do I." He followed her down the hall, Kuisma on his heels. She knocked on a door, then opened it and announced him; he nodded thanks and gave her his best effort at a smile. "This is Officer Kuisma," he told her. "He could use a cup of coffee and maybe a doughnut or something."

Chief Art Brownell, coming forward with hand outstretched, was a square, sandy man with the weathered face of an outdoorsman. "Glad to see you, Gutierrez," he said crisply. "We've been asking around about your people, but I have to say we haven't turned up anything useful. Sorry."

"Me, too." Gutierrez sat down in the chair the other man indicated.

"I had two men out yesterday morning," Brownell told him, settling behind his gray metal desk. "They took the picture of Mrs. Halloran and talked to folks at gas stations and convenience stores on 90 west, and on 35 south; somebody heading for the coast would surely have taken one or the other." He shook his head and sat back in his chair. "No response. Nobody recognized the picture, nobody remembered the van or the license number. This doesn't mean they weren't there, just means nobody noticed."

"I appreciate the effort," Gutierrez said wearily.

"Should be done again today," said Brownell. "Some of the folks who worked Friday were off yesterday, Sunday. But we're up to our, um, our rear ends in local stuff."

"I understand."

"Had something like a riot Saturday night," Brownell went on. "High school kids partying on the streets, smoking all kinds of shit, drinking beer, pissing in doorways. Finally got out of hand, and we had to move."

"Which means you've got parents and lawyers and business people all over you," said Gutierrez, and Brownell nodded.

"I guess one little town isn't much different from another," he said with a sigh. "But I would surely hate to live in a big city. Anyway, we're dealing with that, and then we've got tourists by the dozens running their RV's into each other in this damned rain. What I can do is give you a report on our actions so far, and I think I can pry one officer loose to take you around."

"That would be a big help."

"Just wish we could do more," said Brownell. He frowned at his cluttered desktop, then shot a sad-eyed glance at his visitor. "This is big country up here. Empty country compared to some. Idaho, eastern Washington, central Oregon—unless you're smack in some little town, you're just—out there. Nobody much to notice. Sorry.''

"Yeah.'' Gutierrez took a deep breath and thrust his chin out. ''I have two specific questions to ask you.''

"Shoot.''

"There's a doctor at the hospital I need to talk to, the man who dealt with this,'' he said, and touched his collarbone. ''Dr. Wu, tall Chinese-American and I don't know his first name. He's not on duty until tonight, and the hospital won't release his address or telephone number.''

"Yeah, they will,'' said Brownell, and made a note on a small pad before him.

"And I would like very much to know whether a man named Lawrence Archer has been in touch with you, about his son.''

Brownell sat back in his chair and widened his eyes at Gutierrez. ''Why? I mean, why do you need to know that?''

"The son, Jonathan Archer, has been involved with my niece. That's why Cass was with Mrs. Halloran and me; my sister wanted to get her out of this boy's reach.'' Gutierrez felt a moment's unease at tossing family problems out into public air. ''He's a spoiled-rotten rich kid who's been kept out of serious trouble so far by his father's money and connections. I think it's at least possible that Jon Archer is what's happened to Meg—Mrs. Halloran—and Cass.''

"Um. This Archer's a rich man?''

"A rich *attorney*,'' said Gutierrez.

"That kind of guy, if he wanted help from the Coeur d'Alene police he'd start with the chief. Which he hasn't, not yet.''

"If he does, at least if he turns up in person, I'd appreciate it if you'd tell him I'm here.''

"Sure.''

"Good.'' Gutierrez got stiffly to his feet. ''One more favor. Could you suggest a nice quiet motel, a place where I could put my feet up and make a few telephone calls?''

"JUST GET GOING," he said some thirty minutes later to Kuisma and Officer Christine Mardian. "I have some calls to make, and you'll move a lot faster without me along."

"Yessir. We'll put in a couple hours on 90 west, that's the best bet. Then we'll report back."

Kuisma ushered the policewoman out, sketched a half salute at his boss, and pulled the door shut. Gutierrez nudged a padded armchair close to the desk, sat down with care, and reached for the telephone.

"No automatic teller withdrawals in the last two weeks," reported Will Anders, manager of the Port Silva bank that held Meg's account and had issued her Visa card. "The most recent charges were on Thursday, last Thursday, in Butte. There's one from Butte Automotive Glass, and one from a gas station."

"And nothing since then," said Gutierrez, more to himself than to Anders.

"Look, Chief...look, Vince, some of these little remote gas stations are pretty slow about getting charges in. I've seen a delay of more than a week, even as much as ten days."

"Sure. Thanks, Will. Would you call me, here, or call Hank Svoboda there in Port Silva, if anything more turns up?"

Then Svoboda. "Hey, buddy, I'm real glad you didn't call earlier," said the older man with a sigh. "I just found out fifteen minutes ago that a burned-out wreck in Oregon ain't ours."

"Oh Jesus."

"Yeah. Oregon state police came across this late yesterday, some ways off highway 97 near a little bitty town called Shanko. Van, too burned to tell color or read the plate, been there a day or two. I decided to sweat it out myself, and they finally got the engine number."

About to protest, Gutierrez considered the state of his own nerves, not to mention his digestive system, and decided to be grateful instead. "Thanks. Anything else going?"

"Well, one kind of funny thing," Svoboda told him. "Some guy called the station around eleven-thirty last night and asked for you by name, just Vincent Gutierrez. Dunnegan told him you're on vacation, asked if he could help, and the guy hung up. Probably don't mean a thing."

"Probably not," muttered Gutierrez. He squeezed his eyes shut for a moment, then blinked several times. "Shit. I spent too many hours on a roller-coaster plane this morning; my head's as screwed up as my gut. Hank, I'm at the City Center Motel in Coeur d'Alene." He peered at the telephone and read off the number. "Call me if anything happens, anything at all."

Gutierrez replaced the receiver, clambered to his feet, and inspected himself in the mirror over the dresser. Looked like a mean ugly son of a bitch. Didn't look nearly as bad as he felt. He decided to have a long hot shower before calling Dr. Wu's home.

He set the water as hot as he could stand it, stepped in under the pounding stream, and turned the temperature up slightly. He needed to hurt someone, himself if nobody else was available. Three full days now. Gutierrez closed his eyes and thought about Meg, trying to call her image into his mind, to see her in their best times. Found himself remembering instead the furor and uneasiness as the two of them, two large and assertive people with years of accumulated belongings, tried to fit into his small house together. At the end of the first week, Meg went shopping and came home with four new bookcases and the biggest bed he had ever seen.

Or Meg in the kitchen. She hated to cook, stamped around and swore and burned her fingers. Put dents in his best pots and broke the glass double-boiler he'd had for twenty years. Made about ten gallons of spaghetti sauce in apology.

What the fuck was he going to do without Meg?

The heat finally lost its impact, and he began to feel simply waterlogged. He stepped out, dried himself, and knotted a towel around his waist. His brace had been a bitch to get off, and after several minutes of trying to put it on again, to fasten the hooks somewhere between his shoulder blades, he gave up and threw the thing on the bed. Wait for Kuisma, the cripple's helper. Do something useful and one-handed like making another phone call.

The woman who answered the phone, Dr. Wu's wife or mother or sister, was polite but wary. She would check with the local police first and call back. When she did, still polite, she could say only that her son the doctor was on a fishing trip in his sky-blue four-wheel-drive Subaru and would probably go straight to the hospital, to wash and change there before going on duty at four o'clock.

Gutierrez thanked her, hung up, and looked at his watch. Not quite one P.M. Kuisma would be gone until at least two. Idaho was a clannish kind of place, Brownell had said: people used to their neighbors, used to helping out when needed and minding their own business otherwise. Val's open, eager face was the kind to win sympathy and draw information, whereas his own sterner appearance was more likely to intimidate. Also, he reminded himself, Val was in spite of his funny name clearly a white man in white man's country. No blacks, no chicanos, and damned few Asians, that's one thing he'd noticed about Idaho.

THE WORLD WAS STILL made of water, gray sheets coming straight down with a gentle hiss. "Is this normal summer weather around here?" Gutierrez asked Chris Mardian, turning only his head to speak over the seatback. The two young cops had spent two fruitless hours cruising highway 90, and were happy to break the routine by taking Gutierrez in search of Dr. Wu.

"Not so much of it, for so long," she said gloomily. "This is just incredibly beautiful country; I'm sorry you can't see it when the sun is shining. And under better circumstances, of course," she added quickly, and he thought he could feel the heat of her blush.

"I hope to, some day," he muttered. "Val, there's the hospital. Drive through the lot and look for something blue."

They cruised up and down rows of parked cars, and finally parked their own, a white sedan with the word POLICE on its front fenders, at a spot providing a good view of the back door. They had been waiting only minutes when a bright-blue vehicle slid by them on high tires, and Gutierrez snapped, "Get behind him."

The Subaru parked, its driver's door opened, and Gutierrez stepped out of the police car to greet a tall familiar figure. "Dr. Wu?"

"I beg . . . ah. Mr. Gutierrez. How is your collarbone?"

"Fine. May I speak with you? It's important," he added, and took the doctor's elbow. "Let's go up by the doors, under the roof."

"I haven't much time, Mr. Gutierrez. What can I do for you?"

"Mrs. Halloran is missing. You called her Mrs. Gutierrez," he explained as Wu's brows arched high, "and we didn't bother to correct you, but we're not married yet. She left here Friday around noon, and as you may remember, I left later that same day. No one has heard from her since."

"But I can't . . . I certainly have not heard from her."

"But did you see her leave?"

"No, I . . . ah, wait," Wu said thoughtfully, and looked down at the steps, then out toward the parking lot.

"Yes?" Gutierrez bit the word off short.

"I had come out, for a cigarette. Nasty habit, I always sneak away so no one will see me. And she came by," he went on quickly, as if Gutierrez's clenched muscles had transmitted a warning. "We exchanged a few words, she thanked me as I recall, and then she went on out toward the far parking lot. I remember noticing her walk, that fine free-swinging walk you sometimes see in tall women."

"Did you see where she went?"

"Just a moment, let me try to visualize it." Wu folded his hands together against his breastbone and looked off into the rain. "Not many cars out there. She walked across the empty lot, fast but not hurrying. There was just the one . . . no, there were two vehicles. A van? I think a van, not new. It seemed to me she was headed for that.

"And next to it," he went on slowly, "next to it was something local."

"Local?" Gutierrez's voice was sharp.

"Well. It was, let's see. It was one of those funny hand-made things you see around here."

Gutierrez took a long deep breath and expelled it slowly. "A handmade vehicle."

"No." Wu shook his head impatiently. "A handmade camper—you know, a slide-in—on a very old pickup truck. Brown, with shingles."

It was not, Gutierrez learned, a shingled pickup. It was a no-color pickup, possibly brown or possibly just rusty, with a tall shingle-covered camper. Wu, who was far-sighted but had been paying only mild attention, said that the license could have been from Washington or Colorado as well as from Idaho, because it was green and white. He had seen the vehicles, had seen Mrs. Halloran nearing her van, and had then finished his cigarette and returned to work.

"If you wish," Wu added with a glance at his watch, "I could make you a quick sketch."

"Back to the police station," Gutierrez snapped to Kuisma ten minutes later. "I have to talk to Chief Brownell."

CHIEF BROWNELL FROWNED as he scrutinized Dr. Wu's penciled drawing of a topheavy camper with round windows on the side and another in the rear door. "Vince, those things are... well, maybe not a dime a dozen, but real plentiful around here," he said with a regretful shrug. "There are two guys on the force I know of who built their own campers. And since they don't have to be licensed..."

"This is the first lead, the first thing even resembling a lead, I've had," said Gutierrez, trying to keep his voice civil. "I think I should follow it up."

"Oh, absolutely. We'll make copies of this right away, show it around... Yes?" he said in response to a knock on his door.

"Chief Brownell, there's a Mr. Archer asking to see you."

"I'm Lawrence Archer," came a voice familiar to Gutierrez, and then the high-headed tennis-player's frame pushed past the uniform into the room. "I just got into town, and I need to talk to you."

"Hello, Archer." Gutierrez shoved his chair back and rose, turning to face the newcomer.

"Oh," said Archer, drawing himself tight. He wore corduroy slacks and a leather-elbowed tweed sports coat over a silky-looking dark turtleneck. "*Mister* Gutierrez. And what slanders have you been tossing around in here, cop to cop?"

"Hardly any," said Gutierrez. "I haven't even told Chief Brownell that your big eighteen-year-old boy liked to put heavy moves on fourteen-year-old girls. And there's the information Officer Kuisma dug up in Pueblo, I haven't gotten to that yet, either.

"It seems that Jonathan Archer went to one of these wargames camps in June," Gutierrez said to Brownell. "While he was there he and a buddy took a 'prisoner' and in the process they injured the boy so badly he spent two weeks in the hospital. How much did that cost you, Archer?"

"Quite a lot," said Archer, through his teeth. "Even though I don't believe it was Jon's fault. A man with money and a son is an easy mark, Gutierrez. How much do *you* want?"

"What I want is my fiancée. And my niece. Or somebody's head."

TWENTY-TWO

"Meg?"

She was contemplating suspended animation. Her yoga teacher had been able to achieve something approaching that, greatly slowing her own pulse and respiration rate. First you had to still the mind, eliminate thought.

"Meg, I saved you a sandwich from lunch."

Focus inward. Shut out present reality. Detach from the physical self.

"Here, don't you want it?"

Cass bumped the cot and Meg came back to her physical self in a hurry.

"Oh shit, I'm sorry! You really sure nothing's broken?"

"Fairly sure," she replied in a polite distant voice. She had said nothing to Cass about last night's beating...had said nothing to Cass about anything at all. But her face bore strident testimony to Jay's blows, she'd seen that in the washhouse mirror on her single trip there this morning.

"Well I wish you'd get *up* then, it makes me nervous that you're just lying there like you were dying or something."

What a nice idea. Don't think about it. Meg shifted her position carefully, moving from her side to her back. Hurt quite a lot, but not as much as it would, say, tomorrow.

"Look, it's only bologna because that's all there was; but I put a lot of mayonnaise on and some lettuce. I'll leave it here, okay? And I'll go fill your thermos."

Nothing broken but her spirit. She listened to Cass's departing footsteps and felt tears begin to spill from the corners of her eyes and trickle down her temples. Don't be so nice to me, Cassandra. I had a perfectly good chance to escape last night and I blew it. In the van, keys in the ignition, lights...and the brave heroine guns the big engine in reverse and rips her way out of there. Roars down the road

and even smashing head-on into that bastard in his camper
would have been better than standing there like a rained-on
rag doll and letting him beat me.

Never mind. She sniffed, wiped her eyes with the heels of
her hands, pressed her head more firmly into her pillow,
Vince's jacket. Someone had begun work on the ceiling in
her corner, installing acoustic tiles. When she was in grade
school the perforations were regular, in lines; a bored child
could tip her head back and try to count. The ones above
her now had small holes, larger ones, larger ones still, like
stars of varying magnitudes. No pattern that she could dis-
cern; she unfocused her eyes and still could find no arrangement, no motif.

Sounds of movement intruded, and a thick rough voice
out there somewhere, words just a blur. And a lighter voice,
what was his name, Kev. God, she said silently, politely,
would you please strike them dead, both of them?

"Here's your thermos with fresh water," said Cass as she
knelt beside the cot. "If you're not going to eat this, I am.
You know what he's doing?" she went on quietly, and
paused to bite and chew.

"He's got this big book of pictures, soldiers with all kinds
of guns and stuff, and helicopters, that he's staring at. He
said they're all dead, those soldiers, but Kev said one of 'em
is him, Jay."

He's dead, too.

"And there's a picture of this big shiny black thing like a
wall with writing on it. That's what he called it, the wall. It's
in Washington, D.C., and he says Willie somebody is going
to take him there. I don't know why anybody would take
him anyplace, he oughta be in a cage. Meg, I'm really scared
of him," she added in a rush.

Me too.

"You should see him," Cass whispered.

No thank you.

"It's really disgusting," Cass went on. "He's still got on
that same shirt, you can hardly see the plaid it's so dirty.
And the same Levi's, probably they could stand up by

themselves. He stinks so bad you need to hold your breath around him.''

''I don't want to hear about it, Cass.'' Meg rolled her body over, turning her back on the girl. Pulled her legs up. This position wasn't as comfortable but felt safer somehow. She watched the progress of a drip of water that had come through a tiny flaw in the siding; listened to a soft whispery sound that was soothing if you didn't connect it with the miserable, never-ending rain. Saw a spider scuttle past. Thought of turning and straightening and sitting up to reach for the thermos, but decided against it. If she didn't eat anything and didn't drink anything she wouldn't have to get up from here ever.

CASS AGAIN, smelling of the outdoors. ''Kev's patrolling, and he won't let me come with him. He's getting bossy; he asked Jay for the keys to the gun cupboard and Jay *gave* them to him just like that. Now he's got *two* guns, the long one and then this funny shorter one he says is for deer. He says he saw a deer last night. I'm gonna go have a shower; you want me to get you anything first?''

Meg sighed and straightened her legs. ''There's a bottle in my bag, with a red cap.''

She heard objects being moved around on the floor, the sound of a zipper, and a moment later a hiss of displeasure. ''Gin!'' Cass snapped. ''That's disgusting.''

''I need a drink,'' said Meg.

''Sure, just go ahead and turn your brain to mush the way that asshole out there is doing. He's already on his third bottle.''

''I have only one bottle. Please give it here.''

''I guess you think you're the only woman ever got punched out,'' said Cass. She set the bottle down beside Meg's cot, grabbed her tote bag and left.

You hard little bitch, thought Meg, and felt the easy, helpless tears begin to well once more. Every move hurt, her face was swollen and aching, she wasn't absolutely sure he hadn't broken a few ribs or at least cracked them; how do you tell?

The square bottle was heavy and awkward in her hand, and a trickle of gin ran like ice down her inner wrist as she filled the cap. She tipped it to her mouth, then gave a muffled gasp and swallowed hastily as several cuts inside her mouth sprang to smarting life.

Talk about cause for self-pity, can't even drink. She stared at the bottle with its gold-edged oval picture of Queen Victoria, who looked as if her mouth hurt, too. Lots of things in life were painful. Childbirth. Oral surgery. Playing field hockey and getting run over by Bobbie Mae Jensen (but you were younger then). Falling twenty feet down a mountainside wearing a backpack.

So it's the humiliation that has you whining, lady, not the pain. What we have here is an ego problem. Poor baby.

She clambered painfully off her cot, bent to set the bottle of gin back in her bag, bent again to pick up her big stainless steel thermos. The cool water soothed her poor mouth and reminded her that she had aspirin in her bag, too, no doubt better pain medicine than gin. On his third bottle of rum, Cass had said. That was interesting.

When Cass came in nearly an hour later, Meg was sitting on her cot with her legs tucked up. "He's on his third bottle?" she asked, and gave a slow shake to a plastic vial she held between thumb and forefinger. Less than half full now; either Jay's final punch or her fall had dislodged the cap and poured lots of white powder into her pocket. But not all of it.

"He made me cook breakfast and then clean up the kitchen. There were two of those flat bottles, empty, that I had to take out to the trash."

The dark rum. Looking at the girl, Meg frowned. "Cass, what have you done to yourself?"

"I just cut my hair and colored it, there's this mousse that comes with color." Cass's formerly orange hair was short, wet and apparently black. "Today's Monday the seventeenth, kind of a special day, so I wanted to look different."

"Well, you certainly do," Meg said absently. "Is Jay still sitting out there in the kitchen?"

"Yeah," said Cass, tossing a wary look over her shoulder. "He really stared at me when I came in, spilled some of his booze."

"He probably didn't recognize you. Cass, if he goes out, to the washhouse or whatever, I want you to do something for me."

"What?"

"Bring me the bottle of light rum that's in a drawer under his bed."

"Are you crazy? Did you drink all that gin already?"

"I don't want it for me. I have something here," she said, with a flourish of the vial, "that I want to put in it. For Jay."

"What? Never mind," said Cass quickly, "I can't. He'll see me, he'll kill me."

"Not if you're quick. I can't move fast right now, but you can."

"He'll find out it's gone."

"If he does I'll say I took it." And I hope I have the guts to keep that promise, she added silently.

TWENTY-THREE

"ARROGANT GODDAMNED motherfucker of a *lawyer*!" muttered Vince Gutierrez as he climbed back into the police car. Lawrence Archer had come to Coeur d'Alene in search of his son, and that was all he had to say to Gutierrez or anyone else, except that of course he expected the full and prompt cooperation of Chief Brownell and his force.

Officer Mardian maintained a respectful silence from the back seat, and Kuisma pulled from the parking lot to the street before he spoke. "Uh, we figured we'd go ahead and work 95 south, Chief. You want to come along?"

Yes goddammit he wanted to come along. "No. Just drop me at the motel. Oh—Mardian, do you know where there's a good newsstand? I'd like to get some papers."

He collected five dailies: from Spokane, Seattle, Portland, San Francisco, and just for the hell of it, the LA *Times*. He picked up a large container of hot coffee from a coffee shop adjoining the newsstand—or Officer Mardian picked it up for him. Then the two of them dropped him at his motel and drove away: youngsters on the job, while the old, useless, and impotent sat on their asses.

In the cheerful pine-paneled room Gutierrez settled into an armchair, coffee on the bedside table and his feet on the bed. He read the Spokane paper from back to front, looking for small stories about odd and unexplained events...the car found empty with motor running, strangers whose behavior in passing had attracted attention, the house whose neighbors had heard noises in the night and then been surprised to find the place empty next day. Nothing struck him.

He had just finished his coffee and was reaching for the Seattle paper when a knock rattled the door of his room. "Lawrence Archer," said a familiar voice; Gutierrez snapped "Coming," and struggled to his feet.

Archer wore a tan, trenchcoat-style raincoat. Drops of water glistened on his bald dome and clung to his eyebrows; his eyes were pouched, his shoulders less square than Gutierrez remembered. A six-pack of Carta Blanca beer dangled from his left hand.

"I have some information for you," he said, and turned to glance over his shoulder as if for eavesdroppers. "May I come in?"

Gutierrez dipped his head in the barest of nods and stepped aside; Archer strode into the room, set the beer on the dresser, and peeled off his coat. When the policeman made no move to take it, Archer flushed and draped it over the doorknob.

"On what day did your... did Mrs. Halloran and your niece disappear?"

"You said information, not questions." Gutierrez moved to reach for the door.

"No, wait." Archer took a deep breath and pushed his hands into the pockets of his jacket. "I believe you told me they disappeared from here, last Friday?"

"They left the Coeur d'Alene hospital Friday around noon and no one has seen them or heard from them since."

"I don't know where Jonathan is now, Gutierrez. But I do know where he was Friday night. His call to Doris came from Casper, Wyoming."

"Casper?" Gutierrez cast his mind back over the trip and the maps, seeing the dot that was Casper just before a northward bend in the highway. "I don't believe you," he said furiously. "Casper is a good eight hundred miles from here."

"It was a credit card call," Archer told him, and he nodded toward the desk and the six-pack. "Can I buy you a beer, and we'll talk about it?"

"Talk. Yeah." Gutierrez sank into his armchair and stared at the rug between his boots. Take Jon Archer out of the picture, that meant Meg and Cass had met with either pure accident or random violence. "Thanks," he added, and wrapped his left hand around the cold bottle the lawyer proffered.

"Gutierrez, may I ask another question?"

Gutierrez blew a long breath through pursed lips. "Sure. Why the hell not?" He lifted the bottle and drank.

"Is there any possibility that the girl, your niece . . ."

"She has a name!" Gutierrez snarled. "Cassandra!"

"Sorry." Archer pulled a straight chair around and sat down astride it. "Do you think it's possible that Cassandra could have disposed of Mrs. Halloran somehow? The idea being to get free to meet Jon?"

"Girls her age have been known to pull things like that," said the policeman bleakly. "Not often, but it has happened. They nearly always have a partner, a boyfriend. And in even the few days I spent with Cass, I could see that she was devoted . . . no, obsessed is more like it. Obsessed with your son."

Moisture sprang out on Archer's forehead like fresh raindrops; he avoided the other's gaze and tipped his beer bottle for several swallows before speaking. "According to Doris, Jon definitely has some kind of strong attachment to Cass. But wherever he is now, the boy could not have been here on Friday."

"The thing is, I just don't see Cass taking Meg out all by herself," Gutierrez told him. "Meg's healthy and strong, almost as tall as I am, and Cass is . . . well, you've seen her."

The other man nodded without looking up, and Gutierrez felt his own uncertain temper begin to build. "So thanks for the beer, Archer, and now you can tell me just what the hell you're after."

"I want to find my son." Archer's voice was soft, his head bent. "No one has heard from him, not even Doris. Today, August 17, is his birthday, his eighteenth. I know Doris is baking a cake and all that other stuff she's done every year of his life. Jonathan doesn't give a shit about me, or about his mother, but it's completely out of character for him not to stay in touch with Doris."

"Maybe he sent Cass to friends, or had friends pick her up," said Gutierrez half to himself. "No, that doesn't work; according to Doris he was seriously upset when he called Friday and found no message. Or what about enemies,

Archer? Like people connected with the war-games camp? Somebody who might decide to get even by snatching his girl?''

Archer's face reddened as he shook his head. "I honestly don't think so. I agreed to a very—generous settlement with the family of the boy who was hurt. And he, the boy, was just a ragtag loner, not someone with friends who'd try to even the score.''

Get that, "ragtag loner"; I shouldn't even be drinking this bastard's beer, Gutierrez told himself. "Maybe one of Jon's 'friends' knew about his coming inheritance, and snatched Cass for ransom."

"He'd have come to me for anything involving money," said Archer.

"Never mind, doesn't work. No way you're going to get ransom demands on somebody who's on the road on a motorcycle. I'm afraid I have no useful suggestions for you, Archer," said Gutierrez crisply. "Now I've got things to do, so if you don't mind..."

"It seems clear that he was heading up here to meet Cass," said Archer, words spilling fast. "The police are polite but busy, to me at least. For you, for another cop, they're ready to put out a lot more effort. Just let me in on what's happening, will you? Please?''

Car and driver, thought Gutierrez at once. He could be one more person out on the road with Dr. Wu's sketch of the camper. If Archer wanted to ask questions about Jon at the same time, why not? "You feel like driving around in the rain?'' he inquired.

"I'VE ALERTED THE POLICE in Montana and Wyoming as well as here in Idaho," said Archer as he opened the passenger door of his rental car, a late model Buick. Probably can't *rent* Mercedeses, thought Gutierrez. Good thing, too; nice soft American suspension was just what his aching bones needed.

"But I don't think I'm getting real action from any of them," Archer went on as he settled into his own seat. "The police seem to think that an eighteen-year-old boy with a

BMW bike and plenty of credit cards will come home when he feels like it.''

Gutierrez took a moment's bleak pleasure in the fact that a wealthy attorney could have trouble in the everyday world just like real people. Then he fastened his seat belt, spread a map across his knees, and put his mind in gear. Fact: Meg's van was a gas-guzzler, making twelve to fourteen miles to the gallon. Fact: she'd filled the twin tanks in Butte. Fact: the trip from Butte including the short jaunt up 95 and back probably totaled 325 miles, and the van's range was no more than 450.

"Head north on highway 95," he told Archer. "That's the direction we were planning on, Meg and I; Cass knew that and I think we can assume she'd have told Jon."

Fact: Meg was an experienced traveler who was methodical about preparation; she would not have headed out on the interstate without gassing up. And she always used her credit card. Fact: the van had not turned up, so it probably had been driven out of town. But not far without gas, no matter who was driving it. Conjecture: whoever had grabbed them *could* have driven north, and that direction had not yet been explored. Conjecture: whether they'd been grabbed for themselves or for the van, they were probably dead. Nothing he could do about that except catch the killer and tear his arms and legs off.

Gas station followed gas station, in quick succession at first and then with more distance between. Archer carried an eight by ten folder, one headshot of Jonathan and one full-length picture, the kid with his bike. Gutierrez had a stack of copies of the flyer he and Officer Mardian had put together: picture of Meg, picture of Cass, and the camper-truck as sketched by Dr. Wu. They weren't a bad team for this, the cop and the lawyer; Archer was smoothly ingratiating, while he himself, he knew, wore authority like an invisible uniform. But the return for their efforts was zip; nobody new anything.

"Every goddamned farmer in northern Idaho has built himself a camper," Gutierrez said as he slid back into the

Buick for the twentieth or maybe thirtieth time. "Half of them shingled."

Archer grunted agreement as he pulled onto the highway. "I saw a sign for a campground; let's check there."

"They wouldn't have..."

"Your women wouldn't have," said Archer. "But presumably Jon didn't know that."

"Ah." Gutierrez felt a flash of embarrassment, not because he'd been intent on his own ends, but because he'd forgotten something. "Farragut."

"Huh?" Archer turned to look at the policeman.

"It's a state park with campgrounds, just up the road. During World War II it was a Naval training station; Meg's father went to boot camp there and he talked about it a lot when she was a kid. We planned to stop at Farragut, Thursday through Saturday or Sunday. Cass would have told Jon."

It was three miles to the turnoff and then several more to the park entrance. Gutierrez stared out at the endless rain and cursed himself; he should have insisted they stop and phone, rather than driving out. But he wasn't the one behind the wheel.

Seven o'clock, he noted as he sat in the car and watched Archer slosh off toward a low brick building. Damned near dark already, with no sign that the rain would stop soon or ever. Traffic on the highway was sparse, signs of civilization widely spaced; gas stations between here and Sandpoint, if any, would probably close for the night in another couple of hours. On to Sandpoint? Or back to Coeur d'Alene? He flipped a mental coin and decided to go back, check with Kuisma and Brownell, maybe call Svoboda. Take the search up in daylight tomorrow. At this point he had sad, serious doubts that there was any reason to hurry.

"Jon was here!" Archer dropped into his seat and sat slumped there for a moment before closing the door.

"When?"

"Yesterday, Sunday, mid-afternoon. The young woman recognized his picture; she's absolutely sure it was Jon she spoke with."

"Well?" prompted Gutierrez.

"Oh, sorry. It's just such a relief to have picked up a trail. He told her he was looking for his uncle, aunt, and cousin."

"He expected to find them camping here?"

"That's what he told her. In a Chevrolet van, California license she doesn't of course remember except it ended with an x. Pulling a tent trailer. He said he had planned to meet them sooner but got delayed by engine trouble."

"So he'd had no contact with Cass since the accident, or since Friday, anyway; that's when Meg took the trailer back." Gutierrez marveled that his voice was steady, and was disgusted with himself for making the effort to keep it so. A man should be able to howl and still call himself civilized.

"So it appears." Archer, who'd been leaning back against the seat, straightened and took a deep breath. "But she, the young woman, suggested to him that his family might have decided to stay elsewhere, perhaps on Lake Pend Oreille. She told him there are quite a few nice campgrounds around the lake. I thought we could drive on up there."

"Not me," Gutierrez told him. "I wish you luck, and I'd like you to let me know what you find out. But your son isn't my main interest anymore; it's clear he doesn't know where Meg and Cass are. I need to go back to Coeur d'Alene."

TWENTY-FOUR

"WAIT. SWING OVER and let me off there," Gutierrez said to Archer a few miles south of the Farragut turnoff. "There" was the Haywood Saloon; hangout of cops and cowboys, Brownell had told him, state cops as well as members of the city force. "I'll probably find somebody I know here," he told Archer. "Or at least a telephone. And you can get on up to Sandpoint."

Eighteen or twenty vehicles were parked in the muddy lot before the saloon; at road's edge two dark sedans with double white stripes along their sides were drawn up door to door, engines rumbling as their drivers conversed from behind respective steering wheels. Gutierrez picked his way around puddles, stepped up wooden steps and into smoky warmth. He eased out of his borrowed police slicker, managed on his second left-handed try to hang it on a peg beside the door, and caught the eye of a broad, thick-necked man at the bar.

"Collarbone?" inquired the man as Gutierrez approached.

"Right. And a slug in the ribs a couple months ago," Gutierrez told him, and said "Draft," to the bartender. "Getting too old for the job, I guess. Or too slow."

"Tom Workman," said the larger man. "Idaho State Police."

"Vince Gutierrez. I'm chief of police in a little town in California, Port Silva."

"Hey, I heard about you. You're over here because you got some people missing."

"Right. My lady, and my niece. I've been out in the rain spreading these around." He pulled his stack of flyers from inside his jacket and laid them on the bar.

"Nice-looking woman, real sorry to hear she's in trouble. But this . . ."—he put a large forefinger on the camper-truck—"practically everybody in the panhandle . . ."

"Has one of those. I know," said Gutierrez, and took a hearty gulp from the mug which the bartender had set before him. "But the last glimpse anyone had of Meg, she was walking toward her own van, and a camper like that was right beside it, only other vehicle nearby. It's the closest thing to a lead I've got."

"Does seem to me this one's some different." Workman's eyes were still on the drawing. "Taller, for one. And looks like it has a pitched roof, most times the roof on these things is flat. Shingles?"

"Right."

Workman turned to survey the room. "Ernie? Come on over here a minute, willya? T.J.? Art?"

Within moments nine or ten men had ambled to the bar from tables, pinball machines, the pool table at the far end of the room. Gutierrez was introduced to three state policemen, a city cop, a sheriff's deputy, a truck driver, two ranchers, a breeder of Percheron horses. They passed the flyers around, and the bartender turned on another light.

"Old truck, is it?" asked a lathe-lean man with a white forehead above his tanned face.

"The man who saw it says very old, brown or rust-colored, green and white license plate."

"Used to be a rig like that parked in a pasture near my sister's place in Hayden Lake," offered the horsebreeder, a man nearly as big as Workman. "Fellow was a bee-keeper."

"I pulled one of those handmade jobs over, maybe a week ago," said a state cop. "He was weaving like a drunk; turned out he was an old guy who'd got sleepy. I just told him to get a cup of coffee somewhere, but I put his number in my log."

"You know, there's this guy up by Puma Creek," said Workman slowly. "Me and my brother fish up there a lot. This fellow is a hermit or something, not real old but banged up some; folks figure he's another guy come back from Vietnam, decides he likes the woods better than people. Has a place on some old Diamond International land, and gets around in a rig which as I remember it is a whole lot like this one. But he stays pretty well out, I'd be real surprised if he ever came to Coeur d'Alene. Worth checking, though," he added. "You hang on a few minutes, I'll make a couple calls."

As Workman pushed away from the bar and lumbered off toward the rear of the room, the city cop spoke. "Say, I remember one a ranger told me about. Guy moves from campground to campground around the panhandle, living in this homemade rig with his big old dog. Been doing it for years."

Another suggestion or two, as Gutierrez scribbled notes; then the group broke up and drifted away, each promising to call the number on the flyer if anything turned up. Gutierrez propped a foot on the bar rail and was sipping morosely at his beer when creaking floorboards signaled the return of the state cop.

"Draw me one more, Jerry," Workman called to the bartender. He set his meaty forearms on the bar and hunched over them, turning a frowning, thoughtful face on Gutierrez.

"Well? What did you find out?"

"Guy I remembered is still up there. One ol' boy I talked to thought his camper had a pitched roof; other fella didn't remember it that way but he wasn't sure. He did say he'd heard the hermit, that's what they call him, the hermit...he'd heard there was somebody staying with him the last few weeks, a kid."

"Kid?" breathed Gutierrez, but as Workman added, quickly, "a boy, sixteen, maybe seventeen," Gutierrez registered the earlier words and echoed them: "Last few weeks."

"Right."

Gutierrez pounded a soft tattoo on the bar with his fist. Jon Archer, who then went back to Colorado? No, but what about...some other boy Cass was involved with, and she'd been using Jon as a screen? Or a friend of Jon's, setting things up for the pair? No, that came back to the question of why was Jon himself searching.

"Let's go out there and talk to the guy," he said, and frowned as Workman's burr-cut head moved in a slow negative.

"Why not?"

"First thing, you'd want to have a four by four with a winch to try those old logging roads in this weather; I know two little bridges that's probably out by now."

"So I'll rent one!"

"Next thing, in the dark I don't know as we could even find the place. And the main thing," Workman said with a slow emphasis, "is this guy is not friendly. Guy I talked to in Coolin says he's polite enough when he comes down for groceries and such, but he don't neighbor at all."

"But look here..."

"Word is that he was Special Forces or SEAL or like that," Workman went on. "Word is that he maybe thinks he's still in Nam, sometimes. I think it would be real dumb of us to go helling around out there in the dark, getting ourselves hurt and maybe having to hurt somebody else. Without no more evidence than a little picture some guy drew."

After a long moment Gutierrez unclenched his teeth and said, "I hear you."

"Yeah. But we could head up there as soon as it's light tomorrow," Workman told him. "I'll borrow my uncle's rig. One good thing, the weatherman finally pulled his finger out and says the rain's gonna end tonight. So...you staying in Coeur d'Alene?"

"Yeah. The City Center Motel." He glanced at his watch; better get back there, check with Brownell and Kuisma. "Shit, I forgot I've got no wheels. Would *you* be going to Coeur d'Alene anytime soon?"

"Right about now," said Workman.

TWENTY-FIVE

MEG LUSTED AFTER a gun . . . bit down on the insides of her cheeks and chewed at her grimy, nicotine-flavored fingernails and thought she'd kill for a gun, to get a gun to kill with. Jay dead, stretched out long and filthy and cold: she viewed the picture in her head, adjusted it, rearranged the corpse and daubed it artfully with blood, then slathered it from head to boots with clotted red. If she could have for only five minutes one of those rifles, even the .22 that Kev scorned and had apparently stashed outside somewhere; where the hell was it and could she find it if she could get out?

The bomb might get him, of course, the bottle of pale Mexican rum made somewhat paler by the addition of almost a cup of water. Cass had protested and shivered and complained; but upon Jay's leaving the building she had raced to retrieve the bottle. Meg had a solution already mixed in the cap of her thermos bottle: by her estimation some 3,000 milligrams of what she hoped was poison. Pour a measure of rum out, add the poison, recap the bottle and assume that he won't notice its color, nor the fact that the seal has been broken and carefully pressed back into line.

Cass had scurried to put the bottle back, had preened herself for some minutes, how brave I am; and had then forgotten the whole business so far as Meg could tell. While Meg smoked cigarette after cigarette, Cass brushed her hair, peered into a small mirror to pluck an errant hair or two from her eyebrows, applied an emery board to her fingernails. The girl was no more able to sit still than Meg was; but Cass's restlessness did not seem motivated by fear. More like excitement, anticipation.

In the kitchen a chair screeched, pushed back under weight; Meg pulled her legs up onto the cot and listened to shuffling footsteps. How much of the dark rum did he have left? Perhaps she could go to the bathroom, and in passing the table fall against it and spill the stuff. Yes, and then suppose he decided to switch to tequila, there was still that bottle of tequila in the drawer. Or suppose he responded by beating her again. The thought made her breath come hard, as if a giant hand had closed around her neck.

He was in the open doorway now, just standing there; with a light on in the kitchen and their small lantern set on the floor, he was merely muddy boots and filthy jeans and a shadowy torso, any expression unreadable. Meg couldn't even smell him over the smoke of her cigarette and the acrid bite of the nail polish Cass was applying. She lowered her glance to focus on the tip of her cigarette, said "one thousand and one" inside her head and had reached one thousand twenty-two before she felt him move away.

"What's he looking at, that dickhead," said Cass, but under her breath and without much venom. Sitting cross-legged beside her bunk, she recapped the bottle of polish and spread her fingers close to the lantern to admire her handiwork. She looked up, caught Meg's gaze, and frowned. "Look, I told you I just felt like cutting my hair, okay? No big deal."

"It's still a shock," Meg said quietly. The girl's newly short hair was dry now; thick and straight, it swung like an inky, fluid frame around her small head, setting off tanned skin and strong bones. She was more than ever her Uncle Vince's niece, all the Indian showing. It hurt Meg to look at her.

"He sure thinks so," muttered Cass with a glance toward the door. "He keeps looking at me like I was a ghost or something."

"One little defensive blow doesn't mean we've won the war," Meg told her. "Don't get cute with that man, unless you want your face to look like mine."

Cass shot her a quick glance, winced visibly, and muttered, "Okay, okay."

Meg took a last drag on her cigarette and dropped it into the Coke bottle she was using as an ashtray. "Nail polish, new hairdo; when I was your age my father would have said, Hey, kid, you getting ready for a heavy date?'' August 17. Cass had said it was a special day. In what way?

"Don't be dumb," Cass snapped. "I'm trying to keep myself up here, my mom says that's very important. Personal appearance matters a great deal in life. Actually, she'd like this," the girl added, brushing a lock of hair with the heel of one splayed-out hand. "It's closer to my real-color; she hated that punky orange."

Which is probably why you wore it that way, thought Meg. She'd been diverted, derailed, neatly; whatever plan Cass had she clearly meant to keep to herself. "Does Kev like your hair?"

"Kev? I don't know, I haven't talked to him since I did it." Cass widened her gray eyes at Meg. "Hey, it's getting real late, practically dark. When are we going to have supper? I'm hungry."

It was in fact past eight o'clock, and Meg found herself hollow but not hungry. "I've resigned from kitchen duty," she said flatly. "If you want to offer your services, feel free."

"Well, shit, I don't want to talk to that guy. But I guess if I have to..." Cass spoke without conviction and except for lifting her head to glare at Meg, did not move from where she sat. "But I'm really hungry," she repeated in a near-whine.

"If this is like other nights, he'll be leaving soon." The past two nights he had left the compound around nine or nine-fifteen, to return hours later. "So if you want to grab something from the fridge, you'd better do it now."

"Oh, well. I've got a couple Snickers bars someplace. In the meanwhile, I guess you don't care if I smoke, now that you're doing it too." Cass put the nail polish bottle away in her tote and plucked a fresh pack of Trues from the smaller of her duffel bags. "Kind of too bad, actually. I was almost deciding it would be good for me to quit."

Oh you little bitch. Meg closed her eyes and leaned her head against the wall. Rain still falling, dull noise on a sodden roof, faint splashy sound beyond that as if the compound were a lake. Probably was, more or less. How long could the rain continue without being a danger? What about the creek? she wondered suddenly. The creek that provided their water supply, Puma Creek Kev had called it, had to be nearby; was it big enough and close enough to be a threat?

Behind her eyelids she considered the idea of a flood and found it oddly appealing. She was strong and one hell of a swimmer; even in her present battered condition she'd be happy to take her chances in a flood. Better than dying by inches here in this stinking cabin with this miserable child.

She sat up so suddenly that she nearly tipped the cot. "What was that?"

"I don't know." Cass's eyes had gone round and white-rimmed.

Flood, already? Trees crashing down a watercourse?

A second blast, and Meg realized what it was; Kev was firing the big gun, which boomed like a cannon in the water-heavy air.

Cass got it, too. "That was Kev, with that other gun. I bet he got a deer!"

A deer? Meg had a sudden clear picture of Vince Gutierrez stumbling along through mud and rain with his right arm in a sling. Gutierrez couldn't shoot with his left hand, he could barely scratch his head with his left hand.

Complete silence, here and in the kitchen, as if everyone had suspended breathing. Then came a thump, and a clatter; Meg thought Jay had slapped the table, flung his chair back against the pantry doors. Footsteps heavy with purpose. It was the fastest he'd moved all day, the last *two* days. She heard the back door open, heard it close.

"Kev is gonna be in deep shit, isn't he?" asked Cass. "If he shot a deer? I heard Jay tell him not to, not out of season."

"I heard that, too." Meg moved to the doorway, slid out into the kitchen, stopped. She could hear voices. Jay's bass rumble, the words slow but moving in a chain rather than dropping one at a time. A beat of silence and then Kev, high and fast. Excitement, fear, Meg couldn't tell. She crept past the refrigerator thinking to reach the door and open it just a crack; it opened of itself, and she turned and made a hobbling flight back to the storeroom.

"...out there," grunted Jay. "Until good and late. Good and dark," he added in a near-shout, and closed the door hard. "Dumb shit. Dumb shit. Dumb shit," he muttered as his steps moved across the kitchen. He paused in their doorway once more, and Meg could see raindrops glistening in his lank hair. As he reached in to pull the door shut, Cass said "Hey? Can I go to the toilet first?"

For answer he stepped out of view briefly, and returned to toss something large and hollow into the room. Then he closed the door, slapped the hasp across and put the padlock in place.

"Hey!" said Cass again, but Meg said "Ssshhhh!" fiercely.

"Well what does he expect... What was that he threw in here?" she asked, and stepped cross her bags to the corner where the object had landed. "It's a bucket, a plastic bucket. What's *that* for?"

"Guess," suggested Meg.

Cass set the bucket down and stared at its pale shape in the lantern light. "For...boy, that's disgusting. That's really disgusting, he can't do that!"

"Oh shut *up*, Cass."

TWENTY-SIX

IN THE FAINT LIGHT from the dashboard Elizabeth's face was gray-white as her hair, her profile sharp and haggard. When Ben narrowed his eyes, she might have been an ancient crone hunched over not a steering wheel but a... What do witches crouch over, dead things? No, that was vultures. Elizabeth—he'd wanted her to return to her old name, Maureen, but she had refused to impose yet another confusion on the child—Elizabeth was not cut out to be a vulture; she was making very hard work of it.

"Not much further," he murmured. "Only five more miles to the coast, and then about fifteen south to Cliff-Haven. Do you think you can make it? Or would you like me to take it from here?"

"I drive, or I walk," she said flatly. She'd been queasy all day and violently sick twice, from what she claimed was car sickness. When their route left the freeways for the smaller roads she insisted on taking the wheel. "This is not a road," she said now through her teeth, "it's a trail, for mountain goats."

"Just keep your eyes on it," he said quickly as the right wheels caught a rough edge above what looked like a treacherous shoulder. Two narrow lanes of country road it was, through hills the locals probably called mountains, few house lights visible and no lights on the road itself. The center line was faded and sometimes disappeared altogether.

"You've never been to CliffHaven?" he asked, in his ongoing attempt at distraction through idle conversation.

"The place didn't exist until 1977, the year Michael's father retired," she reminded him. "Michael and I had given up family visits long before that.

"Not that I'd have visited there anyway," she added. "The place is just another hideout for the filthy rich, like Sea Ranch. They sit up there in their half-million-dollar houses and sip chardonnay and 'experience' the Pacific, probably eating crab that honest men risked their lives to catch."

"Well, all the more reason to..."

"Shut up, Ben," she replied without taking her eyes from the road. He shrugged and selected a tape to put in the player. Bach; he couldn't read the rest of the label in the dim light but listened for a moment and was pleased to hear the Fifth Brandenburg. Nice soothing stuff. Shouldn't bother the child sleeping in the back.

At least the *kid* didn't get car sick, thank God. Two vomiting females would be beyond his managing. He laid a wary, questioning hand on his own flat belly; this particular road was beginning to roil even his iron-plated gut. That would be a terrific arrival, roll the Merc into that glossy courtyard and the two of them stagger out gasping and spewing. Breathe deep, he told himself, and think green. No no, gold, much more attractive.

"Here's the coast highway," Elizabeth muttered, swinging left at a sign bearing a green shield and a white numeral 1. "And turn that damned stuff off, I hate Bach!"

Yes ma'am. Ben ejected the tape, pushed himself straighter in the seat, stretched his neck and ran a finger around the inside of his collar. He did a mental inventory of his appearance: slacks a little rumpled but pure wool never really looked bad. Shirt cheap but new, unfortunately still showing fold-lines. Tie that cost fifty dollars last year, not quite clean but dark enough so it shouldn't matter. English hand-lasted shoes, resoled many times but polished just this morning. All in all, if nobody threw up on him in the next few minutes he should arrive looking like a sensible, prosperous attorney who believed in getting good wear from quality merchandise.

A murmur from the back seat caught his ear; he turned in his seat, switched on the dome light, and cast an assess-

ing eye over the still-sleeping child. Clean face, round cheeks
pink against dark lashes, terrycloth jumpsuit clean as well
and relatively unstained. He'd wanted to buy her a dress,
little-girl ruffles or something, but Elizabeth had vetoed
that, too.

"Elizabeth, we should stop and let her go to the bathroom before we get there," he suggested. Elizabeth kept her
eyes forward and her grip high on the wheel; she might have
been frozen in place. Fine, better to arrive with a wet-
bottomed kid than break whatever concentration was car-
rying her.

Occasional lights along the coast now, house lights. Sign
marking a national forest boundary. More lights just ahead,
a bunch: taillights, and headlights, and a cluster of small
flickering beacons on the inland side of the road. Lanterns
and fires, he noted as they drew closer. Michael's old con-
stituency, waiting. So he had not died this day.

Lights in an archway, too, over a lighted gatehouse. Elizabeth slowed as she came up behind a slow-moving sedan,
a pickup ahead of that. Ben saw a uniformed man beside the
road directing cars by. Saw, just past the south edge of the
archway, a row of pale vans with letters on their sides: the
media were on hand. With banks of lights, too, might have
been noontime out here. He checked his tie, stretched his
neck once more; a low, open-topped sports car turned right
and drove past the gatehouse into the development or compound or whatever they called it. Sanctuary by any name.

Pickup and sedan were waved on, gathering speed as they
drew away; and Ben said softly, "Don't look in. Follow the
sedan, give him a little space. Half a mile up is a delivery
gate, no lights; it will be unlocked. Just a little further now,"
he murmured, keeping up the flow of soothing sound as he
glanced in the rearview mirror to make sure no one was close
behind. "Better slow down, there won't be a light. There,"
he announced, pointing to a smooth sidesweep of blacktop. Elizabeth said nothing at all, looked straight ahead, and
stepped on the gas.

"Elizabeth, goddamn it! What the hell are you trying to
pull? You turn around right now and go back there."

"I can't. Shut up, shut up, shut up! Or I'll drive this thing straight into a tree!"

She was coming up rapidly on the taillights of the sedan. Ben tried to keep one eye on the road ahead and another on the woman beside him, a stick figure hunched over the wheel as if she never meant to let go.

"Just take it easy. You'll frighten Tessa: you don't want to hurt Tessa again, Elizabeth." The road was slick from fog, and Ben remembered suddenly that his expensive tires were old and somewhat slick themselves. "Elizabeth, please pull off as soon as you see a place and we'll talk. Take it easy now, just slow and easy and...there, just there, see the sign? Beach parking, three-quarter mile. Please."

She braked a little, then a little more, finally jerked the wheel right; the car bumped over rocky ground and shuddered to a stop. As Ben let his breath out in a whoosh, Elizabeth released her seat belt, flung her door open, and scrambled out. He followed more slowly, turning out the headlights and closing first his door and then hers. She was standing at the edge of the parking lot looking out to sea, hands jammed in the pockets of her jacket.

"I can't," she said without turning as he approached. "I can't go in there. I can't talk to those people, to Michael. I can't *see* Michael."

Ben wanted to hit her... rank, stiff-necked bitch: a good double swing, palm and then knuckles against that set jaw. He took a moment's pleasure in the thought before reminding himself that she was tall and strong and would surely hit back. The two of them would wind up rolling around in the dirt and there would go his good trousers, his last clean shirt.

"Elizabeth. You've seen dying people before. Even dead people."

"Dead aren't as bad."

"True. So we could wait, if you like. But I think, if we wait, the whole thing will be a loss."

"I hate being a ... a vulture."

He winced at this belated reading of his mind. "Not a vulture," he told her. "A sorrowing wife. And a woman with work to do."

"I can work without the money. I don't want to do this. I can't."

Panic was tightening his throat, building into tears behind his eyes; his nose was beginning to run, like an addict's when the poor bastard couldn't get his stuff. Jesus. Maybe, if he pushed her off into the sea, he could appear with the kid in hand and say she'd killed herself. Hope to be named guardian. Some hope. No, he had to...

He had to compose himself, that's what. His moonlit watch told him it was nearly nine o'clock; he had to get this woman to the Tannenbaum place and make sure things were working and then get out to a telephone by ten or shortly after. Threat? Or plea? Both, he decided, blinking to clear his eyes. Threat, and then a plea she could yield to more gracefully. You are not going to get off the train now, bitch.

"Can't get off now," he said aloud, softly.

"I can do whatever I want."

"Oh no. You go back to see Michael or you lose me. Whatever my failings," he told her with a grim smile, "I am a good advocate. I can get you off on the old charge."

"I'll just go back to..."

"Idaho? You think so?"

"Oh," she said, her eyes wide and black in the moonlight. "Over your dead body?"

"Something like that."

"There are other lawyers."

"But you have no money. And when you don't turn up to solace your dying husband, you won't have any claims on the old rads, either. All by yourself, in a very strenuous situation. Think it over," he advised.

"I...I can survive prison," she said, her head up and her jaw set.

Easy, easy. Like riding a rough-broke colt, remember to keep the fucker off balance. God, how he'd hated horses. "I guess you can," he said, his voice tight. "I myself won't have quite the same option." And that was no lie, he told himself bitterly, and felt his eyes fill once more. Jesus fucking *Christ* he had to make this work.

"Ben?"

He blinked and turned away, finding his handkerchief.

"Ben, what's the matter?"

"Fact is, I'm dead too. Dead as Michael, maybe not quite as soon but just as dead."

She gaped at him.

"I've had several very bad years, Elizabeth. Divorce, settlement, loss of all those clients my father-in-law had produced. Bad investments. Bad, bad loans. If I don't get some capital, or at least the promise of some, I'll be found in an alley somewhere with a .22 bullet behind my ear. And brother Sweet will wind up on the street. Oh, yes," he added as she continued to stare, "I used his money, too, and managed to borrow a few dollars against that piece of logged-out scrub he lives on. I had no choice."

"You shit. You miserable, disgusting, unprincipled shit."

"I had no choice," he repeated. "And remember, I didn't make *your* situation, none of it."

"Maybe part."

"No. It just happened. And I think you should have that money, I think you'll do good work with it," he said earnestly. "There's a lot, I won't need much."

"How much do you owe Sweet?"

"Ten thousand on the property, about forty thou total."

"All right," she said, looking past him toward the car. "I'll take care of that, if I get the money. And I'll pay you a reasonable attorney's fee."

"Percentage is the usual way."

"I'll bet," she snapped. "We'll discuss it later. We'll settle on an amount, and you'll live with it or find yourself charged as an accessory, or whatever you call a scheming venal lawyer."

"Elizabeth, I'm not a blackmailer."

"No? Well," she said with a bitter two-note chuckle, "neither am I. I need to change the baby, and wash my face. Then," she added, and squared her shoulders, "I guess we go see Michael."

He took the wheel some ten minutes later, turned the car around and eased it onto the now-empty road. There was moonlight enough; he piloted the big sedan along with no lights, saw the entry-gate lights way ahead, found the delivery entrance and turned in. He got out of the car, tried the gate, was back in seconds to fling himself into his seat and slam the machine into reverse.

"Bitch! Dumb bitch forgot. Or," he added, reaching to turn on the headlights, "or the guard caught it. Never mind, we'll get in; we'll just be public property a little sooner than I intended." Elizabeth's only reply was a wordless, soothing murmur to the child who now drowsed in her arms.

He drove toward the flaring lights, braked at the uniformed man, said "I have Mrs. Tannenbaum with me," and simply turned in under the archway. He glanced in his rearview mirror to catch a glimpse of the guard scrambling out of the way as one media van and then another swung in after the Merc; then he flipped the mirror up and increased his speed, around a corner and along a curving street and around another corner and through a narrower gate into a cobbled courtyard. He braked the Merc to a stop beside a white Cadillac and was out in a flash, to hurry around and open the passenger door. "Out, quick," he said.

A tall house, narrow and gray as judgment, seemed to lean toward Elizabeth, and cobblestones were slippery humps beneath her shoes. She was still twenty feet from the semicircle of front steps when squealing brakes were followed at once by a blare of lights, and voices called, "Mrs. Tannenbaum? Mrs. Tannenbaum, look here!"

She half-turned, heard Ben say "You guys can just hold it," as the child stiffened and drew breath for a cry. "Shh," she whispered, cupping the small head against her shoulder; her feet found a smooth surface, a walkway, and she strode toward the house, up the steps, and through the broad door that had opened for her.

The white-coated manservant nodded and stepped aside. A small woman moved forward from the bottom of a curving staircase; dark-blond hair with frosted tips, soft sweaterlike top bloused over a flaring skirt, slender legs above high-heeled pumps. And the face, sunken eyes and sagging cheeks, thin lips made crooked by poorly applied lipstick.

"Mother Tannenbaum," Elizabeth said in a whisper. "I had to come."

"Maureen," the older woman said. "Yes. And this is Theresa? Michael says you call her Tessa."

The little girl lifted her head, blinking in the bright lights, and Mrs. Tannenbaum blinked in turn, and smiled. "Oh, the precious thing. Maureen, give her to her grandmother. Come to Grandma, Tessa."

She handed her over. "Is Michael... May I see Michael?"

"He's awake now, I think. Yes, go on up. I'll give you five minutes and then I'll bring Tessa."

Ben, standing just inside the door, watched the tall figure mount the stairs as if they were gallows steps. Good girl, good girl. "Mrs. Tannenbaum?" he called softly, and moved toward the older woman.

"Oh. Yes, Mr. Taylor. Ben." She settled the child more comfortably against her shoulder. "I'm sorry, but I don't think Michael will have the strength to see you, too."

"I understand," he assured her. "But may I ask to use a telephone?"

As she peered up at him, he spread his hands and shrugged. "Elizabeth... Maureen... by coming here has effectively given herself up on the old charges. As her attorney, I'd like to contact the appropriate officials and try to arrange for things to proceed as smoothly as possible. So if you have a study or an office where I could make some calls, I'd appreciate it."

TWENTY-SEVEN

DISASSEMBLING AND cleaning a revolver mostly one-handed took concentration, Gutierrez found. Took time. Reminded him of the correctness of Workman's decision not to go after the hermit until morning, a decision heartily seconded by Chief Brownell. Six-inch barrel or no, the only thing Gutierrez was likely to hit left-handed and in the dark was his own foot.

Chief Brownell, informed of the state cop's tentative make on the shingled camper, had made a few quick inquiries of his own. Same results as Workman's: the gaunt six-and-a-half-footer known to locals as the hermit had been coming into the tiny town of Coolin perhaps once a month for seven or eight years. He bought supplies, made no social gestures but caused no trouble, had never demonstrated the least interest in any of the local women or girls. Nobody knew his name, but most people assumed he was a wounded vet, Vietnam vet from his age.

Gutierrez gave the walnut grip a final rub with a soft rag, then put the revolver in its case. Getting off on his war toys, that's what he was doing. Like Kuisma and Mardian, hot to load the shotguns and climb into Mardian's Cherokee and hit the lumber roads toward the hermit's lair. He had counselled them to patience, pretty funny advice coming from him, telling them to go to a movie or something and report back here at six A.M.

He picked up his long-empty glass and got to his feet. Saw in his mind's eye not his eager young colleagues but a gaunt and damaged shape, faceless. Who is the hermit?

Someone who needed to be alone, obviously. But how come, after seven or so years, he'd turned up with a companion, a kid?

Lots of ice, a small slug of Wild Turkey, plenty of water. Maybe the guy was gay and he'd found himself a young lover. Not a very good way to stay anonymous up here, probably. More likely the kid was a relative. Son, younger brother, nephew. Sent to the woods why?

Gutierrez met his own bleak gaze in the mirror over the bathroom sink. Maybe the kid was sent to check up on the older guy. Hermit looks like flipping out even further, family sends a keeper.

Or turn it over: the kid was in trouble, sent up here by a family who couldn't handle him and the hermit was the keeper. In either case, family or close friends involved. People out in the world: who and where?

And what did they create? he wondered savagely. Those string-pullers, did they put together two separate renegades who became an explosive pair, who decided to go marauding, raping, murdering? Gutierrez sank stiffly into the armchair, took a smaller drink than he wanted from his glass, and picked up the *San Francisco Chronicle*, more or less his neighborhood sheet. The paper rattled in his shaking hands as he paged through.

Near the end of the front section he stopped short and frowned at a two-column picture showing a diagonal of road, part of a gate on the right, a blurry group of people to the left, and in the foreground a lanky, uniformed man with longish white hair. Except it wasn't white, it was pale yellow; that was Bob Englund, one of his own men. Gutierrez nodded silent approval of Svoboda's choice; Englund was large and strong but easy-tempered.

"Local lawmen assist rangers in controlling crowds at vigil for dying anti-war activist," read the caption. To the right of that photo were two others: a years-old shot of Michael Tannenbaum, hairy and wild-eyed, and a picture of his wife, flowing black hair and pale eyes and *impact*, even in the grainy newspaper print. Gutierrez had seen this pair a time or two, although never up close; at Cal doing graduate work in 1968-69, he'd been neither a demonstrator himself nor a police officer, just a sad but detached observer.

The story accompanying the pictures had nothing new to say. Tannenbaum was believed to be near death; there was speculation that his wife . . . former wife? . . . might turn up, but no one seemed to know for sure. Tannenbaum had confessed to the killing the pair had been sought for; Gutierrez thought that after all this time, in such circumstances, Maureen Tannenbaum could probably return without much fear of prison.

He tossed the paper aside, stretched out in his chair and turned on the television set to watch the late news. And to think about sleep, call it up; a few hours' sleep would leave him a lot more useful in the morning.

National news, the usual boring summer stuff. He played the machine from one channel to another, taking a momentary small pleasure in such handy things as remote control. Saw forest fires, a storm off the east coast sinking pleasure boats right and left. A demonstration in D.C. by blacks, who had hundred-degree heat to add to their grievances. Some angry Cubans in Miami. Ads for many things, none of which he needed. Several of which he vowed never to buy.

He hitched himself straighter in the chair as a smooth voice announced a segment from the CBS station in San Francisco. It was a background piece on the Tannenbaums, bits of old news film mostly from Berkeley. Gutierrez found himself looking at streets he knew, scenes he more or less remembered. Crowds of young people blocking Oxford Street along the front of the university, singing and thrusting clenched fists skyward. A different day and a larger crowd, many of the young men and an occasional young woman barechested in the sunlight as they streamed out Cal's Sather Gate and down Telegraph Avenue.

Now a film clip he had seen many times; national networks had used it again and again after the Tannenbaums killed a young motorcycle cop late in 1970. Michael Tannenbaum climbing onto a low brick wall and turning to face a throng. Tannenbaum addressing the crowd, hands outspread and face ardent. Tannenbaum being handed down from his perch and turning to walk away, his wife striding beside him.

That fine, free-swinging walk of a tall woman, was that what Dr. Wu had said when he talked of Meg? That's what this reminded him of: Meg striding away, shoulders back and head up. Christ. He flipped channels, found another playing the same tape, closed his eyes and fumbled for the power button.

The name "CliffHaven" caught his ear and stilled his hand. "Here is the scene as our crew filmed it not thirty minutes ago," said an earnest young Asian-American woman, and the film dissolved to a stretch of road, a uniformed man standing guard before an arched gateway in a high iron fence. A bearded man in bib overalls stood by a campfire and talked to an interviewer about righteous actions and righteous people. His face faded and the camera swung away to focus on the dark square sedan turning into the gateway.

Gutierrez watched several uniforms move into place to keep the bearded man and his buddies on their own side of the road. Riot? No, he decided, those guys weren't looking for trouble. They had women and kids with them, and dogs. All looked more sorrowful than angry, even the dogs.

The screen went dark, then bright again, as another fence appeared, another gate. A tall New England-style house, its courtyard brightly illuminated. The sedan there, foreground; beyond that, a woman carrying a child toward the house. She stopped, giving the camera a shot of a sharp profile; then she turned quickly away and set off along the walkway to the front door, long legs moving in purposeful strides, light hair flowing free.

"What the Christ?" Gutierrez said aloud. Dumb, he was simply remembering from the old clips. Okay, maybe, and remembering Meg . . . but there was something else. He sat back in the chair and cradled the cold glass between his hands and stared unseeing at the television screen. His head was bleeding, there was a grating pain high on his chest that brought nausea at his slightest movement. He was peering into the dark, following broadening cones of light, watching for Meg. Seeing her, finally, and a blocky dark shape, a car. A tall man. Then a tall woman, striding. Only for a moment and then she was out of the direct beams, but she remembered that long-legged stride, flowing hair. Blond hair.

On the screen a tall man followed close behind the woman; he turned and waved the television people off, mouth moving in words that were lost in the general babble. Then he trotted up the steps and through the door, which closed.

The camera drew back slowly from the big double door, showing fanlight and semicircular steps and finally the entire front of the house. "We've been informed that the woman you just saw is Mrs. Michael Tannenbaum, Maureen Tannenbaum, eighteen years a fugitive and returning now, we understand, to be with her seriously ill husband. This is Martin Snyder, News Segment Four, from highway 1 just out of Anchor Bay."

Maybe he'd had too much booze. Gutierrez eyed his glass, found it empty except for a few shrunken ice cubes, and got to his feet. Or maybe not enough. He moved thoughtfully about his chores: old ice out, add new, a little more bourbon, good jolt of water. If the television station was here in town, would they have a tape of tonight's news?

Probably not; besides, he didn't need it. In his mind's eye, his old, tired, maybe drunk, but nevertheless cop's eye, he set those images side by side: Maureen Tannenbaum almost twenty years ago, Maureen Tannenbaum tonight. And in the headlamps—same person, he was sure of it. At a distance he'd taken her for blond, reasonable mistake because of the ease of her movement and besides you didn't see flowing white hair all that often.

So. So what? So paths cross by accident, and a day later two of the crosses are missing, and pretty soon a third becomes the focus of national news. Coincidence, he thought, and crunched an ice cube viciously. Bullshit.

Chief Brownell was at a meeting and was not expected home until around midnight. Not an emergency, Gutierrez told Mrs. Brownell after a moment's pause for thought. But he'd appreciate a call from the chief when he did get home, at whatever time.

He set the receiver back in place and stood looking at it. Maybe his eye *was* off, maybe he was dreaming up connections to keep from going crazy. Maybe not.

Okay, Berkeley. There must be somebody on the Berkeley police force who'd been there in the late sixties, somebody Gutierrez knew. He got the information operator in Berkeley and hit paydirt on the third name he dredged up from his memory. Harry Kashiwara was a lawyer now instead of a cop, but he remembered his days on the force well, even a little nostalgically.

"Sure. They called Tannenbaum the Rabbi; some people acted like they thought maybe he was Christ. The guy really did have a special kind of appeal, what they call charisma. Dedicated pacifist, though; I always thought that shooting had to be accidental."

"What about his wife?"

"Ah, the Nun."

"Nun?"

"Rumor was she originally planned to enter a convent after she finished her nursing degree."

"Nursing," echoed Gutierrez. The woman at the accident scene had told Meg she was a nurse.

"Right. In fact, she disappeared from the scene for a while, '68 or '69, I forget which, and everybody thought she'd done it, enlisted or whatever it is they do."

"Harry..."

"Yeah, yeah. Listen, she was...shit, I can't think of a word. I just know every guy who saw her wanted to jump her bones, and word was quite a few did. I never heard she took on any little short Japs, though," he said with a sigh.

"Where was she from?"

"Maureen Gowan? San Francisco born and bred."

"Not Idaho?"

"No way."

"What about Tannenbaum?"

"He was a city Jewish boy, let's see. Chicago, I think. You must be thinking of the Cowboy."

"Cowboy?" Gutierrez echoed.

"Right. Let's see, his name was Tucker, Tanner, Taylor. Taylor, I think. Ben Taylor. From the mountains, maybe not Idaho but Montana or Wyoming. A lawyer like Tannenbaum, few years older, sharp as hell; but he wasn't much of a marcher, more a behind-the-scenes kind of guy. He was tight with Maureen, people said, before Tannenbaum came on the scene."

And what does this all mean? wondered Gutierrez, suddenly very weary. "Thanks, Harry. I'm not sure what I'm after," he said to forestall the other's questions, "but when I find out, I promise to let you know."

Gutierrez put the receiver in place once more, levered himself to his feet and carried his empty glass to the sink. In the mirror there his face was dark and bleak and old; he looked as ancient as his Indio great-grandfather, who'd been ninety or near it the one time he'd seen the old man. If Meg was dead he'd look like this the rest of his life.

One more very small drink. When he'd rinsed out the smeary glass, dried it on an extra towel, and prepared another well-watered bourbon, he gathered the telephone up once more and dropped heavily to his armchair.

"Hank? Anything?"

"Nope." Svoboda's voice was full of sadness. He'd be hurting for himself as well as for Vince; Svoboda liked Meg a lot.

"Okay. There's this funny thing I've found out," he began, and told Svoboda about the three images. "What I want you to do," he went on, "is go down to CliffHaven, ah, well, probably tomorrow early. Ask them, the woman particularly, Maureen Gowan Tannenbaum, about the accident, whether they remember Meg. Try to find out..."

"Vince, I can do all that without you making me a list."

"Oh, shit, I know you can. I just need to be two places at once right now. Maybe they came to the hospital next day and ran into Meg and she recognized them; they might have panicked and killed her. Or they...it could be they grabbed her and stashed her someplace and now they can let her go, now they're public and it looks like they won't be arrested.

What I'd try to do is get the woman on her own, without her lawyer.''

"Right up my alley, old buddy. Ladies tell me secrets without me even asking.''

"Yeah, but this is a tougher lady than most. Okay, I'm leaving here at six A.M., be in the woods and out of touch for hours. Anything urgent, call Art Brownell. I'll call *you* soon as I get back.''

Hank thought he was crazy. Probably Hank was right, Gutierrez decided as he hung up the phone. His mind was full of faces, faces that tipped out from behind barriers like children playing peekaboo, faces that smiled and cried and stared.

His hand was still on the telephone, and the bell jarred him like a shot of electricity. "Hank?''

"Brownell. You asked me to call?''

"Oh, yeah. Yeah.'' The accident, Maureen Gowan Tannenbaum, where to start. Gutierrez licked his lips and said, "Yeah, thanks. Here's what I need to know. I'm looking for a woman, a tall woman with square shoulders and...''

"Yes, I know.'' Brownell's voice was sad. "Why don't you try to get a good night's sleep, and we'll talk in the morning.''

"Listen to me, Brownell. This woman has long hair that's prematurely white. Blue eyes as I remember, very blue. She's a nurse. She's probably involved in some sort of public service but quietly because she's a fugitive. But she's the kind of person who can't help striking sparks, and I think there's a chance she's been living around here.''

There was a long silence and then Brownell said, "Mrs. Brody. Elizabeth Brody.''

TWENTY-EIGHT

Jay paced. Meg huddled on her cot in the embrace of Vince's down jacket and tracked her enemy around his house. Front door and back to the kitchen, the back door. Pause; looking out? Back and forth, again and again. Later he changed his route, to move across the kitchen from the far end by the table to here, right outside their door, and another pause. Back and forth and back.

He made coffee, she heard the pot and the water and finally smelled the brew. What did he put in it? He paced, one path for a while and then the other. Steps slow, but not stumbling. Measured, as if there were so much time to be matched to so many steps and he knew just how to do that. When she realized that she was breathing to the tempo of his pace she clapped her hands over her ears, and found the same tempo in the beat of her own blood.

Drink, she told him. Drink rum, lots of rum. She smelled the coffee again, probably as he reheated it. Later, another odor; he was smoking pot now, the bastard. And pacing.

Cass slept. Resistant at first to Meg's instructions to stay still and keep quiet, she had flounced around the little room or fussed with her bags, pausing every five minutes to ask, "What's happening?" Finally the charged atmosphere had penetrated even her self-absorption, and she had settled sullenly onto her sleeping bag. Was she dreaming? Meg wondered. If so, it was probably not bloody bodies she saw. Meg had finally, belatedly grasped the significance of the date, August 17; it was Jon's birthday, probably their arranged meeting date and Cass expected him to turn up on schedule or near it. And maybe he *had*, a possibility that had not yet, it seemed, struck the girl.

Shortly after ten there was a rattle at the back door, and then Kev's voice, high and querulous: "Hey, can I come in?

What time is it?'' he added, clearly from inside the building. ''Is somebody gonna make supper?''

Jay's front-to-back route brought him to the kitchen. ''Twenty-two hundred hours. Grab a hunk of cheese and get back out there.''

Light footsteps approached the fridge; Meg heard it open, heard it close. Kev's voice, further away now, probably by the back door: ''Guess I'm not hungry after all. Hey, that's ten o'clock. Hey, you're missing the call.''

''Catch the backup at oh-seven-hundred tomorrow,'' Jay said, his voice flat, detached. There was a pause; Meg thought he was probably drawing on a joint. ''So. You think you might like a toke, kid?''

''No. Well, yeah, gimme one.'' A moment's silence, and then a cough. ''I'm really cold, Jay. My feet are wet, my mom always gets real upset if I get my feet wet because I catch cold so easy. Can we go pretty soon?''

''Maybe half an hour. Rain's about to quit, so we want to be sure it's late enough nobody's still wandering around. Here, one more and then you get back on duty.''

MEG ALLOWED HERSELF another cigarette; six left in the pack, and she didn't know whether Cass had more. She drew the smoke deep into aching lungs and examined possibilities once more. They were planning to kill their captives and waiting for the right time. Possible, but why should there be a need to wait? Or they were planning to drive their hostages back to civilization and release them, had to be sure it was good and dark for that. Hah.

Dead deer was a notion she'd discarded at once, not enough of a problem. Dead person was the answer she got every time. Unlucky passerby. Personal enemy of one or the other, probably Jay. Cass's Jon. Vince.

But Vince wasn't dead; she wouldn't *have* it. Would not think about it anymore. What she would think about was escape. Jay and Kev were deep in some plan that from the sound of it was going to take both of them away for some time. Then she would get Cass out, snip snip and out the window. Tools in the garage, Cass could break into the house. Use the wood-splitting axe on this door. Meg made a slow film of this in her head, planning each move, placing each object. Frame by frame, and then back to the start, make it perfect. End with the van driving away down the road, into the sunset. Meg and Cass, Vince and even Jon, singing and waving.

Cass woke, tossed and muttered, finally crept across the room to pee in the bucket. Crept back to her bed as if in shame. Only the softest rain sound now, a gentle whisper hardly audible over the sound of Jay's pacing feet. Finally Jay stopped at the back door, pulled it open, and called softly, "Okay, kid, let's haul ass." Meg pulled out her little flash and turned it on her watch; ten forty-five.

Kev came in and went into the front room; from the sounds that followed, Meg thought he was probably putting on dry clothes. Then a low-voiced exchange, just a word or two, and the pair of them went out the back door. She heard keys; Jay as usual believed in taking all precautions. Just wait, you son of a bitch.

Sloshing footsteps along the back of the cabin, then in the passageway between cabin and garage. Screech of metal, repeated: both garage doors up. She pushed the jacket aside, straightened her bruised and aching body, and slowly, painfully got to her knees and then to her feet atop the cot. Light poured from the garage in a flood of yellow. She watched the shimmery curtain of rain and listened to the truck's engine grind, and grind. Come on! she said silently to the cranky old engine. Come on, you can do it.

She heard Jay cursing. Metal grated; hood raising, she thought. Silence for long seconds, and then, "Okay, try it now."

No. That fumble-fingered idiot couldn't get his own truck started. "Keep trying, it'll catch," she whispered, but the hood slammed. She heard someone say, "You push, I'll steer."

The high-topped contraption came out backwards with both of them pushing, Jay reaching through the window to steer. They shoved it to one side, with much effort through what must have been gluey mud. Now what?

Oh shit, oh *shit* you can't! The nice well-tuned engine caught on the first try and her van backed out, stopped and sat there chuckling along in steady fashion while Kev ran through the rain to turn out the light. Meg squeezed her eyes shut, to contain her tears and to bring back night-vision; and then she sniffed and looked at the dim outline of the old truck. She would by God get it running.

Brake lights flared, and then the white of the backups. Meg put a thumb in her mouth and bit down on it and watched as one of those bastards nudged her van up behind the truck. There was some slipping in the mud, and the whine of increasing rpms. And then the truck moved, and moved faster, and coughed to life. There they went, both of them. She and Cass were alone God only knew where, in the rain and the dark, with no transportation. Nothing to do but cry.

"What's happening?"

Cass's sudden whisper nearly jolted Meg from her perch. "Nothing. That is, Jay and Kev have gone somewhere, in the truck and the van."

"The van, too?"

"The van, too. Cass, you might be able to get away. The rain is easing off, and you have a poncho. If I were to boost you out the window, you could take the lantern, or my pocket flash, and try to follow the road to...wherever it goes."

"By myself? In the dark?" A quaver in the girl's words made her feelings clear. "No, I can't."

"You could get out and get the axe," said Meg, "and break *me* out." Her dream, her plan for their escape, had depended on transportation. So sore that the slightest movement left her sweat-drenched and trembling, she doubted she'd last half a mile on foot out there.

"And he'd come back and catch me chopping up his house! No, I won't, no way! What time is it?"

Meg turned her flash on the face of her watch. "Eleven." Perhaps she should tell Cass her suspicions, her very strong suspicions: that Kev had shot and probably killed Jon or Vince, and he and Jay were out disposing of the body. She weighed the idea for several moments, while the rustle of fabric and the creak of wood indicated that Cass was settling for sleep. Finally she decided there was no purpose in such telling, because there was nothing to be done. Mired in an emotional weariness that approached fatalism, she settled Vince's jacket around her shoulders, leaned her head against the wall, and slept.

SOUNDS OUTSIDE jolted her awake. She wiped the heels of her hands across her gritty eyes, straightened her legs, found her pocket flash. After three.

She turned the flash off and sat right where she was. Idling engines. Garage door. Gears and metallic creaks, engines under load. And cut off. No light through the vent. Garage door again.

She tipped her head back and dropped her jaw, to listen. The rain had stopped and she heard only splashing feet. "Son of a bitch," said Jay, slow and slurred. A thud she could feel; he'd bumped the side of the building.

"Listen, Jay, I don't see what we're waiting for," Kevin whined.

Jay's reply was an indistinct growl.

"But look, look *here*, Jay, listen to me. It's just dumb, I think it's really dumb. I mean, man," he half-sobbed, "we're gonna be like in serious trouble here..." Kev's words ended in a muffled "oof," as if Jay had flung an arm back and caught him in the belly.

"We're grunts. You got that? We wait for word from HQ, tomorrow."

"But..."

"One lieutenant, he'll say no captives, waste of time and effort and he don't want to hear about it. Then the next one, he'll say by God bring 'em in and in one piece, too, or it's your fuckin' head, man." Slow feet squelched along over water-logged earth. "So what you do, you wait for the fuckin' orders, don't even fart without orders."

"Jay, look Jay, we're in Idaho, Jay, and we're in trouble."

"Shut up. Now, you got the watch, remember? Keep your eyes and ears peeled for Charlie, he's out there. What you do, you blast anything that moves. But you already know that, right?" Jay paused for breath, and Kev whimpered.

"And here's another thing. You hear guys crying, just ignore it. Probably it's a trick. Can't do shit about it anyway. Just hang in there. Relief at, uh, 0600 hours."

Thump, thump, thump: Jay bouncing off the building as he made his way around. She heard him fall at the back steps, heard his muttered curses and the clatter of keys. The back door hit the wall; a moment later it slammed.

Shuffling feet, low-voiced sounds that didn't seem to be words, a line of yellow under their door as he turned on the kitchen light. He was coming toward them, she could feel each step. She stood up, then bent to turn on their battery lantern. Whatever's coming at you, light helps.

"Meg? What's happening?"

"I don't know. Stay where you are."

But Cass scrambled out of her sleeping bag and came to stand beside Meg as, outside, slow hands fumbled with the padlock. "Who is it?"

"Who do you think? Get back in your bed."

The door swung wide, and Meg saw Jay's figure for a moment, drenched and muddy. Then the light of his big torch struck her eyes, and she raised a shielding hand.

The torch moved to Cass, who blinked and smiled.

"C'mere," he said.

"Wait," Meg began.

"Yeah," said Cass, "wait just a minute, okay? I need to get my stuff."

With the torch lowered Meg could see Jay's gaunt, wet face, dead eyes, slack mouth.

"C'mere," he said again to Cass.

Meg stepped forward and said, "Please, I'd be better company." She was still wondering with astonishment where the words had come from when Jay's fist exploded against her jaw.

TWENTY-NINE

THE GIRL NAMED Carla sat as close to the kitchen table as she could get, her legs wide apart to accommodate her huge belly. Under the hanging light her short curly hair was the same color as the freckles on her nose and her forearms, the same color as the tea in the cup she set down with a clatter. Around the freckles her skin was the bluish-white of skim milk.

"You okay?" The only other person in the room, a stubby woman whose bleached hair stood up like rumpled feathers, paused for a deep drag on her cigarette. She directed the smoke out the half-open window and tapped ash into the sink.

Carla set her hands on either side of her belly, cradling it. "Yeah, mostly I was just faking, to get those cops off my back."

"Well, I'm sure glad to hear that. I had the doc put me all the way out for both of my kids, so I don't know nothin' about delivering babies." The older woman, Margo, cinched the belt of her pink quilted robe tighter under sagging breasts.

"I still got two weeks to go," Carla assured her, and then shivered. "That dark cop, looked Mex? He's the one scared me. I went with one for a while, a Mexican dude; he was meaner even than Donnie."

"All cops scare me," snapped Margo. "Even good old Art Brownell. My personal belief is, cops decide to be cops mostly so they can hang a gun on their belt and push people around. Specially women; I never knew a cop didn't think women was dirt." Margo turned her head and spat into the sink. She took a long last drag on her cigarette and then killed the butt by running water over it.

Carla stretched a skinny arm across the table to pick up the teapot. "Did you believe that stuff they said?" she asked as she splashed her cup full. "About the missing women?"

Margo shrugged. "Way they moved around, it was clear to me they was definitely looking for people instead of dope or something like that."

"I bet Elizabeth wouldn't have let them in, not without a warrant."

"Don't be dumb, girl. Elizabeth is a tough, smart lady that does whatever she has to do. Otherwise this place would've folded a long time ago." Margo glanced around the room, eyed the sink and then picked up her cigarette butt to deposit it in a nearby wastebasket. "Things is going to hell without her already, you see that? Annie took off with her kids two or three days ago, and that skinny slut Marty left yesterday, God help her poor brats. And whoever was supposed to wash diapers yesterday didn't do it, I had to get Betsy to pick up some disposables on her way home from work."

"You think Elizabeth will be back in time? To deliver my baby, I mean?" Carla's voice was plaintive and not very hopeful.

"Carla, I got absolutely no idea. All she said to me, she had to go away for a while due to sickness in the immediate family. Last time I saw her was Friday morning. That's what I told the cops, *all* I told them. Well, and that she must of went with the tall guy in the brown car. Because they could see for theirselves she didn't take her own."

"I didn't tell them anything. I wouldn't have even if I *knew* anything." Carla edged her chair backwards, set her palms flat on the table and lifted her body upright. "Thanks for the tea, Margo. I think I'll go upstairs and get my stuff together. Soon as it's daylight I'm gonna call Donnie to come get me."

MAUREEN TANNENBAUM stepped from her husband's room into the broad, carpeted hall and eased the door shut behind her. She took a deep breath, stretched and raked her hair back with both hands.

"Maureen?"

She sighed and turned toward the bow window at the end of the hall, where a tall figure was rising from the cushioned window seat.

"Ben, why are you still up in the middle of the night? Couldn't they find a bed for you?"

"I'm quite comfortable here," he told her. "How is Michael?"

"Michael is sleeping. I'm going down to get a cup of tea."

"Come over here for a moment first." He took her elbow to lead her to the window seat.

"How is he really?" he asked in a whisper as they sat.

"Accepting," she said, her own voice near-normal. She turned her head to gaze out at the front courtyard, lighted now only by the moon; her face was serene, mouth easy and brow unfurrowed. "He seems to have come to terms with himself, and with dying."

"How much longer?"

"A few days, a week. I don't really know, Ben. Soonest would be best," she added. "He's experiencing some bone pain. Not usual, but it sometimes happens."

"Has he seen Tessa? How did he react to her?"

"He just looked at her for a long time and then smiled. And she gave him back this big wide grin, she wasn't frightened at all by such a...hollow-eyed skeleton. She was absolutely wonderful."

"That's our Michael, a charmer even on his deathbed," he muttered; he grabbed her arm and said "No, wait!" as she glared at him and moved to rise. "I need to know, is everything going to work out?"

"Money, you mean. Yes, it appears *that* will work out quite well. He's made a will dividing his estate between us, Tessa and me. Two-thirds to her, in trust, one-third to me outright."

"A third?" The sharp words seemed to hit the window glass and rebound; he shot a nervous look down the hall. "What the hell's the matter with fifty-fifty?" he whispered.

"A third is a great deal of money," Maureen said sharply. "Michael actually made the will some time ago, before your visit," she added. "But he wanted to see us, Tessa and me, and he knew that you'd find a way to get us here."

"He did?" Ben's mouth curved in a reluctant smile.

"He felt it was the best time for me to surface...to get the benefit of the grieving widow role, is the way he put it. And he said one more thing," she added, and leaned close. "He said I was to be sure not to let ol' Ben screw me out of more than a few thou."

She straightened, smiled, and stood up. "So I'm going to keep my promises, Ben, because they were promises. And because I probably wouldn't have come without your shepherding, which means I could never have made my peace with Michael. Just don't you be a pig, now or in the future."

"Made your peace with Michael?" he repeated softly. "About everything?"

"Oh yes."

"I don't believe you."

She shrugged. "You've forgotten, even *I'd* forgotten, how difficult it is to lie to Michael. I never could do it, and I still can't."

It was Ben who looked away first, his shoulders sagging. "So it's all up to Michael now."

"It always was. Oh, one more thing I should probably tell you. In the morning, when Mother Tannenbaum comes to take over, I intend to borrow a car and go find a church somewhere."

"Why, to ask forgiveness?"

"To pray for all our souls, Michael's and Tessa's and mine. I wouldn't presume to include yours. Now, I'd better get back; would you go downstairs and order me a pot of tea, please?"

"Sure, I don't mind running the occasional errand. I'll even drive you tomorrow, to church."

"That won't be necessary."

THIRTY

MEG'S EYES REGISTERED only blackness, and she seemed to have bubbles in her ears. Jay's fist had caught her turning face, jaw and cheekbone; the blow had sent her flying and apparently…she pushed exploring fingers through her hair and stifled a yelp as they touched a lump high on the back of her skull. It was soft, sticky; she must have landed against the wooden frame of her now-collapsed cot.

The left side of her face, yes; its shape was odd under her cupping palm, and painful as hell; how do you tell if a cheekbone is broken? Her tongue probed gently and found two loose teeth, upper molars and she thought, she hoped, not dangerously loose.

Had she been unconscious? Maybe not, not completely; she had a vague memory of noises, of doors closing. How long ago?

Her watch was still on her wrist, but it was a stupid quartz thing, no tick, no life. And she couldn't see it. Didn't matter; she didn't remember what time it was when it started, when he came in and hit her.

She struggled on hands and knees away from the wood and canvas of the cot. Groped around on the floor until she found a familiar slippery surface, her security blanket. Pulled Vince's jacket around her again and sat shivering against her drawn-up knees. Gradually the darkness around her took on shades, black lumps against space not quite so black. Must be a bit of light from the vents, stars or moon; she remembered the lantern suddenly and wondered if the batteries had failed.

Get up from there, lady, get on your feet or at least on your hands and knees again, find the light. She brushed a hand against the cot, the blanket. Bags, several. Another cot. A wide-armed sweep and another and there it was. Broken, poor little thing, just like her.

She crawled back to find the jacket, to huddle under it and think and listen. Nothing, nobody out there. They were all of them on their merry way, in the van as she'd imagined it earlier, everybody but her.

Wait. Why had Jay hit her? Something about, yes, about Cass. Cass smiling and Jay's dead face and Meg didn't want Cass to go. But she went. Goddammit to hell. Vince, I'm sorry.

Maybe not, maybe it *was* everybody off in the van including Jon, what it was all about and Cass was fine. She was fine, too, Meg, just maybe a few bruises and some loose teeth and still out in the woods somewhere. No food, after a few days she'd probably be skinny enough to get out through the vent.

Some time later... five minutes, thirty minutes, she had no idea... she heard something. Not voices, just sounds. A door, the back door. Two sets of feet, light and heavy. The familiar noises of padlock and hasp; door open. Cass was a silhouette, tiny, shoulders rounded forward and chin tucked low. The girl put one foot in front of another with infinite weariness, until she was in the room; the door closed and was secured. The heavy footsteps moved away, the back door opened and closed.

She was just a dark shape, unmoving. "Cass?" Meg called softly. "Cass, are you all right?"

"Oh, well, what the shit. No big deal, okay? I mean, I really don't want to talk about it."

"Cass?" Meg came forward onto her knees.

"I know how to do that," the high, tight voice went on, "I've done it plenty of times before. It's not my fault he wouldn't get hard. All I asked him, when he finally let me quit, was could I please go and wash my mouth out. And he acted like he didn't even hear me."

"Cass, here." Meg's own bag was against her foot; she found the square bottle by touch and yanked it out and uncapped it. "Here," she said, and poured the cap full. "Gin. Don't swallow it, just swish it around and spit it out."

Cass gripped Meg's wrist in cold fingers, brought the cap to her mouth and sucked in the liquid. After the girl had gargled and spat a second and then a third mouthful, Meg put an arm across the narrow shaking shoulders, poured gin into her own palm and splashed it against Cass's face. And again, washing her face with gin, washing Jay off.

Cass mumbled something and Meg thought, Enough, don't drown her. She capped the bottle and set it on the floor. "Cass, I'm so sorry."

Cass lurched around and into Meg, wrapping her arms around the taller woman's ribs. "How come shit like that always happens to me?" A big gulp of air, and then she banged her forehead against Meg's breastbone. "Kev was out there someplace, why didn't he make him stop?"

Bang, and bang, and bang, the small hard head going further back each time, coming forward with greater force.

"Cass, that hurts."

"I mean I never did anything to him, how come he can do that to me? Who lets him do that?"

Meg put her arms around the girl, partly to comfort and partly to pull her too close for further bumping. Cass leaned for a moment, limp, and then stiffened and began to hammer with sharp little fists.

"Where were you?" Punch and punch in Meg's sore ribs, and again. "Where was Uncle Vince?" Bam, bam, against the sides of her breasts. "Why didn't Jon come?"

Meg caught the fists and pulled them down, took a crack under the chin from the girl's flung-back head and went weak-kneed for a moment. "All right, that's enough!

"Enough," she repeated more softly. "Come on, let's lie down. In your nice warm bag, Fred's bag. Over here."

Cass was shivering now, and crying hopelessly. Meg pulled her sneakers off, peeled down the muddy jeans, unzipped the bag and rolled her in. Chattering teeth and hard sobs showed no sign of abating: Meg said, "Okay, baby, just move over a little, that's my good girl." Cass hunched backwards, and Meg slid into the bag, edging forward to try to leave a little room between her spine and the cot's rim. She reached behind herself to pull the zipper up, then

THIRTY-ONE

GUTIERREZ WAS STRUGGLING in quicksand that had reached his chest and was creeping higher. On the nearby solid ground, which looked oddly like the front yard of a farmhouse, stood a middle-aged woman and a hugely pregnant girl. They leaned on propped pitchforks, talking to each other and ignoring his cries for help.

Someone rang the farmhouse doorbell, one of the old twist kind, and rang it and rang it. Women and house shimmered and were gone. He pried his eyes open, looked past the bedside lamp to a window still showing only blackness, and fumbled for the telephone.

"Tom Workman," said the voice against his ear.

"Ah." Gutierrez sat up and swung his legs over the edge of the bed. "Sorry, I guess I slept through. I'll be ready in no time."

"It's just coming up on five A.M.," Workman told him. "But the rain's finally quit up there, so I thought we might as well get our ass in gear. Pick you up in five minutes."

Did Kuisma come home last night? Gutierrez wondered as he pulled yesterday's clothes on over clean underwear. He shoved his feet into his boots and went next door, but there was no response to his knock. No sound of breathing inside, either. Goddamn.

He gave his teeth about three swipes with a toothbrush, splashed cold water over his face, eyed the mean old bastard staring back at him from the mirror and said, "Right."

Note to Val: he scribbled a few words on a card. He donned his belt holster and tucked the S & W into place, eased his way into his leather jacket; he put on the sling he had fashioned the night before from two of the motel's towels. Looked silly as hell, he noted, but felt okay. Might even be a handy place to tuck a gun.

Lights swinging into the parking lot raked his window. He closed his own door, stopped to thrust the card under Kuisma's door, and quickstepped down the hall.

"Just like goin' fishing," said Workman cheerfully as he leaned across to open the passenger door. The vehicle was a chunky jeep-type perched high on huge tires; it bore a trailer hitch in the rear, a winch in front. Fortunately it had a step below the door; Gutierrez gripped the frame with his left hand and managed to climb in.

Workman wore a down vest over a flannel shirt and Levi's, with huge lug-soled laceup boots that didn't seem to hamper his driving. "Gonna take us close to three hours," he remarked over his shoulder as he backed the machine out of the lot and whipped it around. "Longer if there's bridges out, but I ain't heard of any, not yet."

"I appreciate your help," said Gutierrez.

"Glad to be of assistance. Gonna be another guy meet us up there, out of the sheriff's office in Boundary County; this here's Bonner. I'm State of Idaho, so I can go anywhere, but I thought a little local muscle was a good idea. Besides, it don't hurt to be polite. You hear anything from California?"

"No," said Gutierrez. The business about the Tannenbaums was too complicated to explain on an empty stomach and an aching head; he wasn't sure it connected anyway. The women at the place called Shelter had insisted last night that their absent supervisor was Elizabeth Brody and so far as they knew that was her real and only name. Like the women in his dream, they were not helpful; didn't like the police, Brownell had said later.

Didn't like men, either, Gutierrez thought now. That pregnant girl had stared at him from behind her big belly as if only its bulk kept her safe from his assault. Maybe later today, if this hermit business turned out to be a bad lead, maybe Brownell would agree to send Mardian out there. They might open up to another woman. If Mardian and Kuisma hadn't disobeyed him last night and blundered into disaster. Gutierrez shifted irritably in his seat.

"Sorry about the rough ride," remarked Workman with a glance at his passenger. "This thing is a kidney-buster unloaded, but we'll need her on the logging roads. Meanwhile, coffee's there, and doughnuts," he added with a nod to the cardboard box tucked between the bucket seats.

As they rumbled through the intersection of I-90 with 95, Gutierrez turned to look behind them at the bright lights of the hospital with its big, well-lighted, nearly empty parking lot. It looked very safe.

SIXTY-SIX MILES to Priest River, according to a sign; an hour's drive in this machine, Gutierrez thought, and longed for his Porsche. The road was painfully familiar, two lanes of blacktop on either side of a wide grassy center strip. He ate half a glazed doughnut, then wrapped the rest in a paper napkin and reached for one of the tall cardboard containers. With a little juggling he managed to pry the plastic lid off and quickly got a faceful of very warm coffee.

Still black out; sunrise should be around six, but the overcast sky would probably slow the coming of light. Eight o'clock, maybe, by the time they reached the hermit's hideout. Full daylight by then, overcast or no, and how would they go in?

"Do you have a loud-hailer?" he asked Workman.

"Got a battery-powered bullhorn in the back, along with my twelve-gauge and my deer rifle. I figured, kind of guy this is, we're not gonna be able to sneak up on him anyway, not the whole way. But we'll try to get close enough to see if there's anything going on."

Gutierrez took another large mouthful of coffee and tried to visualize their destination. There were large stands of timber, Brownell had said last night, as well as pieces that had been clearcut years ago. He figured the hermit's piece would be full of underbrush and young trash trees. Plenty of cover.

Hostage negotiation, that was what they'd be looking at if Meg and Cass were up here. He himself had had some training, but doubted his ability to apply the principles coolly here and now. Kuisma was a better bet; he'd had the training too and was very good.

Stop in Priest River, maybe, and wait for Kuisma? No, he didn't want to stop and wait for anything. Maybe stop long enough to call the motel or Brownell. Then move on, leaving a clear trail. As Workman crawled through the still sleeping town of Sandpoint and picked up highway 2 west, Gutierrez made himself sit back in his seat and sip coffee slowly as he went over the rules, the delicate dance of trust and power, interest and detachment, warm acquiescence and reluctant denial.

"Something's up," said Workman softly. Gutierrez surfaced from deep inside his own head and looked out at a gray dawn, a dark river. Just ahead, where the road made a sweeping curve to follow a bend of the river, he saw a collection of vehicles both personal and official. Two cars were pulled close to the river, headlights blazing over the water.

Workman pulled up behind a county sheriff's sedan, turned off his engine and jumped out. Gutierrez unfastened his seat belt but stayed where he was, rolling down his window. It was cold out there, the air still full of moisture. Ten or twelve men were milling around at river's edge, and someone was in the water, he could hear splashing. No, it was a small boat, a rowboat.

This much action, they have a body or think they have. Or bodies. He reached across to get his good hand on the door, opened it and slid out. He settled his jacket over his holster, took a deep breath and moved slowly across slippery grass toward the crowd.

"What's up?" he inquired of a young man in uniform who waved him to one side.

"We got enough help here," the cop said, and glanced over his shoulder. "Just stay back."

"I'm with Tom Workman, of the state police," Gutierrez said, and then touched his white-towel sling with his good hand. "But I wouldn't be any help one-armed, so I'll try to stay out of the way. Somebody drown?"

"Looks like it," said the cop, relaxing his pose. "Guy came down to the river, on the other side, to check if his boat made it through the storms. He saw something caught on that snag out there, so he called the sheriff."

The splash of oars was clear now above the rush of the river itself. For a moment the boat was caught in the cross-beams of headlights: man in a slicker and a watch cap rowing, figure in a dark uniform crouching near the bow. The river was high and its banks here shallow, so Gutierrez could not see what was in the bottom of the boat.

He couldn't breathe, either, and he had a sudden, urgent need to take a leak. He stood very straight and stared toward the river, at a row of bending backs and reaching hands. There was Workman's broad frame, straightening now and turning this way. Coming this way.

"Male Caucasian," he said to Gutierrez, who found the police language soothing. Distant. And a whole lot better than female Caucasian. "Young, not much more than a kid."

"The hermit's kid?" suggested Gutierrez, and coughed to clear his throat. Or Kuisma?

"Dunno," said Workman with a shrug. "Tall, dark hair. And he didn't drown; somebody blasted him, I'd guess with a deer rifle. Come have a look, see if he's anybody you know."

Workman cleared a path and Gutierrez followed, eyes straight ahead. The body, clad in jeans and a tee shirt and one boot, was stretched out on the riverbank, on a tarp. He noted quickly and with relief that it was too big for Kuisma, heavier and more muscular. The uniformed man kneeling beside the body pushed aside clinging strands of hair, and Gutierrez looked at a pale face still running rivulets of muddy water.

"His name is Jonathan Archer." For a moment he was just a cop again, steeling himself for the impersonal unpleasantness of viewing a dead stranger. Then he remembered this stranger's significance. "His father," Gutierrez said in a rusty voice, "has been looking for him. Lawrence Archer, staying in Coeur d'Alene. Chief Brownell can tell you where."

THIRTY-TWO

"WORKMAN," Gutierrez called, but the state cop, deep in conversation with a deputy sheriff, didn't respond. Gutierrez zipped his jacket higher and stomped his cold feet and swore under his breath. They'd been here by the river for a good twenty minutes, and he was beginning to feel like a goddamned beggar: reach out and tug the coattail and whine, "Please, sir?"

Someone else called Workman's name; he turned, strode to the state police sedan and reached inside for the radio mike. Gutierrez swore again, turned to scan the road, noted Workman's borrowed kidney-buster and remembered that it had an automatic transmission. He remembered next that he was surrounded by law enforcement, probably wouldn't get fifty feet in a stolen car.

Wouldn't know where to go anyway. He shot another look at his watch; after six, their wherever-in-hell destination was some two hours away, and somebody up there, probably the crazy hermit, was using a deer rifle on people. Gutierrez drew himself straight and headed for the state cop, cleaving a path through the gathering crowd by the force of his glare.

"Workman, I have to get going."

"Hey, good," said the big man as he put the mike back. "Got something for you, Gutierrez. Chief Brownell says he got computer printouts of car registrations in Bonner and Boundary counties, checking for old pickup trucks. Lots of 'em around here, of course, but he thought you might be interested in a 1950 Chev registered to a James B. Taylor."

"Taylor. All *right*," said Gutierrez. Family…it was what he'd thought of earlier; the hermit had somebody outside and it could be Ben Taylor, the Cowboy. Who could have kept up his connection with Maureen Tannenbaum.

"Right," he said again. "Workman, can we get out of here?"

The big man shook his head. "Now we got a body, possible connection with your people and maybe even with the hermit, everything gets official. My outfit, sheriffs in both counties . . . we're getting things set up.

"But stick around," he said, and turned at the sound of a siren; a Jeep Wagoneer with a cross on its side was pulling up at the edge of the road, scattering onlookers. "I'll be part of the team, and you can ride with me. Okay, folks, here comes the stretcher, let's clear the way."

"Ride with you. Thanks a lot," said Gutierrez through clenched teeth. A hand touched his shoulder; he turned with a snarl and found himself nose to nose with Val Kuisma.

"Where the fuck have you been? Never mind, let's go. Is Mardian . . . Officer Mardian, you say you know the area well?"

"Chief, we've got a witness," said Kuisma, and Gutierrez saw that Chris Mardian had her hand tucked through the arm of a gangling youth probably seventeen years old. The boy wore a blue service-station jacket and a nervous expression.

"Chief Gutierrez, Jerry Pulaski," said Mardian. "Chief, Jerry lives near Coolin, but he works in a Chevron station in Sandpoint. He has some information for you about a blue van."

Gutierrez reached for the boy, who stepped back, then stepped further back to permit the passage of two men and an obviously heavy stretcher. "Hey," said the boy, "somebody miss the curve and wind up in the river?"

He glanced down at the stretcher, and Gutierrez's gaze followed his. Jon Archer's face was relatively unbroken, still austerely handsome; the ragged wound beneath his breastbone had been washed bloodless by the river. "Hey," Jerry said again, weakly. "That's the guy. He's the one was asking questions."

Gutierrez's reach was successful this time; he closed his fingers firmly around the youngster's upper arm and urged him away from the crowd. "What about the blue van?" the policeman asked, and tightened his grip.

"I seen it last Friday."

"Ah." Gutierrez released the arm and patted the boy's shoulder. "Where did you see it, at what time; and where did it go?"

"It was driving through Sandpoint, right past my station. Must have been about one o'clock, I was sitting on a bench out front finishing my lunch. I guess it was going up to the woods, up there east of the lake."

"Why do you guess that?"

"Because that kid was driving it, I don't know his name but I said hey to him a couple times before."

"What kid is that?" Gutierrez's voice, still soft, had an edge that brought the nervous look back to Jerry's face.

"The kid who's staying with the crazy guy, the one they call the hermit. I seen the hermit drive past, in his camper, and I noticed he was by himself. Then the van came right close behind, and the kid was driving. I waved at him, but he didn't see me."

Gutierrez sighed and rubbed his eyes with thumb and forefinger. "You've been a big help, Jerry. Have you seen either man, or either vehicle, since?"

The boy shook his head. "Not that I remember, anyway."

"And what about him?" Gutierrez asked, and nodded in the direction of the departing ambulance. "The young man they found in the river?"

Jerry looked, too, and looked quickly away, shifting his position to put his back to the road and any dead bodies. "He come into the station yesterday afternoon, on this big black bike. We got talking, and he said he was trying to find this blue van and trailer. I told him I'd seen one, didn't have a trailer but it did have a license plate with an X on it."

"Did you tell him about the hermit?"

"Yessir, he was real interested." Jerry drew himself straight and tucked his chin close. "I guess I shouldn't have. Is that what happened, the hermit got him?"

"I don't know," said Gutierrez wearily. "Jerry, there's somebody over here I think you'd better talk to. You two stay right here," he told Kuisma and Mardian.

Gutierrez herded the boy across the grass toward the river. "Workman?" he called. "Here's a witness who saw the Archer boy yesterday."

"Did you now," said Workman. "I know you, you're Hunk Pulaski's boy from Coolin. How you doin'?"

Gutierrez stepped quietly back, then turned and hurried off to his own troops. "Mardian, do you know how to get to the hermit's place?"

"Yessir."

"We talked to lots of people around Coolin last night, mostly Chris's relatives," offered Kuisma. "Her cousin goes fishing on upper Puma Creek, right past the road to the hermit's property, and he drew us a map."

"We found Jerry because his big sister goes with another cousin," said Mardian. "We were on our way to Coeur d'Alene to bring him to you."

"Lucky you stopped here," said Gutierrez. "Let's go. Ah, Mardian. You have weapons?"

"Yessir. My 20-gauge and my little Savage deer gun."

"I guess they issue deer guns along with birth certificates up here," said Gutierrez. "Never mind. It's damned near six-thirty; let's go."

"DEAR ME, SHE SAID she'd be back by 6:30." The senior Mrs. Tannenbaum gave her frosted blond curls a shake as she glanced at her watch. "And it's nearly seven. May I pour you some coffee, Mr. Svoboda?"

"Thank you, ma'am, I'd appreciate it." Hank Svoboda wore boots, Levi's, and a tweed jacket and should have looked out of place in a flowered wing chair but did not. "I'm real sorry to be intruding on a sorrowing family with my personal troubles, and at such an early hour."

"Time has little meaning in this house presently." Mrs. Tannenbaum filled his cup and set the silver sugar and cream tray within his reach. "And I'm most grateful for the help local police forces like yours have given our security people.''

''Well, I surely wouldn't have bothered you if it wasn't so important, if it didn't involve my granddaughter.'' Svoboda had decided that his quest for information would be more successful if presented from a personal angle.

''Oh, I do understand. I have a granddaughter too, I met her yesterday for the first time. But she's hardly more than a baby, much too young to be running away.''

''I remember when mine was like that. Babies surely are easier than teenagers.'' At a sound from the front door Svoboda set his cup down. When the tall, white-haired woman entered the room, he was on his feet.

''Mother Tannenbaum . . . is Michael . . . ?''

''Michael is sleeping again. I came down and had breakfast, and then Mr. Svoboda arrived, looking for you. Mr. Svoboda, this is my son's wife, Maureen Tannenbaum.''

''Or Elizabeth Brody,'' Svoboda said, with a polite nod. ''That's the name you used in Idaho, I believe?''

Maureen lifted her chin and pushed her hands deep into her skirt pockets. ''What is this, Mr. Svoboda? You look like a policeman; perhaps you should be speaking to my attorney, William Taylor.''

''Oh no, ma'am,'' Svoboda said, with another nod to the tall reddish-haired man behind her. ''That is, I am a policeman, up in Port Silva. But I got absolutely no official position here today, you can ask me to leave any time.''

''Maureen,'' said Mrs. Tannenbaum in a chiding tone, ''poor Mr. Svoboda is looking for his runaway granddaughter who's only sixteen and possibly pregnant. She was last heard from in Coeur d'Alene.''

Maureen Tannenbaum turned with a swirl of skirt and settled into a chair. ''My refuge, Shelter, takes in pregnant women; but not pregnant children, not without their parents' consent. Unless your granddaughter is a very mature-looking sixteen, I can assure you she has not been with us. And I haven't referred anyone that young elsewhere, not recently.''

With a slow shake of his head Svoboda sat down in the wing chair. "Here's the way it went, ma'am. Cass...that's my granddaughter, Cassandra...called from Idaho, and a friend of mine went to pick her up. Meg got there Thursday, called to say they'd be leaving the next morning and would call us every night. We haven't heard anything from them since."

Maureen sighed and made a production of looking at her watch. "Mr. Svoboda, what has this to do with me?"

"Why, the accident." He paused, looked surprised to find that he had picked up the coffee cup and reached to set it back on the side table. "See, several folks remember seeing a blue van like Meg's at that big auto pileup just out of Coeur d'Alene last Thursday night."

Maureen sat straight and still in her armless chair; under the smooth fall of her skirt one knee twitched.

"So we're trying to talk to everybody who was there." Svoboda spread his big hands and gave her a hopeful smile.

"I'm sorry." She came to her feet. "I know nothing about any highway accident; if someone believes he saw me there, he was mistaken. Ben and I had dinner in Washington Thursday night; we weren't on the highway north of town at all. Ben?" she said. Svoboda followed her glance to see the tall man stepping back toward the doorway.

"Absolutely," he said with a nod. "Sorry, but I'll have to excuse myself for a few minutes. There's a phone call I promised to make."

"And I'll go to my husband now," said Maureen.

Svoboda stood up and watched her stride into the hallway, toward the staircase.

"I'm afraid I must apologize, Mr. Svoboda." Mrs. Tannenbaum's mouth drew thin in disapproval. "My daughter-in-law has always been very—political."

"I expect she has a lot on her mind," said Svoboda. "I didn't get that fellow's name straight, her lawyer. Did she call him Ben?"

"William Bennington Taylor," said Mrs. Tannenbaum. "An old friend of my son's."

THIRTY-THREE

"CASS, WAKE UP." Meg knelt beside the cot and folded back the top edge of the sleeping bag. "Come on, get up and get dressed."

She herself had slept not at all, had eased from the bag an hour ago to dress and get ready. To listen. She wore her old soft Levi's, her sneakers, a shirt and long-sleeved sweat-shirt and Vince's jacket, the latter for emotional sustenance and for its pockets. No baggage today, not even a handbag.

"Cass?" She gripped the girl's shoulder for a gentle shake. Cass groaned, stiffened; then she gave a little whim-per and curled herself tight. "Leave me alone."

"I can't. I need you."

"No."

Meg sat back on her heels and looked at her watch. Six-fifteen, and Kev had left just after six. "Cass, listen to me. Kev is gone, and I think Jay is only half conscious; he sounded thick and maybe drunk when they talked. This is our last chance to get out of here."

"No. He'll kill us."

"He's going to kill us anyway. Now you get up or... or here's what I'll do. I'll start throwing things around and screaming and banging on the door. Then he'll come in here, is that what you want?"

"No!" Cass shoved the bag open and sat up, rubbing her face. With heavy, reddened eyelids and down-turned mouth, she looked like a child that had cried itself to sleep.

And this is no time for sentimental images, Margaret. "Jeans, sneakers, sweater," she instructed as the girl got to her feet. "And hurry. Wherever it is Jay goes each night, it always takes him a good two hours; but Kev may move faster." Maybe a lot faster, maybe he wouldn't wait for the call but simply come back and *say* he'd received killing orders. Kev wanted to get this over with.

Cass kept her head down and her eyes averted as she pulled on her clothes. "Maybe Uncle Vince will come today," she muttered.

"Cass, we have run out of waiting time. Okay, here's the plan. I'll boost you out the vent. You look around in the garage and find me the .22, or if that's not there something to break this door down with, a sledge or axe. Pass it in through the vent."

"Then what?" asked Cass. "Never mind, I can't. I'm scared of high places, I'll fall. And suppose I get halfway out and he sees me, then what?"

That picture gave Meg a shudder, too. "He won't. He's in the front room beside the stove; notice how warm it is in here? Even if he goes out to the washhouse, this building will screen you. Help me move your cot over here, to stand on."

Cass complied, head still down. Then she watched as Meg cut the screen up both sides. When Meg stepped down, Cass was still watching, still in her stocking feet. "Cass, get your shoes on."

She shoved her feet into her sneakers and squatted to tie them. "What about the traps in the woods?"

"We'll use the road. Kev took the camper, so we have our van. And if there's a gate we'll just smash through it. Come on, I'll climb up and get my balance and then give you a hand up."

"No, I can't."

"Yes you can. This is our last, our only chance and you simply have to do it. I'm too big for that vent."

"I can't."

Meg yanked the girl to her feet and slapped her hard. "Are you going to be a dumb little *victim* all your life? The two hours or so that's left of it?"

Cass put one hand to her cheek and the other over her mouth as her eyes welled tears.

"Cassandra. *Please.*"

IT TOOK ENDLESS MINUTES and agonizing effort, with Meg finally managing to slide Cass's small but stiff-with-fear body feet first through the vent. Then she held her, eased her out and down, sure that any moment her own tortured muscles would fail or Jay would hear.

A heavy thud, a yelp quickly bitten short, and then in a moment, soft rapid footsteps; Cass might have landed hard, but she'd gotten up. Meg leaned her sweaty forehead, the one part of her that didn't hurt, against the cool metal of the vent frame. What if Cass couldn't find gun or axe? What if Jay decided to come check on his captives?

Or what if the keys had once again been left in the van? If they had, she herself was up shit creek for fair. She closed her eyes, slowed her breathing, and listened. Nothing from the front room, and then she thought she could hear Jay's heavy breathing: good—no, too bad, he should be dead. Nothing from outside, nothing, nothing. Then footsteps again, quick, less cautious. Be quiet, Cass.

There was a soft rap on the wall, and she put her face to the vent.

"What happened to the keys to the van!" Cass's whisper was furious. "There's no keys in this case!"

And what were you going to do with them, sweetie. "I have them," Meg said softly. "What about the rifle?"

"You..." Cass swallowed whatever term she had in mind. "I didn't see any rifle."

"Look again."

One minute, two minutes. Five minutes by the sweep hand on Meg's watch. Then Cass's voice again, shaky. "Meg, there isn't any rifle. Honest. No axe, either."

"Cass..."

"There's this like closet, at the back of the garage. But it's locked."

Two by fours, thought Meg frantically. Screwdrivers from the van? The big lug wrench?

"Meg? Please, you've got to let me have the keys. I promise I'll bring help, I *promise*."

Oh, well. One of two, not bad. "Okay," Meg said aloud, softly, "gas; take whatever is left in the cans against the front wall. Watch, I'm dropping the keys out.'' That done, she eased herself away from the wall, clambered painfully off the cot, she sat down on the floor and leaned her head back against a stud. Nearly seven, oh-seven-hundred as Jay had said last night. Kev would be starting on his way back any minute, maybe he already had. Better be quick, Cass.

She listened for the van's starter. Or the garage door, was it closed? Listened. Listened. What she should be doing, she should be arming herself with a piece of the broken cot or something, for when Jay came in. No, she should find something heavy and get ready to make a lot of noise, to confuse him when he heard the garage door and the van. Get on your feet, Margaret, and do your part.

A quiet distant click, barely audible. Somebody moving in the kitchen, softly, softly, hardly any noise at all. Brush of metal, muffled. Meg sat straighter and stared at the door of the room as it opened slowly.

"I saw him through the window. He's asleep, or maybe dead.'' Cass's words were the barest whisper, her eyes white-rimmed circles in a colorless face. "The lock wasn't closed.'' As she held up the open padlock, there was a groan and the sound of movement from the front room. Cass froze for one open-mouthed second, and then fled noiselessly through the kitchen.

ON YOUR FEET. Step very quietly, but quickly. Pull the door wider. Fridge, stove, counter, and there's the back door, wide open. Probably blowing a cold wind right in on Jay and his woodstove. Hurry.

Out into the kitchen, walk easy don't squeak. Past the fridge past the kitchen stove, another groan from the front room and the creak of chair or bench. Meg lifted the big iron skillet from the stove and took another step toward the door, and another.

"Close the fuckin' door,'' Jay grunted, one slow word at a time.

Not bloody likely. She moved quickly for the door but couldn't help looking into the front room and saw Jay standing wide-legged beside the glowing woodstove. His head was thrust forward, his eyes half-shut, and the .22 hung from his right hand, butt under his arm and barrel pointing at the floor.

"I was...I was going to make breakfast." She turned her back on the open door and moved several slow steps toward him. From the end of her right arm the skillet dangled like a giant appendage; she lifted it a few inches in demonstration: me cook. Bottles on the hearth, she noted, the Myers's bottle lying flat and empty, the bottle of Mexican stuff open. Down almost a third. You're a dead man.

"Unh. I'm sorry. About your kid." He swayed as he spoke; the hand he lifted shook as if with palsy. "I was someplace else, saw this little dink whore...I dunno. Shouldn't've happened."

Happened. Like an accident, accidental rape, so sorry. He was almost within arm's reach; could she take the gun from him?

A screech of metal from outside, the garage door; he lifted his head like a bird dog and the .22 began to rise as well. Meg took two steps forward and brought the skillet across her body as she moved, smooth quick shift to double her grip and then a sweeping rising swing with both hands and all her weight behind it. The flat bottom struck the side of his head with a terrible sound and sent him tumbling against the stove. She heard his scream and thought she smelled searing flesh as she snatched the rifle and ran.

Cass had backed the van out and around, to head for the road. Meg shouted "Wait!" and ran to yank the driver's door open, laying the gun in the back. "Slide over," she gasped as she scrambled in, and Cass obeyed. The road, the gateway...and a heavy pole and wire gate, standing wide. People were certainly getting careless around here.

"Thank you for waiting, Cass." Meg settled more firmly into her seat and eased her grip on the wheel. "And it was brave of you to come in and open the door."

"What did you do to him?"

"I fried him." Meg took a deep breath. She tossed a look at wide-eyed Cass and said, "I hit him with the skillet and knocked him against the stove."

"Wow."

"Yeah. Wow. Now here's what we do. You watch the road, for the tracks, because we don't want to wander around out here for the rest of our lives. The tracks of the truck, see there? And pray, that the road is muddy enough to show tracks but not so muddy we can't get through."

Cass watched, and Meg drove, never out of low gear and never slower than ten miles an hour, faster when possible. The road was red muck, a section of it recently but only partly bladed; a sticky hump ran down the center and once nearly trapped her tires. Stop and you're here for good, she cautioned herself; do not stop for anything. Jay may be dying, but he's not dead; and Kev is ahead there somewhere.

Standing water, careful don't drown the van; and then left and straight again, muddy double tracks. A stretch of gravel, no tracks; Meg moved faster, caught a glimpse of what looked like the camper-truck off the road in a clump of young trees. Never mind, she thought, and said nothing to Cass as she increased her speed. Maybe Kev had drunk some of the rum, too?

She heard the creek before she saw it, a stream not wide but muddy, angry, slapping at the twin heavy planks laid for bridge and making them bounce. Meg, nervous about bridges all her life, ignored Cass's protest and simply drove at the boards, we make it or we don't.

Mud again, and only a single track in the road; a motorcycle was ahead of them or behind them. Last night or today? Never mind.

The road turned rougher, more rock and less mud. She rolled her window down, backed the accelerator off a bit; much over twenty and she'd shake the poor machine to pieces. Almost eight o'clock by her watch and how much further to civilization?

"Something's coming," said Cass, and Meg heard it, too, a loud sharp engine. They made a slow curve left and there ahead of them, coming toward them, was a black-helmeted, black-clad figure on a black and silver bike. Center of the road, get *over* whoever you are. Jon?

Meg slowed, and Cass flung herself sideways, grabbing the wheel and ramming both her feet against Meg's foot on the accelerator. They both screamed, and Meg saw the short rifle slung at an angle behind the black shoulders, saw the white freckled face just as the van smashed into the turning bike and sent it flying.

"Keep going!" urged Cass as she released her grip and sank back to her own place; her breath was fast and shallow, her face greenish.

"Yes, right. I will." Cass had not mentioned Jon since last night, since her howling fury after the rape. Did she know it was Kev they had just run down? Meg wondered.

More mud, slippery stuff on a road that seemed endless; maybe hell is a muddy road going on and on and on. Cass was breathing harshly, probably crying, but Meg kept her attention on driving, consolation later. At least the trees had thinned, letting more light through. She caught the sound of another engine and lifted her right arm in a warding-off gesture. "You stay right there," she told Cass.

It was coming down the road at them like the sun itself, a high square vehicle so red it hurt her eyes. Meg slowed, pulled to the right edge of the narrow road. Saw an unfamiliar female face behind the wheel of the red machine. Braked hard and completely and turned the engine off as she saw the dark furious man who boiled from the passenger door.

She slid from the van into her lover's arms with enormous gratitude, pity, and a distinct twinge of lust. "I have to tell you, Gutierrez, that I don't think much of Idaho."

"Next year you can plan the vacation." He tipped his head back and probed her face with hard black eyes.

"Nothing that won't mend," she told him. "Truly, Vince, it's not as bad as it looks."

"Never mind, I'm going to kill the son of a bitch."

Don't. She shivered, and swallowed against a constricted throat. "The weird thing is, he didn't beat me for fun. He was in charge, I tried to escape, and he did it to teach me a lesson. And Vince, do you know what else he did? He made me *cook*!" Her voice rose in indignation and broke in a storm of tears.

"He was a crazy ugly murderer, Uncle Vince." Cass threw herself at Gutierrez and buried her head against him. "And he killed my cat. But we got him."

Gutierrez looked quickly at Meg, who gulped and sniffed and said, "Oh, lordy, that's right. And not him, *them*. There's a young man with a motorcycle back along the road; we ran him down. And at the cabin, there's a man who has a head wound and probably a bad burn and besides that has swallowed a lot of antidepressant medicine."

"Mardian, call for an ambulance," he told the young woman who had emerged from the driver's seat of the jeep; she climbed back in quickly. "Maybe we'd better have two," Gutierrez added, his jaw still tight with fury. "Cass, what about you? Are you hurt?"

His niece stepped back and said, "I'm fine, I'm okay," with a sideways glance at Meg. "I'm the one who really got us out, I had to climb out a high window and drop a long way. Oh, hi!" She straightened and cocked her head at the approach of Val Kuisma.

"Cass was very brave; and I guess we were both lucky," said Meg. "But I really need to get out of these woods." There went her voice again; she pulled away from Gutierrez and wiped her eyes. "Who were they, Vince? And why did they want us? I kept trying to find that out."

He shook his head as he reached into the inside pocket of his jacket. "I don't have any hard answers, but I think it has something to do with these people. The pictures are almost twenty years old, and the woman's hair is white now. Recognize her?"

Meg took the newspaper clipping, blinked hard and tried to focus. "I don't know."

"Let me see," demanded Cass. She craned her head around Meg's arm for a look. "Oh, sure, I know her. That's the lady with the dead kid."

THIRTY-FOUR

"I'M REAL SORRY, Mrs. Tannenbaum, but I have to insist on seeing Maureen Gowan Tannenbaum and William Taylor."

The senior Mrs. Tannenbaum peered up at Hank Svoboda as if he were a formerly friendly St. Bernard gone suddenly rabid. "Mr. Svoboda, I cannot permit..."

"*Chief* Svoboda this time, ma'am, of the Port Silva police. And temporary deputy sheriff of Mendocino County. If you'll just tell me where I can find them?"

"It appears I have no choice. Manuel!" she snapped at the white-coated man who had let Svoboda in and then summoned her. "Maureen is in the kitchen giving Tessa her lunch. Please tell her there's a policeman to see her and Mr. Taylor."

Mrs. Tannenbaum sat herself down on a highbacked loveseat and pointedly ignored Svoboda, who kept his face bland and polite as he settled into a parade-rest stance.

"Just what is this all about?" snapped Maureen Tannenbaum as she strode into the room minutes later. "Oh, for heaven's sake *hush*, Tessa," she said to the child astride her hip, who had begun to whimper.

The older woman got quickly to her feet. "Give her to me, Maureen. Come to Nana, Tessa," she crooned.

Maureen handed the little girl over and turned a cold gaze on the intruder. "Well?"

"Official visit this time, ma'am," said Svoboda, and recited his titles once again. "Folks in Idaho—Chief Brownell of Coeur d'Alene and Sheriff Erdlatz of Boundary County—asked me to get in touch with you and Mr. Taylor. The idea being it's better for bad news to come in person instead of by telephone."

"Bad news." Maureen's square shoulders slumped, and she sank into a chair. "Has something gone wrong at Shelter?"

"What's going on here?" Ben Taylor burst through the doorway, his face flushed. "Maureen, you do not have to submit to police harassment."

Maureen gave him a quick, impatient glance. "Wait. He asked to see you, too. What kind of bad news?" she asked Svoboda.

"First thing is, a couple of relatives of you folks—a James Taylor? and a Kevin Gowan?—they're both in the hospital in Coeur d'Alene, in real bad shape."

"Oh my God!" breathed Maureen. "Oh, I *knew* Sweet was right on the edge, I knew we shouldn't have..." She looked up at Taylor. "Ben, I can't leave here; you'll have to go."

"I...yes." Taylor's high forehead was beaded with sweat. "What's the prognosis?" he asked the policeman.

"Your brother may not make it. The boy, it's mostly broken bones and concussion. Folks in Idaho hope to keep both of 'em alive; they got these charges see, kidnapping, and murder, and..."

"No." Maureen gripped the arms of the wing chair and pushed herself to her feet. "No, they had nothing to do with it."

"Shut up, Maureen!" Taylor's voice was savage.

"There was no murder," she went on, squaring her stance and lifting her chin. "My daughter's death was completely accidental. I'm sorry, Mother Tannenbaum," she added softly as the other woman gave an anguished cry.

"And there was no kidnapping. Stop it, Ben," she snapped, sidestepping his grab. "We, *I*, took a calculated risk and I don't propose to let anyone else suffer for it."

Svoboda's two easy strides brought him between Ben and Maureen, brought his heavy shoulder into glancing contact with the other man's chest. "Sorry," he murmured.

"No kidnapping," Maureen repeated. "Annie Moss is eighteen years old, she's had three children by three different men and the first was fathered by her own father or her older brother. Lisa," she said quietly, with a nod in the direction of the child, "was her second, the only girl. Annie jumped at the chance to get Lisa out of that life.

"So. That's it," she told Svoboda. "The only thing anyone is guilty of is failing to report a death."

"Now that's real helpful, ma'am," said Svoboda. "Clears up the one little problem, you might say. But see, there *was* a kidnapping. The victims were the people I asked you about this morning, the woman and girl who saw the accident."

"Woman and girl?" Maureen kept her neck rigid and turned her whole torso from the hips, to look at Ben Taylor. Even her lips had gone white.

"I have nothing to say." Ben sat down in the nearest chair and closed his eyes.

"Yes ma'am, they're both real clear about what happened to them, that they got kidnapped and held for about four days and took some bad treatment; and they're real sure it was this James Taylor and this Kevin Gowan that did it. And then there's the other fellow, that got shot dead out there."

Maureen made no sound as her knees gave way; she hit the floor before Svoboda could reach her.

"HANK SAYS HE THOUGHT it was a stage fall, a fake, until he heard her head hit." Vince Gutierrez got up from his canvas chair and went to lean on the deck rail and gaze out at the small cove and sea beyond.

"Um." Meg Halloran, who had spent Tuesday and Tuesday night in the hospital in Coeur d'Alene, most of Wednesday and all of Wednesday night asleep in her own bed, thought this day was a blessing she hated to see end. Pretty blue ocean waving and snapping its whitecaps, sun so brilliant it made her dark glasses a necessity as well as a vanity, fog only a distant possibility: it all turned the last few days into a tale made up to frighten; something by Stephen King. "Does Hank believe her story?" she asked. Maureen Tannenbaum had insisted she had no knowledge of, no part in, the kidnapping. Ben Taylor was saying nothing at all.

"He does, but reluctantly. Hank took a serious dislike to Maureen Tannenbaum. He says any woman who can bury her own child while it's still warm and go right out to promote a replacement is not his idea of your basic good person."

Behind her dark glasses Meg saw the small sprawled body, and the kneeling woman, transfixed by shock or grief or something for just a moment. Then she picked up the dead child, announced in calm authoritative tones that it lived, and drove away. *She started it,* Meg said to herself, finding that most childish of phrases appropriate in its baldness.

"Apparently she never mistreated Tessa," Gutierrez went on. "But she wasn't interested in being a mother. The boy, Kevin, *is* her son; she turned him over to her own mother at birth and went on with her life. So far as she was concerned, he was just one more little brother."

"What will happen to the other child, the substitute?"

Gutierrez turned, propping his butt on the rail and folding his arms on his chest. From Meg's position, nearly horizontal in a lounge chair, he looked like a dark, disapproving statue. "Mrs. Tannenbaum," he said, "—and Maureen too, of course—want Michael to go on thinking she's his daughter. Since he's effectively isolated from the outside world by now, too sick for newspapers or television, they'll probably pull it off.

"So I guess if you're keeping score, you could say that one good thing came out of this mess," he added, his expression softening. "Little Lisa Moss will be spared the shitty, no-hope kind of life her mother has lived."

"I guess," said Meg. (Secretly, guiltily, she counted four days of terror and thought that she and Cass had paid, were paying, a high price for Lisa's rebirth.) According to Maureen, the notion of finding a replacement for Tessa had occurred to her and Ben as they were driving from the accident scene to the compound. Such a substitution had struck her, Maureen, as unorthodox and of course illegal, but not immoral; no one would be hurt. Once at the compound they had buried Tessa, had decided to adopt Lisa Moss from her depressed and not very bright mother and go on with their planned journey to California.

Ben had fretted, had ranted and raved, said Maureen, about that dangerous woman from California... from northern California at that, according to the cards in Meg's sweater pocket. Nasty pushy woman and the only person on earth apart from the four of them who had seen Tessa dead. All this, loudly and repeatedly and fearfully, within the hearing of Sweet and Buddy (known to Meg as Jay and Kevin). But there had been, so far as Maureen had heard and she had been there the whole time... there had been no instructions to kill or kidnap. None.

"Will no one rid me of that dreadful woman?" Meg said softly.

Gutierrez leaned forward to look at her. "What?"

"It may not have been a conscious order, but it was implied. Given what he knew of his brother, of Jay's background and his regard for, his emotional dependence on, big brother Ben."

"Yeah. And even if he did not order it started, he could have stopped it." Gutierrez's fist pounded the rail in rhythm with the last words.

"Well. Probably only by killing us. He'd seen enough of me to guess I'd make a terrible fuss the minute I got free. Public attention was something they absolutely could not risk. I suppose I should be grateful he had enough humanity to keep us alive."

"That wasn't humanity, that was pure calculation." Gutierrez barred his teeth in a grimace of disgust. "If the child substitution failed, he could order his troops to release you and claim to be guilty of nothing more than bad judgment brought on by excessive family feeling. Like, Ben didn't want to pull the plug on his poor loony brother who after all was only trying to help; and Ben really did his best keep things cool by phone until he was free to return to Idaho and straighten things out."

"Ah. And if it succeeded..."

"Then it would have been worth his while, worth the risk, to have you killed. People talk about the Tannenbaum estate as somewhere over fifty million."

Ben and Maureen wealthy enough to do whatever they wanted. Meg and Cass buried anonymously in the Idaho woods. Jay...maybe institutionalized somewhere? And what would Ben have done ultimately with poor dumb Kevin? Meg wondered.

"Meg? Are you okay?" She opened her eyes to find Gutierrez's worried face blocking the sun. "You were shivering. Can I get you a sweater, or another pot of tea?"

"I've drunk so much tea my teeth are squeaking. Isn't the sun well over the yardarm? That's what my father always told my mother when he broke out the bottle early."

"Yes ma'am, it is indeed."

He set off for the door at a near-trot and it occurred to her that he was ready to go back to work. In fact, she planned to insist on it, soon. Gutierrez the solicitous nurse might well prove more exhausting than Gutierrez the testy convalescent.

He was back almost at once with a clinking pitcher and two glasses. "Look, I got olives," he said. He filled one glass and held it out to her; as she stretched her arm out she saw the black and blue marks, fist marks, and she missed the glass and had to reach again.

"Meg?"

"Don't *hover*, Vince," she snapped, and brought the martini safely to her lips. "It's like a flashback, for a minute I'm hurting and I'm *hating*. And right after is this wave of incredible relief: I'm free and I'm *so* glad I didn't kill him." Broken his ear drum and put a dent in his skull, she had, and added more burn scars to his face. But the doctors said the pills were not the cause, or at least not the whole cause, of his present catatonic state. Jay had retreated from the world all the way.

"Yes, be glad," he advised as he settled into his chair with his own drink.

"So. Tell me again that you're sure Ben Taylor will get his."

"Lady, I believe it's going to happen. Kevin is the one who took the last phone call, remember? He says Ben told him to kill you and Cass. The boy is shit-scared, and he's dumb enough to be convincing."

"He was set up emotionally, Vince, as much as Jay was."

"I know that. Lawrence Archer knows that. Lawrence Archer is one mean son of a bitch who plans to see his son's real killer pay."

Jon. Meg had not thought of Jon for a while. First a potential enemy and then a possible rescuer and now she would never know which he was, *what* he was. "Cass hasn't said a thing about Jon's death, hasn't even mentioned his name."

"I think Cass has this agreement with herself, that life started yesterday." Gutierrez had promised to collect his niece from the swimming pool at 6:30; now he tossed a quick glance at his watch before settling back in his chair. "Oh, I stopped by Maldonados' yesterday; would it be okay with you if they come back to work tomorrow? Pete says they need to get moving if they're going to have the downstairs finished by the time Katy comes home."

"Yes, fine; with the bathroom working down there, they won't have to come upstairs at all."

"Then about the study. Their best inside carpenter can come the first of the week, and you'll have your two walls of floor to ceiling bookcases in no time."

"Tell Pete to cancel them. I'll set up a workspace in a corner of our room." Even with one end given over to a small bath, the sleeping-loft-turned-master-bedroom was spacious.

"Meg, you've been lusting after a separate study ever since you moved in here." He frowned at her. "We can afford it, I promise."

"I think we'd better keep that room a bedroom for a while yet. For Cass."

This time he sat up in his chair and stared. "Hey. You don't have to worry about Cass. My mother will be back next week, and Cass becomes her problem."

"Your mother is what, seventy-four years old?"

"Seventy-five, but she's one tough old lady."

"Not tough enough." Meg drained her glass and held it out. "May I have the second half, please?"

He rose quickly, added ice to her glass and then poured pale liquid from the pitcher. "Look, if she doesn't work out with Mama, she can go to her stepfather."

"No. She can't live with a man, a man alone, just now. Especially a man she believes abandoned her."

"Then Mary Louise will just have to..."

"Don't talk to me about Mary Louise. I think women like Mary Louise should be spayed at public expense, like stray cats."

"Jesus, Meg!"

"Sorry."

"Meg," he said, sweetly reasonable. "Cass will mess up your life, our life, totally."

"No. Partly."

"So that's enough. Come on, you don't even like her."

"What does liking have to do with it?" She took her dark glasses off and squinted at the sun-bright sea as she sipped gin. "I understand her. I have a certain respect for the little...wretch. As she has for me. And I can handle her. I think." She took another sip, and pushed away a thought so mean she wouldn't voice it even to Gutierrez. She kept hanging up on the idea of Katy, of bringing messy, screwed-up and screwed-over Cass into Katy's life. Soiled dove and innocent virgin. Gaah.

"Do you really want her around Katy?"

"Oh, Gutierrez, shut up!" She sniffed, and wiped her eyes on her shirttail. "I'm stuck. I owe her, she owes me."

"Well, shit," he said glumly.

"That's a fair approximation of my feeling, too. And we'll have to get married."

"I beg your pardon?"

"Cass has had all she needs of irregular relationships. Not that ours is, really; but I think in her case appearances matter."

"Oh, I agree. I agree absolutely."

THE BRILLIANCE of the afternoon light was too much for his weak eyes; but if he put the dark glasses on, he wouldn't be able to see the little girl who stood on tiptoe to look out the window.

"Pretty, Tessa?" said his mother, from her chair at his bedside. "Pretty blue ocean?"

"Pitty," the little girl said softly, doubtfully. She leaned her forehead against the glass for a moment, in silence, and then said "Gone," in tones of satisfaction.

"No no, baby, it isn't gone."

"She means people are gone, Mother." Michael paused for breath. "She means there's nobody there."

"Does she?" His mother looked at him, and then at the child. "That's very odd. Tessa's a strange child, Michael, but very sweet."

"Yes."

"She doesn't look much like you, not yet. More like me, I think, when I was a child. And she has my gray eyes, you've noticed that?"

"Yes."

"Are you in pain, dear? Shall I take Tessa away and send the nurse?"

"In a minute. Help me sit higher."

She took him gently by the shoulders and helped him up against his pillows. "Better? Tessa, come here and say good night to Daddy."

Tessa spun away from the window and came like a dancer across the carpet. If her words were few, thought Michael, her movements were eloquent. She stopped at the edge of the bed without bumping it, reached out with one hand to touch Michael's hand where it lay limply on the blanket.

"Night, Mi'el."

He smiled at her, and her solemn face broke into its wide grin. "Night, Tessa. Mother? You'll take care of her?"

"Of course, Michael," she said as she bent to pick the child up.

"Promise me."

"I promise that I will take care of her."

As her steps moved away he fumbled for his dark glasses and managed to get them on. The light hurt, and anyway it embarrassed him to be crying even with no one to see the tears. Weakling.

He had not expected to be so instantly connected to a child, even his own. That this was not his own made it even more magical. The newly arrived and the about to depart, in some sort of recognition?

The pain in his chest was bigger, a burning disk with white-hot edges; he groaned aloud but softly, and did not let his hand reach for the button. His mother would send the nurse. He would wait. What did he have yet to do?

The will. He'd done that, dictated the changes one slow sentence at a time into a cassette recorder and given the tape to his attorney's secretary.

He heard a sound, and opened his eyes to see the nurse's face made strange by the dark glasses. "Please," he croaked.

Demerol did not "kill" pain. What it did, for him, was make pain seem far away and unimportant. And compress the passage of time. Remember, remember...what. Yes. Stay clear enough tomorrow to sign the new will. Everything to Maureen.

Ah, easier now, he could get his breath. She had promised to take care of the little girl, and Maureen always kept her promises. She had promised not to let Ben use her, too, but he had less faith in that promise. Ben had something Maureen needed, a permanently stiff cock.

He shifted his shoulders and groaned, looked at the softening blue outside his window and wished himself part of it. Where was Ben? Hadn't been around for a couple of days, or had he, Michael, just lost track? No matter; old Ben could be good company, but he was past the need for company.

He thought the pain was not going so far away this time. Hovering nearby, like an eager friend. He'd have to give up his child soon, his not-daughter; couldn't let his new little love watch pain take him in its teeth.

Well, let it go. He floated above himself, looked down at the wasted disgusting body and tried to pull loose but failed. It will let you go when it's good and ready.

Send Maureen away. Tomorrow. His last strong hope, his refuge and he could not use her. He let the tears fall this time, heard gulping sobs like a child's and put his hands over his mouth. Ugly.

One last terrible temptation lay before him, lifted its head and grinned at him. Go away. What if he asked Maureen to... put him out of his misery. That was the term used for animals, and he was struck by its aptness. Out of his misery.

She loved him. If she were to ease him out of life, and her action were discovered, she would very likely lose the money. The creature grinned wider and blinked, wagged its tail.

He would not ask her. He would try not to ask her.

AUTHOR'S AFTERWORD

THIS STORY and its title were suggested to me by an old ballad that was probably Scots. Called "The Cruel Mother" in the *Oxford Book of Ballads*, it has had other versions, other titles, in other books and on records. The following is a shortened and refrainless version of the song as I remember hearing it somewhere.

She lay down beneath the thorn,
And it's there she had her little babe born.

She's taken out her little pen knife,
And robbed her poor babe of its life.

As she went home all by the church,
She saw a wee babe on the porch.

"Oh little babe, if thou wert mine,
I'd dress thee in the silk so fine."

"Mother dear, when I was thine,
Thee did not treat me then so kind."

MURDER HAS A PRETTY FACE

JENNIE MELVILLE

The raped man had drowned. No one claimed him. Nobody wanted him. Least of all, Police Inspector Charmian Daniels. Why did he have her name and telephone number on a card in his pocket?

Several large-scale robberies of furs and jewels and a mysterious, garishly made-up woman lurking about town add to the bizarre caseload. Charmian is convinced the crimes are connected—but how? A chance visit to a local beauty salon puts her on the trail of a diabolic gang of criminals—and leaves no doubt that even the prettiest face can mask a ruthless heart as cold as steel.

Available at your favorite retail outlet in September, or reserve your copy for August shipping by sending your name, address and zip code, along with a check or money order for $3.99 plus 75¢ postage and handling for each book ordered, payable to Worldwide Mystery, to:

Worldwide Mystery
3010 Walden Ave.
P.O. Box 1325
Buffalo, NY
14269-1325

Please specify book title with your order. Sorry, this offer not available in Canada.

ONLY AVAILABLE IN THE U.S.

PRETTY-R

W❀RLDWIDE LIBRARY
TM

BACKLASH
PAULA GOSLING

Winner of the John Creasey Award for crime fiction

THE TASK THAT FACED GENERAL HOMICIDE SEEMED MONUMENTAL

They had four dead cops from four different precincts, all shot through the head. The headlines were screaming cop killer. Rookies were making sudden career changes, while veterans of the force were anxiously eyeing retirement dates. Panic was growing.

For Lieutenant Jack Stryker, the pressure was coming everywhere: up from below, down from above, and in from the outside. And with each new death, the pressure increased. Was the killer shooting cops at random...or was there a more sinister reason for the murders?

But when Stryker is hit and his partner is almost fatally wounded...Stryker knows it's time to forget procedure and put an end to open season on Grantham's finest...before he becomes the next trophy of a demented killer.

"Gosling's novels have all met with critical acclaim."

— *Library Journal*

Available at your favorite retail outlet in October, or reserve your copy for September shipping by sending your name, address and zip code, along with a check or money order for $3.99 plus 75¢ postage and handling for each book ordered, payable to Worldwide Mystery, to:

Worldwide Mystery
3010 Walden Ave.
P.O. Box 1325
Buffalo, NY
14269-1325

Please specify book title with your order. Sorry, this offer not available in Canada.

ONLY AVAILABLE IN THE U.S.

BACKL-R

 WORLDWIDE LIBRARY

Flight to
YESTERDAY
VELDA JOHNSTON

A NIGHTMARE REVISITED

Dubbed a "young Jean Harris" by the press, Sara Hargreaves spent four years in prison for a crime of passion she didn't commit. Now she's escaped, and she's desperate to clear her name and to see her dying mother.

As her face appears nightly on the local news, Sara disguises herself, and with the help of a young law student she is forced to trust, she returns to the scene of the crime.

The fashionable sanatorium where handsome plastic surgeon Dr. Manuelo Covarrubias was stabbed with a knife bearing Sara's fingerprints looks much the same. But as Sara begins her flight to yesterday, the secrets surrounding the callous playboy doctor who jilted her unfold. Secrets that once drove someone to murder...secrets that could kill again.

Available at your favorite retail outlet in January 1992, or reserve your copy for December shipping by sending your name, address, zip or postal code, along with a check or money order for $3.99 plus 75¢ postage and handling ($1.00 in Canada) for each book ordered, payable to Worldwide Mystery, to:

In the U.S.
Worldwide Mystery
3010 Walden Avenue
P.O. Box 1325
Buffalo, NY 14269-1325

In Canada
Worldwide Mystery
P.O. Box 609
Fort Erie, Ontario
L2A 5X3

Please specify book title with your order.
Canadian residents add applicable federal and provincial taxes.

FLIGHT-R

 WØRLDWIDE LIBRARY
™

A SENSITIVE CASE
ERIC WRIGHT

AN INSPECTOR CHARLIE SALTER MYSTERY

THE BIGGER THEY ARE THE HARDER THEY FALL

The murder of masseuse Linda Thomas was a sticky situation—her clients included big people in high places. It was a case for Special Affairs Inspector Charlie Salter and his chief investigator, Sergeant Mel Pickett. They delicately kick open a hornet's nest of hostile, secretive suspects, including a provincial deputy minister, a famous television host, the tenants of the woman's building, a nervous academic, a secret lover and an unidentified man—the last person to see Linda alive.

A lot of people had a lot to hide—and even more at stake than their careers. To make things more difficult, Salter is worried his wife is having an affair.

It's a sensitive case, both at home and on the job. Charlie's doing a lot of tiptoeing around—with a killer lurking in the shadow of every step.

Available at your favorite retail outlet in November, or reserve your copy for October shipping by sending your name, address and zip code, along with a check or money order for $3.99 plus 75¢ postage and handling for each book ordered, payable to Worldwide Mystery, to:

Worldwide Mystery
3010 Walden Ave.
P.O. Box 1325
Buffalo, NY
14269-1325

Please specify book title with your order. Sorry, this offer not available in Canada.

ONLY AVAILABLE IN THE U.S.   SEN-R

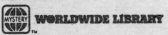 **WORLDWIDE LIBRARY**